H. E. A. R. T. Saga:
The Children

Linna

Adam,
It always brings
smile to my face to see
you online.
Thanks for being my friend
much love

Linna

Crushing Hearts & Black Butterfly

www.crushingheartsandblackbutterfly.com

H. E. A. R. T. Saga:
The Children

ISBN 13: 978-0615614359
ISBN 10: 0615614353

Published by
Crushing Hearts and Black Butterfly Publishing, LLC.
Algonquin, IL 60102

Edited by: V.B. Williams
For Crushing Hearts and Black Butterfly Publishing

Cover by: Para Graphic Designs

For my precious husband Tom

Prologue

The lovely new Ambassador Tatiana sat in the temple office. "I love my job," she mused to herself.

Tatiana's new job was simply delightful. She got to serve the HEART of the world and the HEART's children. Tatiana was now the speaker for the HEART and their Mother, their God. The HEART gave them all they needed to be happy; she gave them life. The HEART gave her energy freely to all who lived on this perfect little world. The energy healed and protected. Anyone could use the energy for help in their daily job; a person could use the HEART's energy to travel anywhere, or talk to anyone anywhere.

The only part of her new appointment as Ambassador that Tatiana dreaded was to punish people who broke the rules of the communities. There had been times when Tatiana had gone to a gathering when she was younger and someone had been mind wiped by the negative energy. Tatiana felt so sad for those people. She knew that they were wrong to speak so blasphemously about the HEART. Tatiana shook her head, remembering the stupidity of someone who would say that a person had a heart in their body. No one could have the HEART in their body. Not only was this kind of thinking blasphemous, but it was illegal science as well.

However, this day the HEART saw fit to bring the joy of a new life into the world, a baby girl. Everyone in the community would rejoice with an extra special energy gathering because all life was precious, but this child was exceptional.

This new baby girl was born to NayLara and NayMichael and had been given the name of Donna. At the age of 18 she would be married to a boy who had been born only a few days ago and given the name of Devon. They would both be given the pre-name of Dra after they were married. It was Tatiana's pleasure to implant the tiny grain of HEART stone in the babies' wrists. They would learn to channel the HEART's energy to use in their jobs, which would be a great service to the communities.

All things about this baby seemed to be normal, but one thing was not. Donna was born with curly copper colored hair. No one had seen a baby born with this kind of hair for hundreds of years. In fact it had been so long that no one could really remember the last person to have that copper colored hair. It was not just little Donna's hair. Tatiana had a feeling that this child was special. She could feel it deep in her soul. Tatiana knew without a doubt that little Donna was going to do something great one day.

Tatiana wondered who it was that last had hair that color. She wondered what that person's life was like. She felt sure that the HEART knew. Tatiana stood from her chair and decided to ask the HEART about it, because the HEART knew all.

Gathering

1

DraDonna loved the energy, but there was something about a negative energy gathering that just didn't sit well with her. She did love the wonderful feeling that special energy gave her. But knowing that the energy had been sucked out of another person made her very uncomfortable.

HarJon, who was from Second Councilor Fredrik's community, had been convicted of beating his wife HarJayelle again. Indeed a very serious crime. The first time he was convicted the HEART's energy had been withdrawn and he was no longer allowed to receive the energy. HarJon nearly went energy mad. He begged forgiveness of the communities. DraDonna felt sorry for HarJayelle. She had been mistreated and would no longer be married. DraDonna also felt sorry for HarJon.

It scared her to think of not having the energy there to heal her, help her sleep, or keep her safe. DraDonna feared the thought of having to remember dreams. To be stuck with remembering something odd that her mind came up with while she slept was just awful, and the thought of not having the energy there for her and her husband every day for everything that they needed was scary.

Today however, HarJon would be stripped of his prename Har, which meant that his wife HarJayelle would no longer be married to him. Then the negative energy would be used on him, wiping his mind and taking any energy out of his body. Then the energy would be re-routed by both of the Councilors into the crowd of people who gathered to witness this man's public punishment. The people who were gathered to witness all of this would partake of the euphoric feeling the special energy gave.

DraDonna sat with her husband DraDevon. He was such a beautiful man. DraDevon was not a big man but he had well-toned muscles and a strong face. DraDonna loved his silky glossy black hair that he kept just a little longer than most people would have said was proper. She knew that he kept it long because she liked it that way.

He was the one of the only reasons she was staying for this gathering. She knew that he loved the feeling of the energy, and she knew the kind of gossip that would ensue if she didn't attend. She had been dealing with the people in this community bullying her all her life, but she didn't want anyone to start in on him.

The other reason was her older sister JorMelony, who was a sweet and gentle soul. She was a petite woman with light brown hair that some said looked to have a little of the cursed copper to it. She had the same amber colored eyes as her little sister.

JorMelony was sitting up front with her own husband JorRobert where all the musicians sat. JorMelony played the tallice; she channeled the energy down to her right hand using the grain of HEART stone in her wrist. JorMelony divided the energy between all the fingers on her right hand, with which she strummed this small instrument. The tallice had a short neck and a box shaped hollow body with various sized metal strings that circled the entire instrument lengthwise. It had a low calming sound that DraDonna loved to hear.

The musicians were now playing a piece of music that had a feeling of doom, typical for this type of gathering. DraDonna knew that just after the energy was re-routed to the people, the music would change to a smooth sensual sound.

DraDonna did not want to miss hearing her sister play her tallice, but she felt like she needed to leave the gathering.

DraDonna didn't like feeling in the pit of her stomach that made her want to run away. She'd had this feeling of wanting to run away so many times in her life. The few people to whom she confided these feelings would tell her that the problem was inside of her and that she should ask the HEART to help her correct her feelings with the energy. She had tried that to no avail. The energy always felt like tingling warmth, but it was always the same, no matter what prayer she used. She wondered why no one else noticed this.

H.E.A.R.T. Saga: The Children

Unfortunately a lot of the people believed that there was something wrong with her and would insinuate that she should have been mind wiped by the negative energy. Even her teachers in school had told her she was a troublemaker.

Most people were polite, but so few were actually nice to her. Her parents and her sister, of course, were kind to her. Then there was her loving husband DraDevon, and there was the former Ambassador Tatiana who had also been kind to her. Ambassador Tatiana had been ordained as the Ambassador just before she was born. But a year ago, just before hers and DraDevon's wedding, Tatiana died.

DraDonna sighed sadly, because she missed her friend. Ambassador Tatiana had told her all her life that she was special in ways that only she and the HEART knew, and it didn't matter what others thought.

It was hard for DraDonna because Ambassador Tatiana died just days before her wedding. Oh how DraDonna wished that Ambassador Tatiana had been the one to perform the wedding. It would have been so lovely to have Ambassador Tatiana, who was one of her only friends, perform the wedding that bound her by the HEART's energy to her best friend.

DraDonna's soul was heavy with sorrow whenever she thought about it. Even the HEART's energy could not heal this pain, but she didn't dare tell anyone. People thought she was odd enough. She didn't want to get mind wiped.

Taking a deep breath, she turned her attention back to Ambassador Symon and his councilors. Ambassador Symon was a fine-looking man. His face had sharp handsome features with large hazel eyes and golden brown hair. The one thing that took away from his good looks was the fact that he always looked like he was either in a bad mood or in pain. But how could he be in pain, and didn't his job give him joy? He was a servant of the HEART, and she took care of all her children.

First Councilor Jude was a small and stunningly beautiful woman with light golden blonde hair and big blue eyes that always seemed to sparkle with joy.

H.E.A.R.T. Saga: The Children

Second Councilor Fredrik was tall and lean with dark hair and dark brown eyes that frequently placed a twinkle of mischief in his animated face. Yet for just a moment Fredrik had a fleeting look of pain when he looked at where HarJayelle was standing.

The three of them talked together at the front of the courtyard, waiting for the meeting to begin. It was a well-known fact that ambassadors and councilors were bonded deeply in friendship, and it was apparent to everyone at this gathering that these three were no exception.

DraDonna looked over at DraDevon and whispered, "I don't think I'm going to stay."

"Why," he asked with concern showing on his face. "If you're not feeling well, the energy will heal you. Maybe you should stay."

"No, it's not that." DraDonna tried to think of something that would give her a good reason to leave. She did not want to cause her sweet husband to worry or give anyone else reason to gossip. "I really feel I need to go back so I can finish making that meal delivery cabinet for the Sol family. I need to have it done so we can deliver it to them tomorrow or they will report me for disrespect of my job."

DraDevon gently took her hand and said, "My wife, you have nothing to worry about. No one really thinks you disrespect your job."

"You know SolKaren doesn't like me. I just don't want to give her any reason to gossip about us." DraDonna said with a pleading look on her face.

"Okay," He sighed. "I will see you at evening energy time, my love."

"You bet." DraDonna replied enthusiastically. "It's my favorite time of day." She said as she leaned over and kissed his lips softly.

Several people gave DraDonna looks of irritation and disapproval as she walked past them to leave the gathering. "I'm sorry to disturb you," she mumbled as she walked past. "Please excuse me. I need to get home and finish a project."

H.E.A.R.T. Saga: The Children

TelAmy, a woman in her early 30's, gave DraDonna a dirty look as she walked past, saying, "It doesn't matter if you leave the gathering early. No matter how much time you spend on that project it will never be good enough."

DraDonna tried to ignore her rude comment. However she could not help but worry. She knew that she had a long way to go before the project was done, and the meal delivery cabinet or MDC was due to be installed tomorrow morning at the Sol home.

As DraDonna walked the short distance from the town center to her home, the sick feeling in the pit of her stomach that she had at the gathering remained. She felt like there was a stone lodged in her belly. She lifted her head and took several deep breaths, hoping that would help her feel better. It did not work. While looking up she wondered about the ever present and ever shifting cloud cover. She wondered why it never cleared up. The people on her world had always known that the light that came up in the morning and set at night was a sun, but none were left alive that remembered ever seeing it.

Deep in thoughts that she knew would get her into trouble, she walked to her home. It was the typical small cottage that married couples would live in the first few years of marriage. It looked simple on the outside with the same nameless trees and flowers everywhere, but as DraDonna walked inside she saw that the house was very different from everyone else's.

It was filled with beautifully ornate furniture that she and DraDevon had made for themselves. She was proud of her work. Even though she did not find the fulfillment in her job that everyone else did, DraDonna always did her best. Most of the time she did not use the energy to do her job as others did. She felt a need to prove to everyone that she could do her job without the energy.

Not long after Tatiana died and Symon had become the new Ambassador, he had asked her to build him a new desk. When it was delivered to Ambassador Symon he asked about the odd design. DraDonna told him about how she did it all by hand. He was irritated, and asked her if she did this

5

with everything she made. After finding out that she did, he scolded her for not using the energy and giving the people in her community the very best. He admonished her to use the energy more in her work and not to be job disrespectful.

DraDonna entered her home and went straight to the HEART stone altar in the center of her home. The HEART stone altar was considered the most important place in any house. DraDonna was very proud of the lovely wood that she had carved herself and the beautiful white stone that brought the HEART's energy to anyone who placed their hands upon it. It was also used for energy travel as well as stone to stone communication when the right prayers were said.

She knelt in front of it and placed both hands on the stone, reciting, "And the HEART provides for them that they hunger not, neither should they thirst; yea and the HEART also gives them strength, that they suffer no manner of affliction." DraDonna held her breath. She saw and felt the blue sparks emanating from the white stone. The energy was running into her hands with a pleasant sensation that felt good and clean. She sighed with relief as the energy made its way throughout her body, easing the queasy feeling in her stomach.

After a few more moments of peaceful communion with the HEART, DraDonna rose to her feet and walked out of her home. As she followed the path to the shop behind the house, she mused on the fact that she was partly wrong. The HEART's energy may not have been different from prayer to prayer, but it felt clean. The energy re-routed from a person getting mind wiped always felt oily and soiled to her.

Although she was in much better spirits when she got to the shop door, the feeling soon changed. The warm dark interior had always felt wrong, like it did not belong to her. She walked in quickly and went right to work.

There was so much to do. She could not indulge in her old feelings of self-doubt. She pulled a stool up to the workbench and began, losing herself in her work. She had all the pieces of the MDC cut and read to go but she still had to assemble them and then do the fine detail work to SolKaren's specifications.

She carefully laid them out in the order that they needed to be assembled. She started with the largest piece, the back, with a standard arched hole at the bottom in the center. She fit the end of the left sidepiece into the left end of the back. DraDonna deftly secured the pieces together with a hammer and nails and proceeded to do so for the rest of them as well.

Once she had it assembled, she then began the sanding. DraDonna always hated the feeling of sand paper. She knew that she could use the energy to do this, but somehow DraDonna always thought that the work was more her own by doing more things by hand.

DraDonna was so involved in this time consuming project that she didn't know that the gathering had ended long ago and it was drawing close to the important evening's energy intake. When DraDonna heard the distant tolling of the HEART stone telling her that the time was soon, she was worried. The cabinet was nowhere near done and she didn't want to walk away from it until it was finished. She also didn't want to miss the most important energy of the day with her beloved husband. Frustrated with how much time it was taking, and going against her better judgment, she put down her tools.

As she had learned in school, she focused her mind on the energy within her. DraDonna gathered the energy to the center of her body, pushing it down her right arm to her wrist using the grain of HEART stone to intensify the energy. She then channeled the energy to her hand, then to her forefinger. Her hand looked as though she was wearing a glove made of blue light, the forefinger bright white.

She bent close to her work pushing the energy that emanated from her finger into the soft grains of the wood, creating a delicate swirling design. She could feel the tingle of the energy in her chest continually run down her right arm into her hand. DraDonna focused the blue sparks on the fine details of the MDC cabinet, making sure that every exquisite detail was perfect.

She was so involved in finishing the MDC with her energy reserves that she did not notice that the final tolling for the evening's energy time had come and gone. When she had finally finished it was well after nightfall.

DraDonna felt very drained from using up so much of the energy; she could hardly think straight as she made her way back to her house.

When she entered through the front door her mind was so clouded with exhaustion that she walked past the HEART stone altar. Even though her body needed more energy, the only thought she had was to go to bed. She needed sleep more than anything.

She stumbled to her bedroom and saw the soft and inviting bed was occupied by her sleeping husband. Without changing into her nightclothes, DraDonna carefully climbed into bed next to DraDevon and instantly fell asleep.

Awake
2

All DraDonna knew was a black cloud of exhaustion. Her body may have settled nicely into the soft folds of the bed, but her mind was sinking into a deep abyss from which she felt she would never escape. Darkness swirled all around her. She felt like she was adrift in nothing. She had no body and her mind could not hold on to a single thought.

The darkness then began to abate and she could see forms and shapes in it. The light grew little by little until she could see that the shapes were in fact the clouds that she had seen in the sky every day of her life. They moved around her, each little cloud having a life of its own and wanting to tell her about it. DraDonna's gaze was drawn to one specific cloud. It was a little brighter than the rest. It sat on her shoulder for a moment and slid down her arm, landing on the ground.

It was then that she noticed she was standing on a mountaintop. Frightened by this, she sat on a nearby boulder hoping to stop the dizziness that threatened to overwhelm her. The one bright cloud settled at her feet.

She looked down at it and said, "What are you?"

The cloud's light pulsated as the form changed and grew. It was just a few seconds until it took on the form of a person. The form answered DraDonna's question: "Not what, but who."

She gasped in surprise. She knew that voice. "Tatiana?" she asked. "Is that you?" Her voice shook with emotion.

The form took its final shape: DraDonna's life-long friend Ambassador Tatiana. "Yes, Donna. It is I."

"How... why?" DraDonna stammered. Normally hearing someone calling her by her child name would have irritated her, but all she wanted to do was to stand up and hug her friend.

Tatiana stopped the young woman's embrace by backing up a bit and placing her transparent hands out in front of her. "I would love to embrace you child, but I can keep your mind here only so long and I am forbidden to touch you."

"I don't understand."

"I hope that you will. All of us need you to be awake. We need you to understand, but I am limited by my oath to the HEART in what I can tell you."

"But..." DraDonna started to interrupt, but Tatiana stopped her again with a wave of her hand.

"I know you have questions, my dear, but we don't have time for you to ask them. I have a pretty good idea of what you would ask, so I will do my best to explain what I can. I know that you have felt all your life that there is something wrong. Most people have tried to say that it is you who are wrong. Donna you are not wrong, but you are different. Special. It's the world. It's..." She stopped for a moment, and then continued. "The world is wrong. You are the only one who has the mind to do what must be done to save us all."

"Tatiana, this doesn't make any sense. Save who?"

"Do you see all the clouds?" The old soul gestured to all of the little clouds that were constantly moving around them. "They are not clouds. They are like me - souls that cannot move on. There are so many of us now that we block the sky." She paused and pointed up. "Look DraDonna, I need you to see."

DraDonna turned her eyes up to the sky and was able to see past all the old souls that were trapped. She gasped sharply when she saw the countless number of precious little points of light. There were so many of them, and it looked as though they were trying with no success to get through the cloud-like souls. "What are they?" DraDonna finally breathed out.

"Those are new souls my friend, the souls of babies. Think about it Donna. Have there been many babies born lately?" Tatiana paused for just a small moment and bowed her head in sorrow. "We don't mean to block them out, but we can't move on."

DraDonna's head began to spin as she realized that this was why there had not been any live births lately.

"That's right, Donna." The old soul confirmed. "We can't move on and they can't get past all of us."

"But what can I do?" DraDonna said. "Why show this to me now?"

"DraDonna, I told you for all your life that you were special, that you were meant for something big. Well, this is it. We need you to free our souls so we can move on and the new souls can be born into the world."

"But what can I do? I'm only a finish carpenter, and not a very good one at that."

Tatiana sighed in frustration.

DraDonna broke in with more questions. "I don't understand how it is you are able to come to me tonight. I am not sure any of this is real. How do I know that this isn't just the first stage of energy madness?"

"You are not energy-mad Donna." Tatiana said with exasperation in her voice. "I was able to come to you tonight because your mind was free of the HEART's energy. In the beginning the energy was used to do good and simple things. Now it clouds the mind and suppresses a person's natural personality traits. I need your mind to remain awake. I need you to know that you are not just a finish carpenter, but also a scientist. If you will look for it, you can find what will set us free. I should also warn you: you must avoid taking energy if you can. There may be times you want or need energy for healing or travel, so you need to start eating a plant called Traveler's Joy." Tatiana leaned over and gestured to a nearby tree with a vine growing around the base of it. "That vine with the white and purple flowers is what you must eat."

DraDonna, desperately trying to keep up with what she was being told said, "I don't understand. Why I would need to eat it?"

Tatiana again sighed, "Traveler's Joy will keep your mind from being affected by the HEART's energy."

"Why do none of those in the communities know about this plant, but you do?" DraDonna asked.

"There are many secrets that an Ambassador needs to keep." The old soul looked desperate. "I need you to not forget your gift of science, so you must eat this plant. We all need you to figure this out, for the good of all souls past, present, and future."

DraDonna felt like she was going to cry. It seemed like such a great responsibility, and she didn't even know where to start. "Tatiana," she addressed the old soul, "how am I supposed to know where I should start? I don't know what to do."

Then another thought came to DraDonna that caused the cold grip of fear to wrap around her soul. "Isn't science forbidden by the HEART? If I start poking around and someone finds out, I'll get mind wiped with negative energy. You know the Ambassadors don't like me; they think I'm bad for the community. I know that even Ambassador Symon doesn't like me. I am sure to be discovered and..." With a shiver she let the sentence drop.

"Child," Tatiana said. "Science was only forbidden because in... in..." she stammered and stopped for a moment, a look of pain crossing her ghostly face. "In times past, science has led to much trouble. But I am forbidden to speak of any of that."

"I just don't know how I can hide something like this from everyone." DraDonna said, feeling fear take over. "Didn't you tell me a story once about a man who was mind wiped just for calling the blood muscle in his chest a heart?"

"That was more a case of blasphemy than forbidden science. I know you have a clever mind and that you will find a way to keep others from finding out." She continued quickly, "I am running out of time, DraDonna, and there is still so much to tell you. I need you to look closely into my eyes. You may not understand at first, but I will need you to remember everything I show you."

DraDonna stood on shaky legs and faced her closest friend. It was an odd thing to look into her eyes. Tatiana was mostly transparent, yet DraDonna could still see the color of her lovely dark brown eyes.

"Hold very still, DraDonna. This is forbidden but I am out of time," Tatiana said. Holding the younger woman's gaze, she placed one hand on either side of her head.

DraDonna felt a warm soft sensation pass from the older woman's hands into her mind, and she began to see an image. It was odd at first, and she didn't understand. She could see the ground as if she were flying just a few feet above it. She could hear Tatiana say, "See child, see! What you are looking for is in the ground. See!"

The landscape that she saw changed from the Ambassador's community to the First Councilor's community, to the Second Councilor's community— but they all looked the same; the communities, the lakes, and the mountains all looked so much alike. The vision flashed by quickly. Tatiana showed her odd-looking animals, strange beasts that she never knew existed.

"What are they?" she asked in astonishment. But her questions were only met with silence.

In the vision she also flew slowly by one of the old solace cabins. This must, she thought, have been an image of the past because the cabin looked new. The vision settled so DraDonna could look in the window. She saw a woman about her age with long, dark blonde hair looking through some kind of tool or instrument. "What is that?" DraDonna exclaimed.

"It is a science tool used to look at things so small that one cannot see them with the eye alone." Tatiana said, her voice sounding weak. "She is using it to see the soil." Then the image began to fade along with Tatiana's face. Before the vision completely faded, she heard her old friend whisper, "See!" one last time.

After seeing her friend's soul diminish, DraDonna found that she was standing again on the mountain. It was quiet and she was alone. There weren't even any of the old cloud-like souls left. She began to shiver uncontrollably as tears streamed down her face. "I just don't understand," she sobbed to herself, suddenly struck by a wave of dizziness. She tried to sit back down on the boulder but felt the ground rocking beneath her feet, and she fell. She did not hit the rocky ground of the mountainside like she thought she would; instead she was again falling through the blackness of the abyss.

DraDonna feared she was going to be doomed to fall disembodied through blackness for eternity, when the jarring feeling of landing caused her to sit up and open her eyes. With tears on her face she looked around the room. "I'm home!" She sobbed.

"DraDonna," a sleepy voice said. "What's wrong, my love?"

"DraDevon, it was a dream. But it was real!" she said with tears still running from her eyes. "I saw so many things, but I don't understand."

DraDevon sat up in bed next to her. He put his arm around her shoulders in an effort to comfort his hysterical wife. "It was just a dream. A dream that was brought on by the fact that you missed the evening's energy."

"I know it was a dream, but we're not supposed to remember our dreams. And she told me I have so much to do!"

"You finished the MDC. You don't need to worry about it anymore," he said, misunderstanding her.

"It was so real," she sobbed. "I saw her and there is just so much for me to do. I don't know where to start."

"DraDonna," he said in a firm and gentle voice, "you need to lay back down and go back to sleep. After daybreak you need to take extra energy."

Still feeling the weight of exhaustion pressing down on her, she allowed her husband to pull her back onto the soft mattress. She snuggled close to him and fell asleep again.

This time it was dreamless.

Change
3

DraDonna woke up but felt as if someone had used wood glue on her eyes, because she was having a hard time opening them. When she did manage to get her eyes open, she wished she hadn't. The morning light assaulted her eyes and a pounding began in her head.

She looked over to DraDevon's side of the bed and found it empty. DraDonna knew that he had already left to do one last check on the MDC and then deliver and install it in the Sol home.

She swung her legs over the edge of the bed and stood up. DraDonna felt a little shaky, but she understood why. Her mind and body craved the HEART's energy. She sat back down on the bed for a moment to try to think. But the foggy headache that throbbed in her skull was making it hard.

"Was it real?" she asked the empty room. "Dare I...?" DraDonna went over everything in her mind. It was all so bizarre. She thought the clouds in the sky are old souls? That couldn't be. Old souls died and were welcomed into the HEART.

DraDonna sat and began to talk herself out of everything that she had seen and heard in the dream. She didn't need this in her life. She didn't want things to change. "Besides, science is forbidden," she said.

She stood up once more and walked over to the HEART stone altar. She was going to take in an extra dose of the clean refreshing energy. She wanted it; she needed it. She wanted to be rid of the pain in her head.

With a sigh of relief, DraDonna knelt at the HEART stone altar and placed her hands on the cool white stone. Just the thought of the little blue sparks making their way through her mind and body made her feel a little better.

"Stupid dream," she said to the empty house. "Who remembers dreams anyway?"

H.E.A.R.T. Saga: The Children

She knew the HEART blocked their minds from remembering dreams. Dreams weren't good for anyone to remember, so the HEART's energy removed the memories. People didn't remember their dreams. But she remembered this one. It would just be more proof that she wasn't good for the community if word ever got out that she had remembered a dream.

Yet there was something that Tatiana had said to her about her mind being clear of the energy so that she could contact her. The logic of this did not escape DraDonna. Her body had been drained of the energy last night by working on the MDC.

DraDonna closed her eyes tight in a futile attempt to block out the memories of the dream, but could not. All she could see was those trapped souls and the little points of light not able to get in.

DraDonna wanted more than anything to block the very painful memory. Not too long ago her sister had given birth to a stillborn baby. The sorrow was still so fresh, and unwanted tears streamed down her face again. They weren't just for her sister. DraDonna had a feeling that if her sister couldn't have a baby, then there was the possibility that she wouldn't be able to have a baby either. She knew that DraDevon was hoping, in the next few years, that the HEART would allow them to have a baby and that it would have her copper colored hair.

She took her hands off the stone and wrapped her arms around herself, trying to shut out the pain of her sister's loss. She wanted to shut out blaring fears of her own as well. "It's true," she sobbed as she sat there at the HEART stone altar. Rocking back and forth, she let the pain out along with her tears.

She took several deep breaths to calm herself before standing up. She wiped the tears from her eyes and face with the back of her hand. She walked into the bathroom on shaky legs with the thought that a shower would help her feel a little better.

H.E.A.R.T. Saga: The Children

After she removed the rumpled clothing that she had worn for over a day, DraDonna stepped into the stream of hot water and sighed with relief. Thinking only of the hot water, she was able to block out any thoughts of dreams and feelings of loss. As she cleaned her work-soiled body, she felt some of the stress wash away, taking with it her raw emotion.

After her shower, she walked to her room with the towel wrapped modestly around her body. She opened the drawers to the dresser that she had made and chose her clothes for the day: a long tan skirt, white linen shirt, and long brown vest. She pulled her work boots on over white linen socks feeling slightly rebellious.

"Let people call me unladylike, I'm going to protect my feet!" she said. As she walked out of her house she decided to set aside all that she had seen in the dream.

DraDonna was determined to make it in time to help DraDevon with the Sol family's MDC, but she had only taken a few steps down the path to the road when she noticed the trees in her yard. Wrapped around the base of the trees were the vines Tatiana had shown her in the dream, the ones with the white and purple flowers.

With trepidation in her step, she walked over and bent down to smell one of the light purple blossoms. It had a clean sharp smell that eased some of the foggy headache she'd had from the time she woke up.

She plucked a piece of the vine with several flowers attached to it. The vine itself was medium green with clusters of six leaves that were slightly darker in hue.

DraDonna took a look around her and made a mental note that the plant was growing everywhere. Some of the blossoms were purple and some were white, but she could tell that they were all the same plant. She mused to herself why she never noticed these lovely little flowers before.

She took a deep breath, closed her eyes and put the plant in her mouth. She chewed cautiously. The first thing that she noticed was the taste: the leaves were sharp, but there was also warm sweetness in the blossom. Very quickly she felt this warmth spread to her head, clearing her headache.

After swallowing, any uncertainty over what Tatiana had asked her to do in the dream began to dissipate.

She knew she needed to do this. Just how she was going to do it she didn't know. Getting caught using science would get her mind wiped. DraDonna knew that if she and DraDevon were ever going to have a baby, she would have to work hard to figure out a way to do as Tatiana had told her.

DraDonna grabbed the end of her skirt, leaned over again and plucked several stalks of the Traveler's Joy, stashing them in the makeshift pocket.

Before she could straighten up she heard her sister's voice. It startled her.

"What are you doing picking those worthless plants?" JorMelony asked.

"JorMelony, spying on other people is a very unbecoming quality in a daughter of the HEART." DraDonna teased her sister. A little worried about what her sister was thinking, DraDonna questioned her carefully. "How long have you been standing there?"

"Just long enough to think you have gone energy mad, little Donna."

"Don't call me that!" she snapped. "I'm a married woman now. Just because you're my big sister doesn't mean you can treat me with disrespect all my life. You will address me with my pre-name," she said with more sharpness than she meant.

"DraDonna, don't get so upset. I'm sorry I didn't use your pre name, I didn't mean any disrespect. I just came over because I was worried about you. I heard that you left the gathering before the energy yesterday." JorMelony continued with a kinder tone in her voice. "DraDonna, please tell me why you are picking those flowers."

Even though she was touched by her sister's gentle demeanor and loving concern, she didn't feel ready to share with anyone just yet what she had seen and heard in her dream... let alone admit that she could still remember it. "Thank you for coming to check on me. I'm feeling a little...

off. But you don't need to worry, as you know I was born off." DraDonna tried to joke.

"You shouldn't say such untrue things about yourself. You are a cherished daughter of the HEART who loves you, and I know you love her." There was great affection for her younger sister in JorMelony's voice. "You shouldn't listen to the idle gossip of the people in our community."

"I'm happy to hear that you don't agree with them."

"You know, I've always loved you for who you are. Don't let anyone in any of the communities bully you into changing, DraDonna."

"Thanks," she said, trying not to cry. "I'll see you later. I've not yet had my morning meal." DraDonna excused herself without looking at her sister.

"May the HEART bless your day." The younger sister said as she headed back toward the front door of her home.

DraDonna glanced back over her shoulder at her sister's concerned face and then walked back in the front door, wiping tears from her eyes for the second time that morning. She walked quickly to the bathroom and took a clean towel from the shelf of the linen cabinet, wrapping the Traveler's Joy in it as she walked back into the bedroom.

Not knowing what to do with the small bundle, she set it on the little nightstand next to her side of the bed. Even though she was hungry, she skipped the morning meal. She needed to hurry so she could catch up with her husband at the Sol home.

Swiftly she exited through the front door. She stopped for a moment and looked around for her sister, but JorMelony was nowhere to be seen. While looking around, her gaze was drawn to the shop that she and DraDevon shared behind her house.

Looking around to be sure no one was watching, she plucked another sprig of Traveler's Joy and ate it. Then with a purposeful stride began to walk toward the shop.

DraDonna did notice how good she felt. It was different from how she felt after taking energy. The energy made her feel like she had been wrapped in a comfortable blanket. The Traveler's Joy helped her feel awake. More awake than she had ever been in her life.

She reached the door to the shop but feared to go inside. She never felt right in her job, but loved that she and her husband worked together. But that might all come to an end.

DraDonna knew that she would have to make peace with this change and somehow find a way to tell DraDevon what was going on, hoping with all of the love of the HEART he would stick by her though it all.

Resolved, she pulled the door open and walked straight to her workbench. She knelt down in front of it, opening the doors to the cabinet on the bottom. She reached inside and pushed all but one of the hand tools aside. She picked up an unremarkable short metal rod with a slight hook on one end. She pushed the hooked end of the rod into an ordinary knothole and pulled.

With just a little force, a small panel came out. She set it aside and reached into the oblong hole in the bottom of her workbench. She felt around for a moment until her hand fell on what she was looking for. She brought it up out of the hole and blew the sawdust off the small elaborately carved wooden box.

She held the box to her chest for a moment, indulging in a memory for which she knew she didn't have time, but she couldn't help it. The emotion was too strong.

She remembered the time her mother had given the box to her. She had told little Donna then of how Tatiana had given it to her just after her birth. Tatiana had told her mother that she was an exceptional child, that such a special child needed a special gift.

DraDonna stood up and placed the box on her workbench and slid the top off. She looked inside at the contents. Two small beautifully bound notebooks and three well-sharpened pencils were inside. She took these out, not wanting to leave them behind, but she also had a strong feeling that they could be of use to her in what she had to do.

She tucked them into the belt line of her skirt and draped her vest down over it, completely hiding this rare prize.

With strengthened resolve, DraDonna turned to head for the door, but DraDevon's workbench caught her eye. She felt a tug on her soul and sat down on the dusty floor of the workshop. She tried desperately not to cry. She loved him so much. DraDonna didn't want to lose the only one who had made her feel like a good person, worthy of love and respect.

"I just have to find a way to tell him," she told the empty shop.

She got up off the floor and walked to the door. She felt her resolve return as she left the shop. No matter what happened, she would be sure that DraDevon didn't get hurt.

Plans
4

DraDonna felt like the mid-morning heat was going to smother her. The heat was also causing her to sweat as she walked. She had the annoying feeling of her bright copper curls sticking to her scalp. She quickened her pace even though she knew it would make her sweat more; she needed to get there before people began to gossip. The last thing she wanted was for DraDevon's name to get dragged down because she didn't show up for an install.

DraDonna's mind was distracted. She needed to find a way to tell her husband what was going on, as well give a good explanation to the community. She did not want to get caught doing anything science-like. She would get mind wiped for sure.

Taking the advice that Tatiana gave her in the dream, DraDonna looked around her as she walked. She was trying to notice everything. She looked up at the squirming clouds in the sky and had an odd feeling she was being watched. She then looked down at the dirt that she walked on. It looked the same as always— rich and dark. It was perfect soil. The plants always grew with no problems.

Next she looked at the trees. There were always the same three all over the community. One had pointed leaves shaped like a hand with branches close to the ground. Another one was tall and slender that had branches that were thin and swept low to the ground. The third kind of tree grew a kind of pinkish white blossoms. It too was low to the ground, but never grew very large and had weak knurly wood. If any of the trees had names, she didn't know what they were.

She finally looked up to the mountain range known as The Ambassadors Mountain. It was a lovely thing to look at. But there was something about the shape of the mountain that bothered her, but she couldn't quite figure out what it was. She was sure it had something to do with the dream.

Looking at the mountain gave her an idea. The solace cabins were just sitting there. No one really took a couples' solace anymore, but she didn't know why they couldn't.

DraDonna could feel a tickly sensation of excitement in her stomach as she approached the Sol home: they could tell everybody that they wanted to take a couples solace. It was a special time that a couple would take in the first year of their marriage to help them bond as husband and wife. The couple would go spend time alone in one of the four cabins that were in each of the communities. DraDonna knew her plan was a good one. She could do all the science she wanted and no one would be the wiser.

She came to the front door and raised her fist to knock, but the door was yanked open before she had the chance. Standing in the open doorway was SolKaren.

SolKaren was a formidable woman of fifty. She was short of stature with gray eyes and mousey brown hair. Her job was that of a PNL energy guide. Women went to her when they were expecting a baby. She used special energy stones that read the status of the baby and projected all information to the HEART, so that the HEART could determine the child's life and identity. The PNL energy stones also monitored the mother and corrected any problems there might be.

SolBruce delivered the babies with the help of his wife and the HEART's energy. But there had been a lot of miscarriages and stillbirths lately. It was a great surprise to everyone in the communities that this was happening and that the HEART could not foresee and fix it.

DraDonna was trying to tell herself that this was why SolKaren and SolBruce had been so ill tempered lately, but she knew better. The Sol family had always been mean to her. She'd heard from her mother that SolKaren suggested when she was born that she should shave her hair off. She said that the copper curls would cause a problem with other little girls. Her mother politely refused and allowed the bright hair to grow.

But SolKaren had been right; DraDonna's hair did cause a problem. Some of the boys at school would tease her, telling her that her hair was a sign of a HEART's curse. There had even been a few times when a girl would be sitting behind her in class and would snip off a few of her curls. Her teachers, in the interest of classroom bliss, would make her wear a hat and seat her in the back of the classroom.

"HEART's greeting SolKaren," DraDonna said in a bright formal manner. "I trust that DraDevon is installing the MDC, and that it is to your liking?"

"Yes, DraDonna." SolKaren's voice was so cold that the words froze inside DraDonna's ears. "DraDevon's work is adequate," she said briskly.

"Happy to hear it. I should go in and see if my husband needs any help." She hoped SolKaren would step aside and let her in with out any confrontation.

But SolKaren held her ground. "You know, DraDonna," SolKaren began, "it is job disrespectful of you to not show up to one of your own installs. I could report you to the Ambassador for this, but I won't... this time."

With all the good manners she could muster, DraDonna bowed slightly and said, "Thank you for your patience and indulgence SolKaren. I am sorry that I was late this morning, but I was up very late last night working on your MDC, so as you can imagine I was not feeling very well when I woke up."

"Just don't let it happen again when you are on a project for me or I'll see to it that you're mind wiped." SolKaren huffed and stepped aside to let her pass.

DraDonna walked through the front door and looked around the main living area of another typical home, only this one was a little larger to accommodate a family that has had children as well as grandchildren. In looking around, the young carpenter couldn't help but feel a sense of pride, spotting pieces of furniture that she and her husband made.

She found her husband in the kitchen putting the last screws through the MDC into the wall, as SolBruce held the cabinet in place. "HEART's greeting SolBruce. I hope you find your new MDC to your liking," she said as she approached.

"It will do," he answered.

Looking at him, DraDonna suppressed a smile of amusement. SolBruce was indeed his wife's perfect match; he looked just like her. He was short and round with gray hair and gray eyes. "I'm sorry that I was not here earlier SolBruce, but I was not feeling well at daybreak."

"I'm happy to see that you're feeling better, my wife," DraDevon broke in with a dazzling smile.

"Much better, thank you. Are you finished with the install?" She walked over to inspect the cabinet.

"I just put in the last screw and I think I'm ready to go," he said, putting the screwdriver in his tool belt. He put his arm around her shoulders and directed her toward the open front door. "I hope you enjoy the new MDC, SolBruce. It has been our pleasure to serve your family."

With his loving arm around her, they walked out the front door and down the path to the road.

"I'm sorry I didn't get up in time to help you with this," she said. "But I have an idea. Something that I think would be good for us."

"What do you mean?" He replied with a curious look on his face.

"Well," DraDonna began. "I think that you and I should go on a couples' solace."

DraDevon stopped short and looked at her. "Are you serious? That sounds great, but I don't think anyone has done that in a long time."

"Yes, I am very serious. Sure people stopped doing it, but I don't think that it has been forbidden."

"Well my love, I think it's a great idea. But we should probably go and clear this with Ambassador Symon first," he said with a grin.

DraDonna agreed, and they walked excitedly up the road to the temple office, where they hoped to find and speak to Ambassador Symon.

DraDevon knocked softly on the door to the small office. After standing there for a few moments with no answer DraDonna said, "Maybe you should knock a little harder."

"I don't think he's in there," DraDevon replied. "Perhaps we could come back later."

The couple turned to leave, but to their surprise the door was yanked open and a rumpled looking Ambassador Symon was standing in the doorway.

"HEART's greeting..."

"What do you want?" the Ambassador interrupted tersely.

"Sorry to disturb you Ambassador, but we have something that we would like to ask you about," DraDonna said, hoping he would be a little nicer. She needed him to approve their couples' solace.

"Well, what is it DraDonna? I have lots of things to do," he said, letting the impatience show in his voice as well as on his face.

"Ambassador, if you would approve it, my wife and I would like to go on a couples' solace," DraDevon said, jumping right in. "I know that no one has gone on one for a long time, but we would really like to go so we can bond further as a couple and commune with the HEART."

The Ambassador's handsome yet tired face hardened as he looked closely at the young couple in front of him. "Well, people haven't felt like they needed to do a couples' solace for quite some time. Is there some kind of a problem of which I need to inform the HEART?"

"No Ambassador," DraDevon answered quickly. "It is very much the opposite; we are very happy together. We would just like a little bit of time alone away from the gossip of the community.

"DraDonna would not have a problem with gossip if she would follow the rules of the community a little closer," he said rudely. "In any case, the cabins have not been used for a long time, so I don't know what shape they're in."

"Oh we don't mind fixing the cabin up. After all, you know that we have skills in this kind of work. Besides, it will be another great way that we can serve the HEART," DraDevon said with excitement in his voice.

Ambassador Symon stood there glaring at the both of them, his face as hard as ever, yet not saying anything.

"Please, Ambassador." DraDonna begged. "This would mean a lot to us."

Her pleading seemed to cause something to snap within the Ambassador. He said in an angry retort, "Couples haven't needed to do this for a long time, so I will have to commune with the HEART before I can give you an answer." With that he pushed past them in a huff, looking back over his shoulder at DraDonna as he reached the temple door. "Just because my predecessor Tatiana thought you were special DraDonna, doesn't mean you can do whatever you want. Our communities have rules that everyone has to follow, special or not." He yanked open the temple door and quickly closed it with a bang when he had walked through.

"Don't mind him you two. He's in one of his moods again." A lovely feminine voice came from behind them in the office.

They turned around to find First Councilor Jude standing in the doorway. Her golden hair fell around her face.

"Councilor Jude!" they both exclaimed happily. "We didn't know that you were in the Ambassadors community," DraDonna said. "What brings you here?"

"I used energy travel just now. I actually need to speak to Ambassador Symon about a local matter," the First Councilor explained. Looking a little closer at the hurt look in DraDonna's eyes Councilor Jude went on to say, "Hey, you two, don't worry about him. I knew Ambassador Tatiana. She did believe that you were special DraDonna. I agree with her; you will do great things."

Their friendly conversation was interrupted by the sound of the temple door opening. Ambassador Symon emerged from the dim interior looking even more irritated than he did when he went in.

He walked swiftly over to the waiting couple and formally said, "The HEART, our MOTHER, has granted your request for a couples' solace. Be sure that you finish up any projects before you leave tomorrow. And be on time tomorrow for a send-off gathering. Now if you will excuse me, I have other business to attend to." He then greeted Councilor Jude with a slight nod, barely placing his hand at her elbow to direct her back into the office.

He shut the door with an aggravated thud.

"Wow," said DraDevon. "I don't think he took a breath during that whole speech."

DraDonna giggled a little and said somewhat jokingly, "Don't be disrespectful DraDevon. He's letting us go on a couples' solace!" Their jovial spirit continued as he draped his arm across her shoulders and they began walking down the road to their home. "Well, young lady, we'd better get going. We have a lot to do."

DraDonna stopped and turned to look at DraDevon's face. "I really feel like I should go back and check with Ambassador Symon about who our work will be rerouted to. I would hate to be accused of being job disrespectful again."

DraDevon chuckled a little bit, and called to her as she jogged back up the street, "Don't worry about that. I would worry about him. He looked like he was going to mind-wipe First Councilor Jude."

When DraDonna approached the tiny office building, she saw that the door was closed but could hear raised voices inside. She raised her hand to knock, but stopped, mesmerized by the sound of the Ambassador and the First Councilor having a heated argument.

Councilor Jude's voice was muffled with the sound of her tears as she said, "Symon, You can't kiss me like that again and just pretend that it didn't mean anything, because it does!"

DraDonna carefully peeked around at the window by the door and saw Councilor Jude lovingly reach up and caress Ambassador Symon's face. At first he smiled and closed his eyes as he relished her soft touch, but then he reached up in a firm yet gentle manner, pushing her hand away.

"Jude," he said, "we are servants of the HEART, so you know that we cannot let this go any further. We should have never have kissed in the first place, and what just happened a few minutes ago was wrong. It was just taking us down a road that you and I know we cannot travel together!"

"But I love you, Symon." Jude sobbed. "I have loved you all my life and I know that you love me too." He opened his mouth to say something but she stopped him. "Please hear me out Symon. You know that I learned the truth last year, and I have come up with a plan so that we can be together. It's so simple…" She let the sentence drop at the tormented look on his face.

"Jude, I do love you. I have always loved you. That's why I have been avoiding you for the last few months. It hurts me to be near you and not be able to express my love for you. There have been many generations… other Ambassadors… before me. They managed to keep everything on this world running smoothly, without being married. I will not let it all fall apart on my watch."

"But I have a plan," Jude said with desperation in her voice.

"I told you before I don't want to hear it, Jude!" he said with firmness in his voice. He turned his back on her and walked over to his desk. "You'd better get back to your community now, and tell them about the special gathering tomorrow just after daybreak." He dismissed her. "If you will excuse me, I have to make my own preparations so I can properly handle this… Dra situation."

DraDonna was horrified at what she had just witnessed, terrified of being discovered. She quietly backed away, and then ran as fast as she could down the road toward her home.

Understand

5

DraDevon did not look up from his EDUstone as his wife rushed through the front door, slammed it behind her, and then leaned up against it so she could catch her breath. She pushed herself off the door and leaned over the window, looking out.

"DraDonna, you missed the midday meal." He looked up at her and asked, "What happened? Did Ambassador Symon snap at you again?"

DraDonna looked out the window as she tried to catch her breath, ignoring his question. After she managed to get her breathing under control, she walked on shaky legs to where DraDevon was in the main living area. "What are you looking at?" DraDonna asked, looking at the EDUstone in his hands.

"DraDonna, please tell me what happened. You look like he told you he was going to mind wipe you."

"No, no. It was nothing like that. I umm, will tell you about it later," she stammered. "So is this a map of all the solace cabins?"

"Yes," he said as he handed her the EDUstone.

On this stone was the image of their world with all the cabins marked by little red triangles. In each of the three lands there was a mountain range and large lake. There were two cabins in each of the mountain ranges and two by each of the lakes.

"DraDevon, would you think I was energy mad if I said that it would be fun for us to visit each of the cabins?"

"No," he replied in a teasing manner. "Not if we go by energy travel."

At this she handed the EDUstone back to him. She pulled the notebooks and the pencils out from their hiding place in the belt line of her skirt and began writing down where each of the cabins was on the map.

"But DraDonna, why would we need to go to all of them?" he asked her as he spied the small treasure in her hands. "Wait, where did you get those?"

"Well my husband, a few days after my birth, Ambassador Tatiana came to visit my mother and me. She brought a gift, as Ambassadors or Councilors usually do at the birth of a child. But she had heard of my umm, special hair. The gift that she brought my mother was different. It was a small wood box and inside was notebooks and pencils. She also told my mother that a special child deserves a special gift."

DraDonna looked up at him and said in an anxious voice, "Almost every one I have ever known has said that I was wrong in some way, but Ambassador Tatiana maintained that I really was exceptional. It has always been hard for me to believe that I'm anything other than a mistake made by the HEART..."

DraDevon was worried by her emotional story. He stood from his chair and dropped the EDUstone on the seat. He walked the few paces to where she stood and put his arms around her and pulled her into a tender embrace. "My beautiful wife, Tatiana is not the only one who believes you are special. I also understand how you feel. People in the community bullied my mother quite a bit because of the pre name that the HEART gave her when she married my Dad."

He tenderly slid his hand up her back, stopping for a moment on the back of her neck, then cupping both hands on either side of her face. "I know how fantastic you are. I always have." He gently pulled her face to him and tenderly kissed her.

The sweetness of his lips moving on hers sparked a growing heat inside her soul. DraDonna matched his kiss with her own growing passion. She twined her arms around his waist so she could pull herself closer to the man who made her feel like her soul was on fire.

His kiss grew even more intense as he slid his hands down to the small of her back, pressing her body even closer to his own.

"I love you so much, my beautiful wife," he said, his lips leaving hers. He then left a hot trail of kisses on the side of her face, down to her neck, causing her to her gasp with the tingling pleasure of his heated lips on her skin.

The young lovers' intimate embrace was interrupted by a quick decisive knock at the door.

"DraDonna, DraDevon! Open up!" said a sharply pitched voice. "The HEART's daylight is waning."

Both of them laughed a little as DraDevon walked to the door. He opened it with a smile. "HEART's greeting, MayEdna! What brings you to our home?"

The thin older seamstress smiled brightly and walked right in. "HEART's greeting DraDevon. HEART's greeting DraDonna. I heard the news. You two are going on a couples' solace, and you will need travel packs. So, I need you to tell me if you will be doing any traveling on foot, or if you will be doing all of your traveling by HEART's energy?"

DraDonna wondered if MayEdna was going to fit any more words in that one breath. "HEART's greeting to you too, MayEdna," she said with amusement in her voice. "I'm surprised you know. I didn't think anyone had been told yet."

"Oh, my dear," MayEdna laughed a little. "You know, I have my ways of finding things out."

DraDonna smiled at the kindly older lady. "I think we're going to do most all of our travels by energy, but if it's not too much trouble we could use some special packs that would hang at our belts for carrying some of our tools."

"Why in the HEART of the planet would you need tools? Judging by what I saw the two of you doing when I knocked on your door, I am sure you two will find better things to do than to fix things with your tools," she said with a little wink. "Nevertheless, MayJordan and I will have the packs ready for you before the evening's energy."

With a nod and a smile to each of them, MayEdna turned and briskly walked out the door, leaving a lighter mood in her wake.

After hearing the door close, DraDevon burst out laughing. "She is so wise, DraDonna. We will have plenty of other things to do." His tone was playful. "Why don't we leave these tools behind and…?" DraDevon let the sentence drop and smiled at her in a suggestive way.

"DraDevon," DraDonna said, feeling the heat of a blush in her face, "You and I being alone with nothing else to do but make love sounds so wonderful, but we did promise Ambassador Symon that we would fix up the cabins. Therefore we will need our tools, so we had better start packing them."

They spent the next several hours in their stuffy dusty shop going over what they needed and did not need on such a trip. DraDonna went through all of their tools with nervous energy, not sure what they would need.

Each of her carpentry tools just didn't seem right to her. She knew none of them would help her with what she needed to do. But with the reason that DraDonna had been giving everyone, she knew that she needed to choose some of them.

She grew more nervous about what she was going to tell DraDevon at the evening's energy time, but she was getting very hungry and wanted to go back to the house and have the evening meal. She struggled with the idea of having to tell her husband that she wasn't going to take the evening energy with him.

"DraDevon," she called out across the shop.

"Yes, my wife?"

"It's getting close to evening meal. I think we should finish up."

"You're right, I'm hungry." DraDevon stood up with a large wooden box in his hands and grunted under the weight of it. "I'm not sure how much of this we'll need, so I'm going to take all of it up to the house. I'll choose what I'm going to take when I see what packs the May's give us."

"Why don't you set it on my work bench?" she suggested. "I need to add some of my own tools to that box and then I'll help you carry it to the house."

"Good idea," he said, grunting as he set the heavy box down with a thud.

DraDonna stood up from where she had been kneeling on the floor next to her workbench, trying to choose the tools she would need to bring. She looked in the box and then dropped the few of her own tools that she picked out into the box with a chorus of metal clangs.

"Is this the box that Tatiana gave your mother?" he asked, reaching across the top of her workbench and picking up the ornately carved wood.

"Yes," she said with a hint of melancholy in her voice.

"That reminds me, DraDevon. I don't know why I haven't shared this with you before, but..." DraDonna reached into the belt line of her skirt and pulled out one of the notebooks and pencils, then handed them to her husband. "I want you to have these."

"I don't..."

"No, DraDevon, I should have told you that I had these when we were married. I'm sorry."

"DraDonna, you don't need to apologize to me, you were right to hide them. The HEART hasn't made paper and pencils in a long time, so they're a rare gift. I don't know what I would do with them."

"You're a smart man," she said with a twinkle in her eyes. "After all, you married me, didn't you?"

Matching her playful tone he said, "Yes. Well, I didn't have much of a choice, now did I?'

She laughed, "Put it someplace safe, welder man, and help me get this box to the house."

Amongst a lot of grunting, groaning, and sweat, they managed to get the box across the yard to their house and just inside the front door where they dropped it with a loud clang of tools. Before either of them had a chance to complain about how hard the box was to carry to the house, they heard MayEdna's distinct rap on the door.

With a little bit of a sigh, DraDevon pulled the door open for the cheerful seamstress. "HEART's greetings once again!" She called brightly as she crossed the threshold, extending the bundle in her left arm to DraDonna. "I hope that they're all to your liking. We did have to rush things a bit," she said, as if she was excusing shoddy workmanship.

The packs were anything but shoddy. They were beautifully made out of a strong woolen weave that had been dyed light brown and had been monogrammed with a vivid blue DD on each bag. There were two large knapsacks with drawstring tops, two medium sized packs with straps that tied around the waist, and a smaller bag that also tied around the waist.

"Thank you MayEdna! These are fine packs!" DraDevon exclaimed.

"We are just doing the HEART's work DraDevon. You two have a nice trip and don't work too much." MayEdna turned on her heel and bounded back out the front door and down the path to the road.

DraDevon closed the door and suggested that they have their evening meal. So, DraDonna deposited the bundle of packs on one of the chairs in the main living area. They both walked into the kitchen and got their meal out of the MDC. DraDonna questioned if they should take some other working supplies, but DraDevon just shrugged his shoulder and said, "No, the HEART will provide."

"Speaking of the HEART," he said as he stood from the table. "It's almost energy time; I think I hear the first toll now." Proving him right, they both heard the decisive toll announcing that it was almost time for the evening's energy.

Having no thought of what she was going to tell him and feeling a little flustered, she stood quickly and said, "Excuse me for a moment." She quickly walked to their room and retrieved a sprig of Traveler's Joy from the folded up towel on her nightstand and began to eat it.

Not knowing that DraDevon had followed her into the room, he startled her when he said, "You'd better hurry, it's almost time."

She whipped around in surprise, too disconcerted to say anything.

"What are you eating?" He asked in confusion.

DraDonna swallowed and started to say, "I don't…"

"Come on," he said, interrupting her and grabbing her by the wrist. He quickly pulled her with him to the HEART stone altar.

"DraDevon, I can't." She told him.

"You can't? Do you mean you can't take the energy?"

"No."

"I don't understand, come on and kneel with me. We can talk about this after the energy."

"I just can't, DraDevon." She said with tears in her eyes. "I'm sorry."

The second toll rang, announcing that it was now time for the HEART's energy. DraDevon hurriedly knelt down and placed his hand on the HEART stone, quickly saying the ritual words just in time to receive the special strong evening's intake of the energy. After about 30 seconds of blue light running through his body, he stood up, looking calm and even a little sleepy. He saw that she was still standing where she was before the energy time. He looked at closely and saw that tears were running down her face.

"Please tell me what's going on. Did Ambassador Symon revoke your right to take in the HEART's energy?"

Without saying a word, she motioned for him to sit on one of the chairs in the living area. She quietly followed him and then moved the packs from the seat of the chair to the floor before taking the remaining seat.

She took a shaky breath, wiped her face with the back of her hand for the third time that day and began to explain. "My oddly colored hair has always been trouble for me. Because of it, I have been marked all my life as a troublemaker in the community whether I was one or not. But my family and Ambassador Tatiana always told me not to listen to anyone. They said that The HEART our Mother loves me the way I am, and that I was made special for a reason. In fact, just this morning, JorMelony lectured me on this. I don't know that I have ever truly believed any of them. It seemed that their voices were outnumbered by everyone else who continued to treat me as though I was some kind of blasphemous mistake that the HEART had made. But after you and I were married last year, I saw that you did love me. Not because you had to, but because in your eyes I was perfect the way I am. I started to think that if you could see me this way, then maybe there wasn't anything wrong with me."

"Of course there isn't..." DraDevon started to say, but DraDonna interrupted him.

"Please, let me finish." She went on. "Last night I was working really hard on that MDC for the Sol family. I know that they don't like me, and I was trying so hard to impress them, not so much for my sake as it was for yours. I didn't want them to think badly of you if we didn't deliver the MDC on time. I was also trying to hurry because I didn't want to miss the evening's energy with you. So I used up all my energy reserves, and I still didn't make it in time.

The peculiar thing is that when I got in bed, I had this dream. I can remember all of it, even now. In the dream I saw Ambassador Tatiana's soul. She told me that my mind was free of the energy's clouding effects and that was why she was able to contact me. She showed me a plant called Traveler's Joy and said that I should eat it, to help my mind get over the energy. She also told me that I was a scientist in my soul—not a carpenter. She told me that there was something wrong with the world and that it was in the ground and that I had to find it in order set free all the souls of those who have died." Another tear trickled down her face.

"I'm not sure," she said, "what all of this means. And that's not even the worst part of all this. Tatiana also showed me that these trapped souls were blocking new souls from being born, and that's why there haven't been any babies born lately." She stopped and waited for him to say something.

He was silent at first, turning his head to look out the window at the mountain and the lake. More than a little overwhelmed by everything that his wife had told him, he continued to look out the window, trying to sort out all the complicated thoughts and feelings that he had swirling around in his head. He just didn't know what to say.

H.E.A.R.T. Saga: The Children

The longer he stayed quiet, the more nervous DraDonna felt. Tears filled her eyes. She had so many fears, but the strongest was the fear that someone might try to stop her; that she would be convicted of community upset— or even worse, science—and be sentenced to negative energy... Mostly, though, she feared that DraDevon would not go with her, would not love her anymore.

"Please say something, DraDevon," she begged. "It would mean everything to me if you would help me with this. I know that this is something I have to do for the good of everyone in all of the communities. But mostly... for us... so we can have children." Again she stopped, waiting for him to say something.

He turned his head back to look at her with a little sadness in his eyes. "What about the couples' solace? I have to say, I'm disappointed you're using that as a cover and not to draw us closer as a couple." He stopped for a second as a new thought came to him. A look of deep concern crossed his face as he asked, "Could this all be just energy madness? I'm guessing that instead of taking energy since last night, you have been eating that plant. Couldn't all this be just a part of the depression and madness?"

She stood up from her chair, walking over and kneeling down in front of him. She looked him in the eye. "Look at me closely," she told him. "Tell me, do I look mad to you? A little more emotional than normal, sure, but do I really look mad to you? I know this all sounds very odd, but it's true and I need you. I need you to help me do this. You would know better than anyone if I was energy mad."

Again he was silent, but only for a moment. He looked in her eyes and said with a look of good humor in his own, "You must be energy mad if you think I wouldn't follow you anywhere you would go for the rest of your days."

DraDonna sobbed, leaning forward and hugging him around the waist. Then she put her head on his chest and said with her voice muffled by his shirt, "I thank the HEART everyday for you!"

"Well just so you know... Tatiana isn't the only one who thinks you're something special."

"Oh!" DraDonna exclaimed as she got to her feet. "You just reminded me. Come with me, I need to show you something." She grabbed his hand and pulled him to his feet. "I can prove to you that this is all for real."

"I believe you, DraDonna. You don't need to prove anything to me."

"I know, but just the same I need you to understand," she said as she took him out the front door.

Even though it was evening time and the daylight was waning, they could still see the sky. She pointed to the misty cloud cover that completely covered the sky in all directions.

He shrugged his shoulders and said, "I don't understand what you mean. It's just the sky. The same cloud cover as always."

"DraDevon, don't you remember hearing from some of the older people? They told tales of patches of blue in the sky. But now no one does. It's just clouds all the time all over the world. Look closer my friend, those are not clouds. They're old souls that cannot move on. For some reason they're trapped, and if we don't find a way to set them free, there will be no more babies."

DraDevon looked into the evening sky and gasped, "I swear by the HEART that one of the clouds has a face and it's looking at me." A little shaken by what he saw, he pulled her back into the house with him. "Those clouds are the old souls aren't they?" He wrapped his arms around her and whispered in her ear "I'm so sorry I didn't believe you. It all sounded just so..."

She hugged her precious husband and said softly, "It's okay. I had a hard time believing it at first myself. I'm just so happy that I have you."

He pulled back just a little and gently placed his hands on either side of her face. "You have me, DraDonna. Body and soul forever!"

He stroked her lips with his thumb and then kissed her passionately. She melted into him and matched his desire with her own lips, kissing him back just as hard while gripping the back of his shirt, pulling her passion heated body closer to his. DraDevon's kisses had always made her heart race, but this time the heat of him made her feel like she was on fire and the very pulse of her soul depended on the movement of his lips.

The heat of their passion was so intense that DraDonna was sure they had melted in to one being. She knew when they expressed their love for each other in such a sensual way that their souls were intertwined for all eternity.

Later that night they were snuggled up in bed, their clothing scattered all over the room.

DraDevon stroked her hair affectionately, saying very tenderly, "You know we will be cleared to conceive a baby in the next two years. I hope that when we do have a baby that it's a girl and that she will have your beautiful copper hair."

"I hope so, too," she replied, melancholy in her voice.

"Why do you sound so sad, my love?" he asked her with concern.

"I was just thinking about my sister. Almost two years ago JorMelony and JorRobert conceived a baby boy and he was stillborn. No one could figure out why. No matter how many prayers were said to the HEART, they just could not figure out why it happened. It was so painful to see this perfect little baby boy laying in my sister's arms with no life in his little body. This pain just didn't go away for me no matter how much energy I took in. But at least now I know why. It's all the old souls. They're trapped. They're blocking the new souls."

"Well, I'm not going to worry about it too much," he told her. "If anyone can find out what's wrong with the world and fix it, it's you."

DraDonna giggled a little at this. She relished how safe she felt in his arms and she snuggled closer to him. It didn't take long before they both fell asleep.

Advice
6

For the second time, DraDonna's body rested comfortably among the soft folds of the blankets and in the strong arms of the man she loved, but she felt her mind falling into that familiar dark abyss.

Just as it was in the first dream, DraDonna found herself standing on the same mountaintop surrounded by the cloud-like souls. But unlike before, Tatiana was standing in front of her in full transparent form.

"Tatiana!" DraDonna exclaimed with surprise.

"Hello child, our time is short." The old soul greeted her.

"I'm a little surprised to be here again, but I'm happy to see you. I need your help, Tatiana. I just don't know where I'm supposed to start."

"Notice everything, Little Donna. It will give you clues, but mostly what you need to find is in the ground."

Again hearing her old friend use her childhood name gave DraDonna comfort in this odd dreamscape. "I don't understand what you mean by that, Tatiana. What is in the ground?"

"I can't tell you that, I am bound by my oath to the HEART."

"Well then why did you bring me here?" DraDonna asked in confusion.

"I have brought you here to warn you that there is not much time. You have to hurry, and there is someone among you that is not who they seem. This person is plotting something and will try to stop you to be sure that their plan is successful; by then it will be too late." Tatiana hurriedly went on with her warning, her voice sounding weak. "Be careful in whom you confide, and do not wait for the gathering. If you do so, this person will stop you from leaving."

"But who is it?" DraDonna called to Tatiana's rapidly fading figure.

"Free us..." was the only reply as the darkness once again gathered around DraDonna.

The dizzy sensation took over again, making her feel as though she was falling into nothing. DraDonna gasped and opened her eyes to find that she was still in bed with her husband close beside her.

She had the urge to get up to place her hands on the HEART stone altar, take in a large dose of the energy, and then go back to dreamless sleep. But instead of doing that, she got up and packed the small bag with the Traveler's Joy and began to dress.

Even though DraDonna tried not to make too much noise, her sudden activity woke up DraDevon. In a half-sleepy but suggestive voice, DraDevon called to his wife, "Hey, beautiful lady. Come back to bed."

"DraDevon, I saw Tatiana again."

"What did she say?" he asked, suddenly very much awake.

"Well, she told me again that what I need to find is in the ground, and she begged me to free them again. But there is something else. She told me that someone we know is not who they seem to be and that they have a plan, and they will try to stop us from interfering in their plan."

DraDevon sat up in bed, "Someone has a plan?" he asked astonished. "Did Tatiana tell you who it was?"

"No, she didn't." DraDonna answered him. "All she told me was that there isn't much time."

"Well, then who do you think it is?" DraDevon asked her with worry.

"I'm not sure." she replied. "But I have a feeling that it is Ambassador Symon."

"What makes you think it's him?" DraDevon inquired.

"You need a better reason than because he is ill tempered towards you. DraDonna, he's ill-tempered to everyone." DraDevon said with a little disdain.

"There's more to it, DraDevon. I haven't yet told you what happened yesterday when I went back to talk to

Ambassador Symon." She took a deep breath to steady her voice.

"When I got to the office, I heard two people fighting. It was First Councilor Jude and Ambassador Symon. I didn't mean to spy on them really, but I heard Councilor Jude say that he can't kiss her like that again and just pretend like it didn't mean anything. Councilor Jude went on to say that she knows the truth now and she has an idea for them to be together; he tells her no, that he can't. He said he has a responsibility to all the HEART's communities.

"I peeked through the window and saw Councilor Jude reach up and touch his face like I would touch yours. Ambassador Symon firmly pushed her hand away. He told her that she knows he can't. She said she knows he has feelings for her, and that she knows a way for them to be together. He confessed his love for her, but said that it doesn't matter. He doesn't want to know what she is up to.

"He said that there were a lot of Ambassadors before him, and that he will not be the one to let it all fall apart, not even to be with her. He kind of turned cold on her and said that she needs to get back to her community because that they all need to prepare for tomorrow. He said he has to handle the Dra situation."

She paused for a moment and then went on. "I don't know what he has planned for us, but I just don't have a good feeling about this gathering."

DraDevon sat on the bed, stunned to hear of such a forbidden relationship. He turned and swung his legs over the bed, and said, "I think that we need to get moving. It sounds to me like Ambassador Tatiana gave you some good advice, but I just don't see how anyone can know what we're up to. We haven't told anyone."

"You have a good point," DraDonna responded. "And you're right. I don't see how anyone would know or how they could find out what we're doing. You and I are the only ones who really know what's going on, but still... there was something in the tone of Ambassador Symon's voice when he talked to us yesterday… the way he said he was going to take care of us. I felt, I don't know, scared I guess."

DraDevon cleared his throat before speaking, "For sure, we will not tell anyone what we're really doing. That's just the smart thing to do. The fewer who know what we're doing the better. I agree with you; we should not go to the gathering. It could be dangerous if Ambassador Symon is planning something. We need to leave before anything does happen.

"But wait," he said. "DraDonna, something else is bothering me."

"What is it?" She asked him.

"Well you said you heard Councilor Jude say something about how she had a plan for the two of them to be together. Do you think that it could be Councilor Jude that's a danger to us?"

"I don't really think so," she answered him. "She has always been nice to us, and Ambassador Symon just brushed her idea off."

DraDevon had finished dressing now and walked out of the bedroom with DraDonna close at his heels. In a very casual way, DraDevon knelt in front of the HEART stone altar.

"What are you doing?" DraDonna asked him with a sense of alarm.

"I need it!" he stated in a demanding tone.

"No, my friend, you don't. I haven't had any energy for almost two days. That plant you saw me eat last night is called Traveler's Joy, and it will help you. You will not need the energy when you eat it. I know this sounds strange, but when I take it my mind and body feel more aware than ever. It's as if I have been asleep all my life, but now I'm awake."

DraDevon was quiet for a moment to think about what she said.

DraDonna continued, "I understand if you need it, but take the Traveler's Joy. Tatiana said that the plant would work even if we took the energy for travel and other things." With this DraDonna reached into the small pack at her belt and pulled out two good sized sprigs and showed them to him.

Without another word he stood up, snatched one of the plants from her hand and ate it. "I know that you're tough, but I'm not a wimp either. If you can do it so can I. We need to get packing fast, my wife."

DraDonna laughed a little and pulled the notebook out of her other pack tied at her waist. Opening it, she had a list of things they would need, standard things. She read off the list as DraDevon hurriedly gathered the items, bringing them to the bedroom and spreading them out on the bed. DraDonna chose some of her small hand tools to put in her pack with her notebook and pencil.

"DraDevon," she said, "do you think that we will need to pack food?"

"I'm sure that the cabins we go to will have MDC's. So I don't think that we'll need any."

"I hope so, because I don't think that we'll have room in the packs for food," DraDonna told him as she looked over their packs.

"Hmmm," DraDevon said. "I just had a thought. Does anyone know where the food comes from that we find in the MDC?"

"I don't really know. I haven't ever thought about it." DraDonna said, and then recited the evening prayer, "And the HEART provides for them that they hunger not, neither should they thirst; yea, and she also gives them strength, that they suffer no manner of afflictions." DraDonna continued thoughtfully, "I guess like everyone else, I've never questioned it."

It was close to daybreak when they finally had their bags packed. They were ready to go, but they got a surprise knock at the door. Feeling a little apprehensive, DraDonna looked over at her husband. He whispered to her not to worry.

With a deep breath, DraDonna opened the door.

First Councilor Jude was smiling at her. "HEART's greeting, DraDonna and DraDevon, it looks like you're ready to leave. You aren't going to miss the gathering are you?" she asked them. Before they could reply she went on." It's going to be an exceptional gathering with special music. I know that most everyone on the planet will be coming to see you off. I think that you two are going to restart this old tradition. I always knew that you were going to do something great, DraDonna, and now you have."

DraDonna and DraDevon exchanged knowing looks.

"Of course we will be at the gathering First Councilor Jude," DraDevon answered her. "May I ask why you have come to visit us so early?"

"I have a gift for you both," she said, handing them each a small cloth bag. Inside each bag was a matching necklace. The pendant was a small oval shaped piece of white HEART stone strung on a strong fabric cord. "Go ahead and put them on," she instructed them. "Keep them next to your skin and the HEART stone pendant will help you bond with each other and with our MOTHER the HEART in a more… umm… meaningful way." She finished with a little knowing smile.

"Thank you so much, First Councilor Jude," DraDonna said as she and DraDevon put their necklaces on.

"As much as I would like to take credit for this gift, I can't. These are from Ambassador Symon. He found a lot of these stones when he was a small boy, and then fashioned them into necklaces. He sends these with his apologies, and he told me to tell you that he is sorry for his behavior, that it was unbecoming of a servant of the HEART."

A little taken aback by this, DraDevon managed to stammer out, "Umm, convey our thanks to, um, the Ambassador."

"I will do that," First Councilor Jude said brightly. "I will see you at the gathering. Be sure to be on time." She turned and left through the open front door.

DraDevon turned to his wife and asked, "Do you think we should go to the gathering?"

DraDonna took a moment to think and remember what Ambassador Tatiana had said to her about someone not being who they seemed to be. DraDonna told him, "No. Remember Tatiana's warning. We need to leave now."

"Alright then." They put on their knapsacks.

"Where do you think we should start?" she asked her husband.

"I think we should start at cabin number one in the mountain of the Ambassadors community."

"Why should we start there, DraDevon?"

"Well my wife, we have to start somewhere."

DraDonna had been feeling a little apprehensive about what they were getting into. DraDevon saw this and tenderly took her hand in his own.

They walked together, hands and souls entwined, to the HEART's stone altar. DraDevon opened a little drawer under it, pulling out two smaller round HEART travel stones. He handed one to his wife and they each clutched the travel stone in their left hand while placing their right hand on the HEART stone altar.

They both recited the prayer for energy travel: "Yea we travel from house to house, relying upon the mercies of the HEART. Solace cabin number one, Ambassadors Mountain."

The altar stone glowed with a steady blue light, and the light traveled from their right hand to the stone in their left. When it reached the stone in their left, the energy pulled them through the stone to Cabin number one on Ambassadors Mountain.

They found themselves standing in cabin number one on the Ambassadors Mountain with their right hands on the HEART stone altar.

Gone
7

JorMelony sat at the center of the courtyard. She had the temple and The Ambassadors office at her back, and a rapidly growing crowd of people in front of her. She had never been one to get nervous in front of a crowd of people. She had been playing the tallice all her life so normally it did not bother her, but this morning something was wrong. She could feel it in the pit of her stomach and it made her feel like her morning meal was going to come back up.

She looked over at her husband JorRobert, who was the lead HEART stone percussionist. The HEART guided him with his percussion stone through each piece of music, and he in turn guided the rest of the band with the rhythm he played. This job required him to take in and then use a lot of the energy, which he happily did while properly using the grain of HEART stone in his right wrist.

Her job in the band was a little simpler. She played the small and subtle notes with her small tallice. She loved it. JorMelony loved the sounds it made, and the tickly feeling she had inside when she channeled small streams of energy through the grain of HEART stone in her wrist to enhance those small notes. However, today she didn't feel right. JorMelony was afraid that with her not feeling right, her music would not sound right either.

JorMelony looked to her husband for some sign that everything was normal, but she just could not seem to catch her husband's gaze. JorMelony still felt sick, like she needed more energy. She did take some with her morning meal, but she felt like it was not enough energy today. All JorMelony could think about was going home and soaking up large doses of the HEART's energy.

JorMelony looked out past the growing multitude of people, hoping to see the brightly colored curls of her younger sister; instead she spotted the faces of her parents. The both of them glowing with delight to see one daughter play and another one restart an old, yet cherished tradition. JorMelony feared the growing sensation that something was going to go wrong would prove to be true and dash her parents delight.

It was now daybreak and the band began to play a light and happy tune. Ambassador Symon, First Councilor Jude, and Second Councilor Fredrik walk out from the temple office to the midpoint of the tiled courtyard of the community's center. The gathered throng applauded in excitement to see all three of the HEART's servants, as well as in anticipation of the strong dose of the energy that they would all get from this gathering.

Ambassador Symon looked more refreshed than usual. Second Councilor Fredrik slapped the Ambassador on the back and looked as if he had just said something that was funny as First Councilor Jude laughed at what he just said. Ambassador Symon stepped forward with a dazzling smile on his handsome face. He raised his arms with both hands glowing from the energy, so the large crowd of people would know to be silent for his speech. In respect for him, the band stopped mid-tune.

"Children of the HEART," he began. "This is a very special day today. We have not seen a gathering like this for more than a generation. There is a newly married couple, a couple that I, myself, bound in marriage with the HEART's energy, who wish to take a couples' solace." The sound of his voice was obscured for a moment by cheers and more applause from the people he addressed.

"The HEART of the planet, our MOTHER, is very pleased to see this happening again, and she would like to re-extend this offer to any couple who is newly married to take a couples' solace. All couples need this time to make their bond stronger as husband and wife by communing in solace with the HEART."

He paused for a moment to see if DraDonna and DraDevon had shown up yet. Ambassador Symon looked around. Seeing that they had not yet come, he nodded to Second Councilor Fredrik and the taller man quietly left the gathering with a worried look on his usually happy face. Ambassador Symon saw that he still had the multitude focused on his words, so he went on.

"While we wait on the happy couple to join us, I would like to tell you a little bit about them." Although no one noticed, Ambassador Symon was beginning to feel irritated at DraDonna and DraDevon for not being on time.

"DraDonna is the daughter of NayLara and NayMichael, who are both schoolteachers. DraDonna has an older sister, JorMelony, who played the tallice in our band here this morning with her husband JorRobert, who leads the band. DraDonna has been raised as a carpenter and is now serving my community by fulfilling our needs for furniture in her own unique way.

"She was married to DraDevon less than a year ago. He is the second son of BriMarie and BriHenry, who both work as glaziers making the windows for our community. DraDevon's older Brother is NulSam, who is married to NulJena who both work in home maintenance, and NulJena is going to have a baby soon."

With this announcement the gathered crowd applauded enthusiastically. After waiting a moment, Ambassador Symon continued his narration about the lucky couple. "DraDevon is a detail welder who services this community with his HEART enhanced skills at the forge."

As he finished speaking, Second Councilor Fredrik approached him with a grim look on his face and quickly whispered something in his ear that the crowd could not hear. He turned to face his Second Councilor. "You're joking, right?"

"I wish I were," Councilor Fredrik replied.

Ambassador Symon quickly turned around and dismissed the band. He drew his two councilors close and said quietly, yet with teeth clenched, "Councilor Fredrik, you and I are to stay here and give these people a high dose of energy with a small voltage of negative energy mixed in, and with any hope they will all go home and sleep for a few hours and forget what has happened here this morning. Councilor

Jude, I want you to take JorMelony and JorRobert with you back to the Dra house and see if you can find any clues to where they went. Report back to me. If I am not in the office, use my EDUstone on my desk."

Turning back to the crowd, he put on a fake wide smile. "Let us all link up and take joy in the energy that the HEART our MOTHER gives us!"

Councilor Jude quickly found where JorMelony and JorRobert had joined the crowed and motioned for them to follow her. With some disappointment, the couple turned away from the large gathering and followed Councilor Jude down the road toward the Dra home.

JorMelony had hoped that the awful feeling she had clinging to her from the beginning of the gathering would be washed away by the clean sensation of the HEART's energy. Instead, she and her husband were following First Councilor Jude down the road. And she knew it was to her sister's house.

"You know, JorMelony," JorRobert started, "I am not at all surprised that your sister and her husband didn't show up."

"Why do you say that?" she asked her husband with a confused look on her pretty face.

"I just mean that this is the type of thing she would do. Being late or not showing up to her own gathering. She has been doing things like this all her life." JorRobert put a hand on his wife's small shoulder to slow her anxious pace.

"You know I don't like her very much, I have not hidden that from you. But I have always wondered what happened when she was inside your mom. Was there some kind of mistake?"

"JorRobert," she broke in angrily. "How could you say such a blasphemous thing? The HEART of the world, our MOTHER, does not make mistakes. My sister is not a mistake!"

"I'm sorry JorMelony. You don't need to get so upset. I was just wondering like a lot of people do. You have to admit that your sister is an odd one. I have heard people in the

54

community say that they don't know why the HEART matched her and DraDevon. He's a good and normal person and she is so…"

"Special!" JorMelony interrupted him. "There is nothing wrong with my sister and you should not be listening to idle gossip, such things are unbecoming of a son of the HEART."

"I am sorry to be the one to have to tell you this, but a lot of the people in our community think that she should have been mind wiped a long time ago."

"I can't believe you just said that." She shook his hand off her shoulder, turned and walked with a quickening pace down the road after First Councilor Jude.

JorRobert watched his wife's back with frustration for a few moments and then jogged to catch up at the Dra home. He arrived not long after his wife and entered the house through the open front door. He found JorMelony standing just inside the door with a shocked look on her face.

"What is it?" he asked her with a small touch of concern in his voice. Then he looked around in the main living area. He saw a room that had been ransacked. "Who did this?" he asked.

"I did." piped First Councilor Jude, "I'm looking for anything that would tell us what happened to them; where they went. Why don't the two of you go check in the bathroom and the bedroom? Let me know if you find anything at all."

Without a word, the once quarreling couple walked, with hands clasped, to the small bathroom and looked inside. Nothing seemed out of place.

"Did you find anything in there?" Councilor Jude called out to them.

"No, nothing," JorRobert answered her. "Just a few personal things missing, but nothing out of the ordinary."

"Well, keep looking. Check the bedroom. I'm almost finished out here."

They went into the bedroom and found a rumpled bed and a few articles of clothing scattered about, which did not seem out of place for someone like DraDonna.

JorRobert was checking the blankets on the bed, not knowing what he was looking for when his hand felt cold hard steel. He pulled it out of the tangled blankets to reveal one of DraDonna's screwdrivers.

"This is odd," he said, showing it to his wife.

Upon further inspection of the bed, JorRobert found several more tools belonging to one or the other of them.

JorMelony walked around the other side of the bed from her husband, wanting to look at her sister's nightstand. JorMelony admired the unique craftsmanship that was singular to her sister. She loved the look of the sleek legs of the bedside table that ended in a blossom design. While she was admiring the beauty of the feet of the nightstand, she saw something green on the smooth hardwood floor. Curious about what this may be, JorMelony bent over to pick it up. She found that it was a leaf from that plant that she saw her sister picking the other day.

"Have you found anything at all in here?" Councilor Jude asked from the doorway.

"I found some tools lying on the bed here, but not much else." JorRobert told her.

"JorMelony," First Councilor Jude inquired gently. "Have you found anything?"

Casually, she closed her hand to conceal the small leaf that she found. "No, Councilor Jude, I'm sorry."

"Please let me know if you do find anything or hear from them. We're very concerned about them. The Ambassador will be in contact with you through your home HEART stone." She smiled at them both saying, "HEART's blessing." Then she turned and left.

With a pleading look in her eyes JorMelony searched her husband's face, "JorRobert, I know you don't like DraDonna, but she is my sister and I love her."

"I know, my wife."

JorMelony opened her hand and looked down at the small green leaf in her palm. "Whatever trouble they've gotten themselves into, I hope they will be okay."

Surprised
8

It was a breathtaking feeling to travel by the HEART's energy. The cold and sweet feeling of the energy running through the body from the right hand to the left, the energy connecting the two stones caused an odd mix of pain and pleasure. This odd feeling of pleasurable pain intensified as the body was pulled by the energy through the travel stone to the location that was stated in the prayer.

All these feelings swirled through DraDonna's body, followed by a dizzying sensation as they found that they were standing in the solace cabin.

DraDonna and her husband took their hands off the HEART stone altar, slipped the travel stones into the packs at their belts, and looked around the cabin in surprise. What they had expected to find was a small cabin that was dusty, dirty, and run down.

However, the scene that was in front of them was so very different. The cabin was twice the size of their home. It was not dirty or in disrepair. It was clean and neat with not a nail out of place.

"I have a very bad feeling about this, DraDonna," DraDevon stated.

"So do I. These cabins haven't been used for more than fifty years and look at this place. It is so clean, and in perfect shape." DraDonna mused out loud. "I wonder who has been here."

"This is really creepy," DraDevon said with a shiver. "Maybe we should have a look around to be sure that no one is here."

"Good idea. I will take a look around the bedroom and the bathroom and unpack our stuff as well. You take a look in the eating area and make sure that the MDC is working." She held her hand out for DraDevon to hand his knapsack to her.

"Sounds good. While you're at it, make sure that bed is in good working order." He winked, planting a playful slap on her backside.

"You naughty boy!" she called back to her husband as she lugged all their packs to the other side of the cabin.

DraDonna looked around at the large bedroom, with a big bed right in the middle of it and a window just behind the bed with wispy white curtains draping down either side that were tied back by beautifully knotted ropes. The bed had an intricate iron frame that had lots of lovely twists and knots that must have taken the welder weeks to create. The bed was made up with lots of soft fresh white linens that were tucked neatly around the fluffy inviting mattress.

Her pulse quickened when she thought about her husband's suggestion of putting the bed to good use. Oh how she wished that they really could just spend some of this time expressing their deep love for each other. He was one of the few people in this world that didn't treat her like she was some kind of joke that the HEART was playing on the community. With him by her side, she felt like she could do anything. DraDonna knew that he believed in her. Knowing this helped her to have the confidence she needed to free all the trapped souls.

Looking at this bed made her think of how talented DraDevon was at welding the amazing detail that he carved into each and every scrap of metal. She thought of how hard it must be to weld, trying to channel the energy into just two different fingers and then to make cold hard metal look nice. It was amazing to her.

DraDonna thought about how easy she had it because she got to work with soft wood. To turn hard iron into something beautiful was incredible to her, just like him.

With a sad sigh, DraDonna resigned herself to the fact that they probably would not have much time for romance. She knew that they would have to work hard to find out what was wrong with the world. Just what they were supposed to be looking for, she didn't know.

DraDonna opened the knapsacks, pulled out the clothing, and walked over to a beautifully carved dark wood dresser with a lovely framed mirror mounted behind it. She bent down and pulled out the well-made drawers, admiring how smoothly they slid in and out, thinking of the work that went into the fine piece of furniture.

The young carpenter raised her head just a little and looked in the mirror. She saw a quick flash of brown fur disappear under the large bed.

"DraDevon!" she yelled as she spun around, running the few steps over to the bed, and dove under it.

"What is it?" he called as he dashed into the room, only finding the bottom half of his wife's body sticking out from under the bed with her legs kicking.

"What are you doing?" he said, unable to hide the laughter in his voice.

"Ah, just a moment," came the muffled sound of her voice as she wriggled backwards from under the bed on the smooth hardwood floor.

She stood up and DraDevon burst out laughing at the comical sight of his wife's wild copper hair and rumpled clothes. He took a big step forward and scooped his left arm around her hips drawing her to him. Then with a twinkle in his eyes, he tried to smooth her wild curls down with his right hand. "My wife, you are the most amazing creature on this planet," his husky voice filled with love and admiration.

Not able to resist her charm any longer, he drew her head to his. Slowly, and ever so gently, he caressed her lips with his own.

His sweet and loving mood was infectious and the feel of his lips on hers was intoxicating. Her entire body tingled like she had just taken a big dose of the energy, and her mind was so muddled all she could think of was where his soft sweet lips would kiss her next. She wound her arms around his back and clutched his shirt tightly in her hands, holding onto him, pressing closer to his warm body. DraDonna could feel how their souls were bound as one; she wanted to melt into him again. All she wanted, all she cared about at that moment, was for them to be one body and soul forever.

He called her an amazing creature. He is probably the only one in all of the communities that would say such a thing. His sweetness filled her soul with so much love that DraDonna felt like she was going to burst with happiness.

Ignoring the yearning need in her soul to express her love for her husband, DraDonna pulled away from him just a little and took a deep breath to clear her passion filled mind.

"DraDevon," she said breathlessly, "there was some kind of creature in here. I saw it quickly run under the bed."

"Oh?" he asked his voice still husky with passion. "Is that what you were doing under there? Did you find it?"

"No, and I wasn't able to see where it went either. It just vanished."

"Well, what did it look like?" he asked, still stroking her copper curls, unable to resist his wife's beauty.

It was incredible how much just his stroking her hair affected her ability to breathe. "Um…" she said, trying unsuccessfully to think clearly.

"It was little, brown and furry. But I didn't get a very good look at it." Drawing a shaky breath DraDonna suggested, "Maybe we should have a look around and see where it went."

With reluctance he released his wife and asked, "So you didn't see anything at all under the bed?"

"Not so much as a speck of dust." she replied, longing for him to put his arms around her again.

They spent a few moments looking around the room, but there were not that many places to hide. "I'm sorry my wife, I don't see anything. I don't know what to tell you."

"Well, I don't know what to think DraDevon, this place really is creepy." DraDonna said with a frustrated sigh, "Whatever it was, I just hope it doesn't come back. Let's go see if that MDC is working and get something to eat. I'm hungry."

"That's a great idea my wife." He put his arm around her shoulders so they could walk to the kitchen together. "I think we also need to find more Traveler's Joy so our minds stay fresh."

"Well, I already have a supply of it; I keep it in my small pack." She pulled out two large sprigs, giving one to him.

"Mmm!" He grunted while eating the sweet flowered plant. "This makes me hungrier. Why don't I get us some food, and you use your new scientist brain and figure out what we should do next."

"Sounds good, welder man," DraDonna said affectionately, as she sat down at one of the chairs by the lovely kitchen table.

DraDonna's mind was sharp and clear from the effects of the plant; she pulled her notebook and pencil from the small pack, and reviewed the few things that she had written down about the area that she and DraDevon lived in. She made a few more notes about the look of the ground and the dirt itself— after all, Tatiana had told her 'it' was in the ground.

She was so absorbed in her thoughts and the notes she was reviewing that she did not notice the plate of food that her husband placed in front of her for some time, until he said, "Eat my love. You need to keep your body strong, too."

She looked up from her notes with a smile for the man she loved, said a quick thank you, and began to eat without giving too much thought about what she was eating. She saw that DraDevon had a notebook out as well.

Looking across the table at it, she saw that he had something very different in his. "May I?" she asked, before pulling it toward her. "Sure, I... um... don't know why I did that. I was looking out the window as you were working with your notes and started to write this image down," he explained.

DraDonna looked closely at the simple yet elegant sketch of the mountain range just outside the kitchen window.

"How long did it take you to do this?" she asked.

"Not long."

H.E.A.R.T. Saga: The Children

"It's very beautiful, DraDevon. I think that this might be a gift you have in your soul like I have the gift for science in mine," she said with wonder. "You can make images on paper, but what is that funny looking mark in the lower right corner?" she said with a confused look.

"Oh that's something my father's father told me about. He said back in the days when they used paper more, you would press one of your fingers in the paper, concentrate a little bit of the energy and then it makes this energy stamp. Someday when we have children, I will show them this image and the energy stamp. It will show them that I was here."

His story filled her soul with hope. A hope that everything would be okay, that they would get to have children. DraDonna smiled as she handed the notebook back to him.

DraDonna picked up a piece of fruit to eat and the happy couple settled down into a comfortable silence.

While eating, DraDonna once again took up her pencil and began to write down all she remembered of both dreams. Following her lead, DraDevon picked up his pencil and began to work on the image of the mountain in front of him, but their peace was interrupted by a rustling sound outside.

They both looked up at each other in alarm. "What was that?" DraDonna asked in a hushed tone.

"It may just be an animal, but we shouldn't take any chances." he said, matching her quiet pitch.

"You're not going out there, are you?" she asked, suddenly terrified that something might happen to her beloved husband.

"I'll only be a minute. You stay here."

"Please be careful, my friend," she said, fear showing in her light brown eyes.

"Oh I will. The HEART is with me." He smiled reassuringly.

He quietly left the cabin and DraDonna watched with dread as the door closed behind him. Her food now forgotten, all she could think of was what he might find outside.

The moments passed by at such a slow pace that it seemed as if time had stopped altogether. She strained to hear something, anything, when she thought she heard a rustling noise, and then it got louder. She stood from her chair when she heard what she thought might be her husband crying out in pain.

Standing there in the kitchen, she debated on whether or not she should go out and help him when the door burst open and DraDevon came flying in with a strange man on his heels. Out of instinct, DraDonna tried to tackle the man.

They toppled to the floor, knocking into DraDevon, causing him to fall and hit his forehead on the side of the HEART stone altar.

She wrestled with the man for what seemed like an eternity, until the guy, using his brute strength, grabbed her shoulders and shoved her hard backward, flipping her over and landing on top of her. Gaining the advantage, he pinned her under him.

Straddled on top of her, he said in a murderous voice, "I know who you are DraDonna. I was sent here to do whatever is necessary to keep you from interfering in our work."

"I don't know what you're talking about. We're on a couples' solace!"

"Do you think I am an idiot? We know what you're up to. We know it has to do with science." He sneered at her.

"We? We who? Who sent you?" she gasped, out of breath. "Get off me, I can't breathe."

"Ha!" He laughed at her. "I'm not going to let you just walk out of here, when you might go tell…"

His speech was cut short.

DraDevon, standing over them, said, "Get off my wife!" He smashed a chair over the attacker's head and he instantly fell unconscious.

With a grunt and a great heave, DraDonna shoved him enough so she could squirm out from under him.

"You're hurt!" she exclaimed, seeing a shallow bloody gash on his left arm, as well as his bruised forehead.

"I will be okay. We need to gather up our stuff and get out of here fast," he told her as he strode quickly into the bedroom, pulling the cords that held the curtains back off the wall.

"What's going on? Who was that guy?"

"I'm not sure, but I don't think he was alone," DraDevon grunted as he tied the guy's hands behind his back.

"What happened out there?" DraDonna asked him, as she ran around the cabin gathering up their things.

"There's no time to explain. All I know is that I was lucky to have gotten way from him. He had a big knife and wasn't shy about using it." He stood up, done binding the dangerous man's hands and feet. "Do you have everything?"

"Yes, but where are we going to go? We need to look at an EDUstone."

"No," he replied quickly. "I think they might be able track us with it, so wherever we go it has to be a random decision."

As both of them hurriedly took the travel stones out of their packs and placed their hands on the HEART stone altar, they could hear a light female voice calling for someone.

DraDonna hesitated for a moment and then said, "Cabin number two, Second Councilors Lake." They hurriedly said the prayer for travel.

The blue light of the HEART's energy began to take them as a woman with long blonde hair burst in the front door, running toward them. She made a futile attempt to stop them, but was just a few moments too late, ending up with only a handful of blue energy.

Help
9

JorRobert, a big man, sat uncomfortably in a small chair in the main living area of his home. He had the HEART percussion stone in front of him. Normally when he played, he didn't even notice the small chair; he got lost in the music. But today, he couldn't focus enough to channel the energy to the grain of HEART stone in his wrist. He should have been practicing some of the pieces for upcoming events, but his mind was not at ease. He kept going over everything that had happened just a few hours ago, but the sound of his wife throwing up again was really distracting.

He stood as the bathroom door opened and his wife walked out looking wan. "Are you sick JorMelony? Maybe you should go see the energy PHY."

"No, I'm alright. I think that you and I just need to take some energy together here at home and then practice," she said shortly.

"Fine." JorRobert held out his hand to his wife and they knelt together at the HEART stone altar. The unhappy couple placed their hands on the cool white stone and together they recited the prayer, "And the HEART provides for them that they hunger not neither should they thirst; yea, and she also gives them strength, that they suffer no manner of afflictions."

The white HEART stone began to glow with a soft blue light that gathered around their hands and then traveled up their arms with smallest sparks of blue light running in and out of their bodies. They took sharp breaths in and exhaled, sighing as the energy soothed their physical and emotional problems. The light withdrew from their bodies, leaving them with a feeling of warmth and happiness.

"I feel badly about the way I spoke to you earlier. It was unbecoming of a son of the HEART," JorRobert confessed to his wife.

"I'm sorry I snapped at you, my husband." JorMelony stood up first, leaned over, and kissed her husband on the top of his head. "I really think that I should go see an energy PHY because I still don't feel well. Is it ok if we practice together a little later?"

"That's fine," he said with a smile. "I need to commune with the HEART about the upcoming music events and how our band can best serve the community."

"Sounds good," JorMelony said and kissed him on the lips this time. She hurried through the front door before JorRobert had the chance to stand from the altar.

JorRobert knelt for just a few moments more, enjoying the warm sensation of having just taken energy, when he saw the flash of a message appearing on the HEART stone.

"JorRobert. HEART's greeting. This is an urgent message from the Ambassador. Councilor Jude told you that I would be in contact with you. There is a big problem with which I need your help. Your wife's sister DraDonna and her husband DraDevon have gone energy mad in the worst possible way. I will need your help to stop them from what they plan to do."

With concern wrinkling in his forehead, he placed just his right hand on the far corner of the HEART stone.

"Ambassador, HEART's greeting. This is JorRobert. What has happened? I will do what I can to help, of course." He knew that his words would appear on the Ambassador's HEART stone.

"There are things that the HEART wants you to do to help fix this situation and you will have to do them without question. Please come to my office and I will give you more details at that time. HEART's blessing."

"HEART's blessing," he replied, as the glow of the stone faded.

Now even more concerned, JorRobert got to his feet, walking quickly out of his house and up the road. He passed the Dra home on his way to the Ambassador's office. He stopped for a moment to look at the house and the shop, wondering why they went energy mad. Everyone loved the energy. Who would voluntarily give it up? He reminded himself after all that this was DraDonna and she was the only one he knew of who didn't like to use the energy in her work. Why she did things the hard way was a mystery to him and everyone else who knew her, including the Ambassador.

This thought reminded him that the Ambassador said that this was urgent, so he jogged quickly up the road to the temple office, a little scared and a little excited about what he was going to hear. He approached the office door with a tingle of anticipation of the things he would be told to do. He made up his mind to do whatever the HEART asked of him as he knocked.

"Come in," called the unexpectedly high voice of First Councilor Jude.

JorRobert opened the door looking surprised. "HEART's greeting First Councilor Jude. I received a message from the Ambassador to come here to discuss an urgent matter."

"Yes, you did JorRobert. He called me here from my community as well on the same matter."

"Did he explain to you what's going on?" JorRobert asked the First Councilor, his curiosity heightened.

"Yes, it's all very sad that two such talented and cherished children of the HEART can go so wrong. The HEART has not seen such madness in hundreds of years."

"I mean no disrespect First Councilor Jude, but why is the Ambassador not here?"

"No disrespect has been perceived JorRobert. Ambassador Symon is in the temple communing directly with the HEART on this. So he called me here to help handle this." The First Councilor continued, "He told me all the details and asked me to tell you everything... as well as give you this." She held out a necklace much like the one that was given to DraDonna and DraDevon. Instead of the HEART stone pendant strung on a fabric cord, it was strung on a lovely chain made of a yellow ore that he didn't recognize. "Please, put it on," the First Councilor said with a smile.

He took it from her hand. "Why has he given such a rare gift to me?" JorRobert asked in awe of this beautiful endowment.

"This necklace is a gift from the HEART and her servant, the Ambassador, to a good and loyal child of the HEART," she said, walking around behind him. "Let me help you with it."

He pulled the chain up around his neck, holding the ends so she could take them.

She pulled the ends a little closer to her, putting them together. She then focused and channeled the energy down to both arms, intensifying the energy with the grains of HEART stone that she as a Councilor of the HEART had implanted in both wrists. The energy channeled to the thumb and forefinger on each hand, she let out a short intense burst. This fused the two ends together, causing a small wave of energy to travel down the chain to the HEART stone pendant hanging just below the hollow of his throat. It warmed up and glowed slightly.

"AH!" JorRobert called out in surprise.

"Keep this close to your skin at all times. This necklace is gift, but wearing it is also an oath of obedience. Serve well and it will give you a special link to the HEART's energy," First Councilor Jude explained sweetly.

JorRobert took a deep breath in. "Again Councilor Jude, I mean no disrespect. But I was told that everything would be explained. Just what does the Ambassador think that DraDonna and DraDevon are going to do?"

"I will explain everything in its proper order," she began to sound a little irritated. "First of all, you need to do something special that will strengthen your body and mind." She reached into one of the pockets of her black robe that marked her as a servant of the HEART and pulled out the sprig of a plant, handing it to him. "Eat this plant. It is called Traveler's Joy. It is a gift of the HEART and will enhance the energy. Eat a good sized sprig of it every time you use the energy for any reason."

"What does it taste like?" JorRobert inquired, looking closely at the plant.

"It is sharp, then sweet. Go ahead JorRobert."

He put the plant in his mouth, chewed quickly, and swallowed. Then Councilor Jude continued her explanation.

"So, the rest of what I was told to pass along to you is that DraDonna and DraDevon have, for reasons unknown, stopped taking the energy and have gone energy mad."

"I know this already." JorRobert felt a little irritated at her for repeating this information again, but one look from her and he ducked his head in embarrassment for having spoken so impolitely to a servant of the HEART. "I'm sorry. Please continue."

"Yes," she said, not sounding as offended as he thought she would be. "Ambassador Symon has uncovered a plot that the two of them have come up with in their madness. They plan to force the HEART to let the two of them rule or they will kill her."

"What!" Shocked at this news, JorRobert said, "I admit that I have thought that DraDonna is a bit off, but for her to even think of doing this..."

"I know, JorRobert. I myself am shocked by this. I really care for DraDonna, but I know it to be true. Her madness needs to be stopped."

"But the HEART, she is our MOTHER, our GOD. No one can kill her, not even the maddest person on our planet can do that!"

"Of course she cannot be killed! But that doesn't mean that DraDonna and DraDevon will not do irreversible damage to all our communities with their plan. This is why we need your help. They must be stopped," she said fervently.

"You can count on me, Councilor Jude. Whatever you need me to do," he promised with the light of conviction in his dark eyes.

"You are such a good, dedicated son of the HEART," she said soothingly. "We have a couple out there by the name of TynLexa and TynTomus, also good dedicated people like yourself. They are watching and will try to stop them if need be, but we need someone here to monitor what is going on out there with this special EDU stone." She handed him the smaller version of what all families have in their homes. "Please, make yourself comfortable here in the temple office and let us know if anything happens through energy message."

"I will be happy to, but what is it that they might be doing? I'm not sure what I should be looking for," he said, feeling a little unsure of his new task.

"Don't worry, JorRobert. You will know it when you see it. Don't hesitate to message me. I am needed in my community, so message me there." The lovely First Councilor walked over to the small HEART stone altar, pulling her traveling stone out of the pocket in her robes. With a singsong voice, she enthusiastically recited the prayer for travel. She disappeared in a flash of blue energy.

At the sight of the First Councilor's departure, a hot feeling began to grow in his chest. How could she leave him to a task that he had no idea of what he was really doing? *"DraDonna and DraDevon have gone energy mad; it's all their fault. Now JorMelony will be even sicker when she hears this,"* JorRobert thought bitterly to himself.

The more he pondered on the whole situation that he was mixed up in, the more this hot feeling grew, and the pressure of it inside his chest needed release or he felt like he was going to explode.

Without thinking about it, he picked up a large yellow ceramic cup that was on the desk and threw it against the wall where it smashed into a thousand pieces. The cup, much like the pressure in his chest, was smashed... but it was still there, only now it was in a thousand sharp and dangerous little pieces in his soul.

News
10

JorMelony left the office of the PNL and started on the path to her home. She did tell her husband that she was going to the PHY office, but she had a feeling that she needed to go see SolKaren in the PNL office. The HEART's energy showed that the reason for her sickness is because she was with child again.

SolKaren had been coldly polite, but JorMelony didn't care. The energy helped her with the sickness and the thought that she was with child again brought her so much joy. JorMelony hoped with all her soul that this child would live. She was told by the HEART that she and JorRobert could still have two children. She wanted more than anything to have both a boy and a girl. She loved her sister very much, but she had secretly wished that she had a brother as well.

Feeling much better and bubbling over with excitement, she entered her home. "JorRobert, I'm home. I have good news!" she called excitedly. "Hello?"

She looked in all the rooms of her home for her husband. He was nowhere to be found. His percussion stones were still by his chair along with his music, so she knew that he had not gone to practice with the other members in their band.

"I wonder where he went," she said to the empty house.

Wanting so much to share her good news with someone, she decided to tell her parents. She also wanted to tell DraDonna her happy news. The last time she tried to have a baby, it had ended in a stillbirth; DraDonna took the loss of her nephew very hard.

Thinking of her younger sister reminded her that she needed to tell her parents about how DraDonna and her husband were missing. JorMelony wanted to be sure that she told them herself and not let them hear it from idle gossipers.

H.E.A.R.T. Saga: The Children

She walked over to the HEART stone altar, knelt down and placed her right hand on the stone, reciting the prayer for sending energy messages: "I strengthen my parents NayLara and NayMichael in all my conversations, through the HEART."

The light gathered around her right hand but stayed on the stone. It flashed once to signify that one of her parents was at the HEART stone altar in their home.

"HEART's greeting. Hello Mom and Dad; it's me, JorMelony." She waited for a reply.

"HEART's greeting. Hello JorMelony. This is your Mom. Your Dad is in a class with young men. I hope all is well with you today."

"Mom, it has been a busy day. I have some news for you; good news first. I have found today that I am with child again. I hope with the grace of the HEART our MOTHER, this one will make it. But SolKaren said that there is a good chance that this one will die, too. She told me that there hasn't been a live birth in several years."

"JorMelony. SolKaren is fine PNL but she has never liked our family. This is truly a blessing of the HEART. I know that this child will live. I feel it in my soul. Have you told your husband yet?"

"I have the same feeling. Please share this good news with Dad. I have not told JorRobert yet. I could not find him. Have either of you seen him?"

"No. We have not seen him since yesterday at the punishment gathering. Is anything wrong?"

"JorRobert is fine. But there is something wrong. DraDonna and DraDevon are missing. After the solace gathering, First Councilor Jude, JorRobert and I went down to their house and they were just gone."

"Where did they go? What solace gathering? There has not been a solace gathering in more than 50 years."

"Don't you remember the solace gathering this morning? DraDonna and DraDevon decided to go on a couples' solace and the gathering was this morning. How could you forget that?"

H.E.A.R.T. Saga: The Children

"I remember there being a gathering. You played your tallice beautifully. I remember a very strong energy from the Ambassador and Second Councilor Fredrik. But that's about it. Your Dad and I went home. We took a nap. Then we had classes. DraDonna is missing?"

JorMelony was beginning to feel frustrated with her Mom. She wasn't getting anywhere. Her Mom just didn't remember the reason for the gathering. It was so odd, but JorMelony didn't have time to think about it. She wanted more than anything to find her husband so that she could share the good news with him.

"Don't worry about it, Mom. Don't say anything to Dad about DraDonna being missing because I'm sure everything is fine. She and DraDevon probably were so excited about going on their couples' solace that they left early. It's so odd that you don't remember that."

"Well, don't you worry about it either. You know DraDonna; she has always done things her own way. Besides, worrying isn't good for you or the baby. You need to take lots of the energy and get lots of rest. Do what SolKaren tells you."

"I will, Mom. I just wish there was another PNL in our community. SolKaren says the meanest things about DraDonna and DraDevon. You're right about DraDonna. They probably were just excited about going on their couples solace."

"I have to go soon JorMelony. I have a class of little ones to teach."

"I need to go, too. I need to see if I can find where JorRobert is so I can tell him the wonderful news. Give Dad my love."

"I will do that. I love you. HEART's blessing."

"I love you, too. HEART's blessing."

The words and the light of the energy retreated down inside the stone. JorMelony stood with renewed joy in her soul. She was going to have a baby and this time the baby was going to live.

She had such a strong desire to find her husband and tell him all about the good news.

Looking over at their musical instruments, JorMelony thought that the best thing to do would be to check with all of the people in the band. "I hope this doesn't take too long," she said to the empty house. "I'm hungry."

Notebook
11

DraDonna and DraDevon removed their hands from the HEART stone after energy travel for the second time that day. Looking around they saw that they were in another perfect cabin that was identical to the first one.

DraDonna took a deep breath and said, "I don't think that we should unpack anything. We should keep our packs here by the altar."

"Good idea," DraDevon agreed. "I also think that we should err on the side of caution and have a look around outside."

"While we're out there, I need to get to work and see if I can figure anything out," she said as she pulled out the small notebook from her little pouch. "We also need more Traveler's Joy, my friend. There isn't much left in my pouch, and we need to keep eating it so our minds stay clear."

"That's my wife, always thinking. Let's go," he said as they walked out of the cabin together.

The lake was right in front of them when they walked out the door. It was beautiful and still. The surface of the lake was as smooth as glass with nothing to disturb its perfect surface. Even though there was no direct light on it, the lake's smooth surface shimmered.

"Beautiful," DraDevon breathed out.

"But too quiet."

"Well, we are kind of far out from all the communities."

"That's not the kind of quiet I was talking about," she said. "I just thought that there would be more animals and insects, and the plants... they all look the same as they do in our community." DraDonna's voice revealed her confusion.

"Speaking of plants my love, don't forget to pick us some more Traveler's Joy while you are figuring out why things are too quiet. I'm going to have a look around and then maybe sketch the image of the lake and the cabin in my notebook."

"Here. Take this," she said, reaching into her pack. She pulled out a small sprig of the vine. "This is all I have left. I will bring you another bigger one in a few moments."

"Thanks, my beauty." He took the plant from her, kissing her lightly on the lips. DraDevon reached up to caress her copper locks.

Unable to resist his sweet gesture any longer, DraDonna stepped closer to her husband and reached up to run her fingers through his silky black hair.

"You know I love the feel of your hair, too, my welder man," she said with playful affection.

"Oh really?" he asks her with an impish grin on his handsome face. What else is it that you like the feel of?" he asked, grabbing her hips and pulling her against him.

"Your lips are quite nice," she said softly, channeling the little bit of energy she had left in her toward her right hand, running her fingers across his full lips.

DraDevon drew in a ragged breath and said with eagerness in his voice, "I love it when you do that."

"Yes, I know. That's why I do it," she replied with a bright smile on her lips.

"Well… you'd better stop or we're not going to get anything done," he said without much conviction in his voice just before kissing her firmly on the lips.

Even though she knew that she needed to get to work, DraDonna wanted so much to indulge in the addictive heat that her husband sparked in her soul, kissing him back with enthusiasm. She slid her hands around his neck, then down to his well-toned shoulders.

Reluctantly DraDevon pulled away from her, kissing her ever so lightly on the forehead. "I love you so much lady, but we'd better get to work."

"You're right," DraDonna said with a sigh. "Besides, I'm not sure I'm comfortable doing this with you outside."

"Oh? Have you suddenly developed a shy side after nearly a year of being married?"

"Well kind of," she answered him as she gestured at the sky. "I have the feeling that we're being watched by a lot of people."

DraDevon laughed and released her hips, "Remind me not to make love to you outside."

Laughing, she turned to walk away. "I love you, my welder man. I'll be back with more Traveler's Joy in a few moments."

"Sounds good, my lover wife." He walked toward an embankment by the lake.

Not far from the cabin, DraDonna spotted a small thicket of trees with the pointed hand shaped leaves. She walked over to see if she could find any Traveler's Joy. Just as she suspected, she spotted the vines winding around the bottoms of most of the trees, vines with white flowers and vines with purple flowers. She picked one of the vines with the purple flowers and ate it right away. The sharp sweetness spread quickly to her head. DraDonna picked more, enough to fill the small pouch at her belt.

She picked two extra vines, one more for each of them to eat. As DraDonna walked in the direction that she last saw her husband go, she looked up in the sky. "I'm trying," she told the squirming mass of cloud-like souls. "Please help me. Tell me something, anything that will help me free you."

She kept walking, feeling a little silly for talking to the clouds even though she knew what they truly were. The silence made her feel like a fool. She approached the cabin and saw DraDevon sitting on an incline next to the lake. "Did you find anything?" she asked as she approached him.

Looking up from his notebook, he smiled at his wife and said, "No, I think we may be in the clear."

"Good to hear," she said as she handed her husband a large sprig of the vine with white flowers on it.

Looking at the flowers he said, "Do the vines with the white taste any different?"

"Not that I've noticed."

"Good," he said as he ate the vine with a sigh. "I think that I actually am getting to like the taste."

DraDonna spotted the notebook in his lap and asked, "May   I   see   what   you've   sketched?"
"Of course, my love."

Looking at the image on the page, she once again felt amazed at the talent it took to do such a thing. "DraDevon, this is so beautiful."

"It needs more work, but I'm mostly pleased with it."

Handing the notebook back to him she said, "You should be pleased; it looks great. I, on the other hand, am not getting anywhere. The only thing I've noticed is that everything is the same everywhere. It's all the same kinds of trees and plants and bugs. I was hoping if we went to different cabins we would see different things." She cleared her throat. "Anyway, I am going back to that small thicket of trees to see if anything else comes to me. I'll come and get you shortly for our afternoon meal."

"Sounds good, my beautiful lady," he said with affection in his voice.

DraDonna walked back to the thicket deep in thought. Tatiana told her to notice everything. But she also said that what she needed to find was in the ground. DraDonna looked up into the clouds and asked, "What is in the ground?"

Again, her answer was silence. She sat down on the ground just outside of the trees. Once again, she took out her notebook and wrote down how all the trees and plants were the same. She set the notebook down on the ground next to her.

"It's in the ground; it's in the ground," echoed over in DraDonna's head; it was all she could think of. She ran her hand over the ground. Finding a soft spot, she dug her hand in and let the soil fall through her fingers. She scooped up a big handful and brought it closer to her face to get a closer look.

It was the same as everything else—just like the soil back in her community: perfect dark soil that makes all the perfect plants grow. But it was too perfect. How could this world be too perfect?

She retrieved her notebook and wrote this down, feeling like she was close to something. *"How can the world be too perfect?"*

She began to feel her stomach rumble to tell her that it was time to eat. With a sigh of frustration, she pushed herself off the ground and began to walk to the cabin, thinking that she might check to be sure that the MDC was working properly before getting DraDevon.

The advice that Tatiana had given her kept playing in her mind. It's in the ground. Almost automatically, she looked down at the ground while she was walking and then stopped. Coldness gripped her soul. There was another set of footprints just outside the cabin door. She was pretty sure that those were not there earlier... and that they didn't belong to her or DraDevon.

Quietly, she backed away and ran behind the cabin, then toward her husband who was sitting on the other side of the lake, hoping maybe it had been DraDevon who was looking for her and making extra footprints in the dirt.

"DraDevon!" she called when she reached his spot on the incline of the lake. "Have you been looking for me?" she asked.

"No, I've been here since you left," he replied. "Why do you ask?"

"DraDevon, I don't think we're alone anymore. I was heading back to the cabin, and I found another set of footprints right outside the door."

A look of urgency and alarm flared in his eyes as he quickly placed an energy stamp on the image and snapped the notebook closed. "Let's check this out. But carefully," he said, standing up.

They walked swiftly and silently to the side of the cabin and carefully looked in the window to the main living area of the cabin. "It's her," DraDevon said. It was the same woman, the one with long dark blonde hair, who had tried to stop them from leaving the last cabin.

"What do we do?" DraDonna whispered back.

"Let's wait and see what she does first."

H.E.A.R.T. Saga: The Children

Kneeling at the HEART stone altar, the woman placed her right hand on the right corner of the HEART stone.

They heard her recite the prayer for communication with the temple office.

"I wanted to report to you that I have found them again. Tracking them was fairly easy with the stones. They're not in the cabin at the moment, but I went through their packs and I'm pretty sure they're doing what we've thought. What have the stones revealed to you?"

She paused silently for a moment as she read the message that appeared on the HEART stone.

"Then it's confirmed," she paused again for a few moments more. "I found him in cabin number one of Ambassadors Mountain. They had beaten him up pretty badly. He was bound hand and foot, but he's now resting comfortably there."

She was quiet as she read what was written on the HEART stone.

"No, please don't do that. You know that my loyalty to you goes deeper than that. I will stop them this time, but please send me some help." She paused again. "Okay, good. I can use the help. HEART's blessing." She ended the message.

Before she got to her feet, blue light surged and ran up her arm as she took in a dose of energy.

"DraDonna, I have an idea," DraDevon whispered.

"What is it?"

"It will take too long to explain. Follow me to the front door and play along."

DraDevon grabbed her roughly by the shoulders and began to yell, "So you're the one I've been looking for! Where is your husband?"

"I don't have to tell you anything!" she yelled back at him, understanding what he was planning.

He winked at her and mouthed the word sorry, and raised his hand to strike her.

DraDonna snapped her head back at the precise second he landed the slap on the left side of her face; it was all sound and no pain. "You can do whatever you want to me! I will not tell you anything; not for all the HEART's energy!"

The noise of their fighting drew the woman out of the cabin, brandishing a large sharp knife. "What's going on out here; who are you?" She stood in front of the cabin door at DraDonna's back.

DraDevon looked down at his wife before saying anything. She silently mouthed the words: Just do it. He then grabbed her left arm in his right hand, twisting it around her back and spinning her around, gruffly pushing her forward. He addressed the blonde woman. "My name is NorRobert and I have been sent to help you," he lied.

Still skeptical, she questioned him further. "Where is your wife?"

Thinking quickly, he answered, "She is resting at our home in the Ambassadors community because she is with child." The woman still appeared to be unconvinced, so DraDevon went on with sarcasm in his voice. "Are we going to stand around here all day exchanging family stories or are we going to go inside and get this energy mad woman to tell us what she knows?"

"Very well," the woman said. She lowered the knife and turned for the cabin door.

"Get moving," DraDevon said gruffly to his wife. He released her arms and then shoved DraDonna so hard that she collided with the blonde woman. Using the element of surprise DraDonna flung out her arms and wrapped them around the other woman.

"Hurry DraDevon, get the knife!" she said urgently.

He yanked the knife from the woman's pinned hand as she squirmed in DraDonna's arms. "Let go of me!" the woman screamed as she struggled and fought.

"Hurry DraDevon, get something to tie her up with! I will get her into the house but move fast; she's hard to hold onto." DraDonna groaned under the struggles of the hostile woman.

Running into the cabin, he snatched up the first thing he could find: their knapsacks. He whipped the ties out of the tops and dashed back to help his wife drag the woman inside, where they tied her to a chair.

"So are you two going to beat me and leave me for dead like you did my husband?" she sneered at them.

"No, we're not going to beat you up. Your husband attacked me first," DraDevon answered. "I was just defending myself and my wife. Besides," he went on, "we need you to be aware of what is going on. We need you to answer some of our questions."

"Ha!" She laughed at them. "There isn't anything you can do to me that will make me talk! Do your worst."

DraDonna looked the woman in the face and said, "Oh no, we will not have to do anything to you. We'll just not let you have any energy. After a while that little jolt you just got will wear off and you'll tell us anything."

"Ha!" she laughed again. "You are such a fool. Just like everyone else on this stupid planet. The energy helps me some, yes, but it doesn't affect my mind like it does yours. I could go the rest of my life without it. You see, there is this special little plant that grows around and all I have to do is eat a little bit of it, and I'm free. I'm smarter and stronger, unlike everyone else who walks around like they're asleep."

DraDonna smiled as she pulled a small sprig of the Traveler's Joy out of her pouch and asked, "Is this the little plant you're talking about?"

A look of surprise entered the woman's eyes.

"Yeah, we know about it. You see we are getting the best of both, too—energy healing and travel—but clarity of mind and strength from this wonderful vine."

A little worried, the woman asked, "How do you know about the vine?"

"Oh, I think I will be the one to ask the questions here, and you will be the one to answer them."

"Not likely," she scoffed at DraDonna.

"Look, we don't want to hurt you. What's your name?" DraDonna asked her, but she was met with silence.

"You know... something I've learned about this sweet little plant is that it doesn't really last very long," DraDonna continued. "You have to keep eating it, especially after using the energy for any reason. You'll get confused, dizzy, you will get headaches, and it makes you hungrier. So before too long, you will be willing to tell us anything."

Still the woman remained silent.

"Would you like some? All you have to do is tell me your name."

The woman stubbornly refused to speak.

"Well you think about it while I go through your packs and see what they will tell me."

The woman began to struggle harder, to no avail, as DraDonna picked up one of the woman's packs that were monogrammed with a 'T.'

"Get out of my stuff," she yelled.

"Oh, sounds like your Traveler's Joy is wearing off; would you like some energy?"

"Get mind wiped!"

DraDonna set the pack down and pulled out a piece of Traveler's Joy and sniffed it with a smile on her face, then placed the plant under the other woman's nose so she could smell it too, but for just a second.

"Would you like some?" she asked as she ate a piece. "Mmm! It's sweet, and it is so nice to have a clear head."

The blonde woman licked her lips as a sweat broke out on her forehead. She began to feel throbbing pain in her head. "My name is TynLexa."

With this, DraDonna pulled another sprig of the plant out of her pouch and held it to TynLexa's mouth so she could eat the plant.

DraDevon, who had been standing behind his wife watching her get the woman to talk, was beginning to feel more and more nervous.

"DraDonna," he addressed his wife, "we need to move this along. Didn't she say that someone was coming to help her?"

"I know, but we need to get as much out of her as we can," she whispered back to him. DraDonna turned back to the other woman and asked, "Are you hungry or thirsty?"

85

"Yes, I am."

With just a look and a nod, DraDevon went into the kitchen and got a small glass of water from the MDC. He held the glass to TynLexa's lips and she drank deeply.

Then she said a little sarcastically, "I thought that you were going to withhold food and water from me. You guys don't know much about torturing."

"That would be because we don't know anything about torturing. We're not like that. We would not deliberately hurt another person. But it wouldn't actually hurt you if we didn't give you any Traveler's Joy because you don't actually need it. I will only be giving you some if you tell me what I need to know."

TynLexa was thoughtfully silent, but DraDonna went on. "I must confess that we don't fully understand what is going on here. We know that something is wrong with the world. But I promise you this—we will figure it out and fix it—with or without your help."

DraDonna picked up the first pack, pulling out clothing and personal effects, setting it aside. Then she looked in a smaller softer pack which she found to be full of Traveler's Joy. Then she moved on to the larger, heavier third pack.

She gasped when she saw what was in it. She pulled out something she'd seen before: a science tool with two long barrels on it. They were for looking through, and a plate was under them holding something very small, something for looking at. Along with the science tool was a notebook full of observations. DraDonna exclaimed in delight as she realized what was in its pages. "TynLexa, what were you on to with your observations?" she asked.

TynLexa was perspiring again and seemed to be in a lot of pain. "I would love to share what I have found with you, but I can't," she said in a strained voice.

"Why can't you tell us? And why would you share it with me? After all you were sent here to kill us..."

"It's because you have been a lot nicer than I was told you would be. I was told that the two of you were energy mad and treacherous, so I was supposed to stop you," she said through clenched teeth.

"Then tell me what you have found in here, TynLexa."

The woman's face was turning red. DraDonna, not fully understanding what the problem was, offered her another sprig of Traveler's Joy, but TynLexa turned her head and spit. "That…won't…help!" TynLexa gasped in pain one more time, and then slumped forward, unconscious.

"DraDevon… I think it's time for us to go."

"You're right, but I think that we should untie her and lay her down on the bed. We can't leave her like this."

As they untied her, they noticed that she was wearing a metal chain with another piece of the same HEART stone hanging from it, that there were burns around her neck and on the hollow of her throat where the stone rested.

They looked at each other, a little scared.

DraDevon carried TynLexa into the bedroom and laid her on the bed.

"I hope she's going to be okay. I don't think she was a bad person, just that she was being controlled by the Ambassador," DraDonna said, feeling bad for the other woman.

"DraDonna, do you think maybe we should try to take her necklace off?"

"That sounds like a good idea to me," DraDonna replied with a smile.

DraDevon reached behind her neck, but could not find any kind of clasp or any way of taking the chain apart.

"What's wrong? Why won't it come off?" DraDonna asked.

DraDevon slid it around on her neck so he could see the back. "Looks like whoever gave this to TynLexa didn't intend on her ever taking it off. The links are fused together."

"Can you cut it off with the energy?" DraDonna asked him, knowing that his skills might work better than hers.

"I think so," he replied as he focused what energy he had in him down to his right wrist, splitting it like he would for an arc weld. Bringing his thumb and forefinger together, DraDevon leaned in close and sliced through the chain with the hot spark of energy emanating from his fingers.

He released the energy and stood up straight. He then reached into his shirt and yanked his own necklace off. "I'm not wearing this thing anymore," he said as he tossed it on the floor with the one he cut off TynLexa.

"Neither am I," said DraDonna, pulling her necklace off as well. "It's probably how they have been able to follow us and how they know what we're doing."

"In that case, we need to get out of here now," he said, taking his wife's hand and hurrying to their packs by the HEART stone altar. "Do you need to take any of that stuff?" DraDevon asked, pointing to the bag of science equipment near their feet.

"All I need is this," DraDonna said, bending down to pick up TynLexa's notebook. She placed it in her small pack with her own notebook.

"Where are we going to go this time?" he asked her as they both shouldered their knapsacks.

"Well, how does cabin number one of the Second Councilors Mountain sound?"

"Quiet," he answered her as they both placed their hands on the HEART stone altar. Together they said the prayer for travel.

Control
12

JorRobert began to feel like his back was cramping. This chair was just too small for him. He set the EDU stone on the desk so he could stand for a moment to stretch. The fact that his back hurt from sitting in a chair too small for him, and the fact that he was hungry was adding to the shards of anger inside him.

Watching the images on the special EDU stone was giving him a better idea of what was going on, but he still felt those dangerous shards of anger tearing at his soul. Councilor Jude was not telling him everything, and this amplified the hot rage that kept burning in his brain.

JorRobert sat back down and tried to calm himself by picking up the EDU stone and looking closely at it.

"I wonder how this works," he mumbled to himself. He guessed it was somehow linked by the HEART's energy to the small stone pendants they wore. But anything beyond that, he just didn't know.

Thinking about the necklaces and how they were linked to this EDU stone made him think of the one he now wore. With his left hand he felt the smooth, cool stone. JorRobert knew he wasn't an exceptionally smart man, but he wondered: shouldn't the stone warm his skin? Still the thought that his stone necklace could be linked to an EDU stone, that someone else was watching, left him fuming in paranoia.

What gives her the right to spy on people? Was First Councilor Jude watching him, too? He hoped not; he was trying to help her after all.

He clenched his left fist and smashed it on the desk, causing him to lose his grip on the stone in his right hand, dropping it to the desk. Just before the three different images faded, he finally saw something that caught his eye. He quickly picked up the stone again so he could closely watch the scene that was unfolding before his eyes.

H.E.A.R.T. Saga: The Children

It looked as though DraDonna and DraDevon were fighting, and then TynLexa came out of the cabin— fooled by their ruse— and then she was captured.

He watched, fascinated, as the three images played out the same scene from three different points of view. He forgot his anger and suspicions for a few moments, fascinated by what he was seeing.

At first DraDonna tried to get TynLexa to talk, but to no avail. TynLexa needed more of the Traveler's Joy to help her mind stay strong. JorRobert's dislike of DraDonna increased when he saw her tease TynLexa with the plant, getting her to talk before giving her some.

TynLexa was so weak, giving in and almost saying too much, but on some level, obviously wishing she could say more. He could understand what was going on.

Just as she began to talk, he could see that she was in pain. He saw sweat pouring off her and her eyes bulge with the pain. He wondered what was causing this woman's pain. As much as he didn't like DraDonna and her husband, he knew that it wasn't anything they had done. He was watching their every move and could hear everything.

Sometimes, he thinks, he can almost hear their thoughts.

So… who was hurting TynLexa?

JorRobert saw her slump over and then the other two carry her into the bedroom, laying her down on the bed. He looked closely as DraDevon removed the necklace; one of the images went dim. JorRobert then watched from the other two perspectives and saw the burns all around TynLexa's neck were the necklace had been.

There was cold fear in the pit of his stomach when he realized that her necklace was just like his and that it was the necklace that had caused those burns. Then, cold fear was replaced by burning rage.

With his free hand, he reached up and tried to yank his own necklace off, but to no avail. He felt trapped struggling with it on his neck and this made him so angry he felt once more like he was going to explode.

Although the anger remained hot in his soul, his eyes were once again drawn to the EDU stone as DraDonna and DraDevon ripped their necklaces off. The last two images on the stone went dark.

"HEART's curse!" he hissed. "I'm going to have to report this!"

Barely able to manage his anger, he walked over to the HEART stone altar and quickly said the prayer for communication to First Councilor Jude. "HEART's greeting First Councilor Jude. This is JorRobert. I have news. The Dra's captured TynLexa and managed to get her to talk a little. They also took her notebook so they could know what she was working on. I'm not sure what happened to her, but TynLexa is now unconscious. For some reason DraDonna and DraDevon took their necklaces off and I can no longer track them on the EDU stone you gave me. Please advise."

"HEART's greeting JorRobert. This sounds more serious than I thought. I will be there in a moment to advise you further on the situation. HEART's blessing."

"HEART's blessing," he mumbled.

JorRobert stood up and backed away from the HEART stone altar, knowing she was going to arrive by energy travel.

In a quick flash of blue light, First Councilor Jude was standing in front of him, poised and lovely wearing a long black skirt, a white linen blouse, and the long black outer robe of her office.

The spectacle of her beauty did nothing to calm the rising anger in his soul. It began to bubble up and expand until it took over his rational mind. Without any warning, he charged at First Councilor Jude and caught her by surprise.

Out of instinct and self preservation, she raised her left hand, still gripping the travel stone, and struck the enraged JorRobert across the face with it, hoping that this would knock some sense into him.

No such luck.

Her efforts to defend herself and subdue JorRobert only served to fuel his irrational anger. He charged her again, this time barreling into her side, knocking the stone from her hand and knocking her off her feet.

"What has gotten into you?" she gasped, trying to catch her breath.

"Why won't you tell me the truth about what's going on?" he yelled as he grabbed the front of her shirt with his left hand, heaving her to her feet. "Tell me!" he said, shaking her so hard that her teeth rattled.

She sputtered, stunned and frightened by his unreasonable outburst. She was unable to say anything.

"Why don't you answer me?" he screamed, raising his hand and slapping her. Her head snapped backwards, banging it against the wall behind them.

JorRobert began to scream unintelligibly, not with anger but with pain. He dropped Councilor Jude to the floor, falling to his knees, tearing at the necklace at his throat—now glowing malevolently in yellow light. "Make it stop!" he gasped, writhing on the floor.

Councilor Jude stood up and straightened her clothing. She walked over to the HEART stone altar and said the quick prayer for a small jolt of the energy that healed the rapidly forming bruise on her face.

"Please!" JorRobert begged.

Walking back over to where he writhed in pain on the floor, she calmly said, "I told you when I gave you that necklace that wearing it was an oath of obedience."

"I thought that you meant obedience to the HEART," he choked out.

"Ha!" she laughed mirthlessly. "You assumed wrong. It is an oath of obedience to me."

"Please stop. You're killing me!" he gasped.

Without another word, Councilor Jude stood up and pulled a necklace similar to his own— only with a bigger stone— out of the collar of her shirt. She grasped her stone with one hand and focused the energy within her for a moment on his stone. The angry yellow glow in JorRobert's stone then faded along with the burning pain.

H.E.A.R.T. Saga: The Children

The stone and the chain began to cool, and JorRobert heaved a sigh of relief.

"You see, I found these stones a few years ago. I remember that day so well. I was alone in my home. I had been practicing my channeling. I was practicing too much and was weak from lack of energy when I stumbled on my way to the HEART stone altar and tripped. I was on the floor for quite some time feeling weak and barely conscious when I saw that some of the floor boards were loose. I pried them up and found a hole under the floor. In that hole was an odd metal box that was very rusty and old. I had a hard time getting the lid off the box because the hinges had rusted shut, but I kept at it. I had a feeling that there was something wonderful in there." There was a gleam in Councilor Jude's eyes.

"When I did get it open I found that the box had treasures in it made from the HEART stone. There were HEART stone pendants along with several other things inside the box. Some of the stone pendants were strung on yellow metal chains and some were loose in the box. They were all dusty. Then I saw this larger one among them, I picked it up and put it on and it felt cool and smooth against my skin.

"Somehow I felt stronger, strong enough to go to the HEART stone altar and take in a large dose of the energy. I could feel it react to the energy that I had within me and it began to pulsate with an unusual yellow light. I later found the larger one that I am wearing now controls the smaller ones.

"You see, JorRobert... it responds automatically to my emotions in a defensive manner." She stopped for a moment, letting her words sink in. "But I haven't always worn it. I knew I would have to keep them hidden. It was less than a year ago that I thought it would help me and I was right. They have been... handy." She smiled, self-satisfied.

"I don't understand how they are linked to that EDU stone," JorRobert said, his voice still raspy from the pain that was inflicted on him.

"Oh that's simple," she said lightly. "Another thing that was in that box was a note written on some paper that was so old and frail that it crumpled when I breathed on it. It was instructions on how to link the stone pendants to an EDU stone. It is really very easy. In any case you will have to obey me. You will not attack me again!"

"I'm sorry First Councilor Jude, please forgive me. I don't know what came over me. I was just so angry."

"Have you had any energy or Traveler's Joy since I left you earlier today?"

"No I haven't. I have spent the day watching the stone like you asked me to."

"Ah... you fool." She sounded amused. "Your little man brain needs either one or the other to stay balanced." She pulled some Traveler's Joy out of the pocket in her black robe. "This should help you keep in control of yourself. Just don't forget— eat it often. It grows everywhere, so you should have no problem finding it."

He sat up and gratefully took the plant and ate it, instantly feeling the clarity that comes with eating the plant.

"Now get over to that altar and get those wounds healed. We don't have much time."

JorRobert got to his feet and stumbled over to the HEART stone altar, quickly saying the prayer for healing. He gasped as clean blue light and sparks went right to the burns on his neck and the injury to the side of his face, healing them fast.

With an unexpectedly overwhelming feeling of dizziness, he fell backward from the HEART stone altar onto his back again. He could do nothing but wait for the room to stop spinning. "Why do I feel dizzy?" he asked. "That has never happened with a healing before."

"That's because your silly little man brain has the Traveler's Joy fighting to keep the fogginess of the energy out of your mind. You need to get up off your back and eat more Traveler's Joy and stop wasting my time," she said with impatience, handing him another sprig of the white flowered vine.

He ate the vine she offered and sat up. The dizziness began to subside.

"Feel better, JorRobert?" she asked.

"Yes."

"Good, and if you don't mind we have a lot to do," she said briskly.

"Councilor Jude, what is it that you need me to do?" he asked, a little apprehensive.

"I need you to bring DraDonna and DraDevon back here to face energy punishment for their crimes against the community. And I need you to bring me those notebooks, both TynLexa's and DraDonna's. They have information that I need. You will bring these things to me, as well as DraDonna and her husband.

"But most importantly, bring DraDonna to me by any means necessary, even if you have to kill DraDevon to do it."

Deep malevolence was in her voice that made JorRobert want to hide. He was stunned by what the First Councilor had said; he was speechless. How could he kill another person? He knew that he had to obey her or he would die; but could he do it? "How would I do it? I mean, kill him... if I have to. I wouldn't know how to get them to come with me," he said, feeling overwhelmed and confused.

"Well, JorRobert, I think I can help with that," she said, pulling her robe aside, revealing something tucked into the beltline of her skirt. She pulled out what looked like a small carpenter's square with rounded off edges, one end a little longer than the other. It also looked to have been made from HEART stone. She handed it to him, showing him to grip it at the bottom.

"This is what I call an emitter," she explained. "It will emit short, hot bursts of the HEART's energy. You focus the energy inside of you on the emitter, and it propels the energy out of the emitter so fast that it's hot enough to melt metal. You'll need to eat lots of Traveler's Joy and then take in a lot of energy before and after its use because it will drain you."

"Where did you get this thing?" he asked, feeling a little trickle of excitement creep into his soul as he held the weapon.

"It was among the treasures that I found in the metal box," she replied simply. "Do you have any more questions for me before you go?" she asked him.

"I have a few," he admitted worriedly.

"What are they?" she said, impatience in her voice.

"I was just wondering what will happen to TynLexa and her husband. Do you want me to go get them and bring them back to you?"

"No, I don't. I will take care of them. Your top priority is to get DraDonna and those books. Is that all?"

"Just one more thing if you please, First Councilor Jude," he said with as much respect as he could muster. He didn't want a repeat of what had happened earlier. "I'm not sure where to find them. They left cabin number two of the Second Councilors Lake and I was not able to hear where they were going."

"I have a pretty good idea what they're up to and what information is in that book. I think if you go to the Dra's house sooner rather than later, one or both of them will come to you.

Copy
13

The stunning feeling of energy travel receded from their bodies, leaving them feeling a little breathless. DraDonna and DraDevon took a look around them and saw another perfect cabin.

"Let's go have a look around outside," DraDonna suggested as she dropped her knapsack on the floor.

"Good idea," DraDevon agreed and grabbed her hand as they walked out the front door of the cabin.

The young couple gasped with shock at what they saw. Everything looked the same as the first cabin. It wasn't just the cabin that was the same, but every contour of the mountainside as well. It was an exact copy down to the last tree and flower.

"DraDonna, did we make some kind of mistake? Are we at cabin number one of the Ambassadors Mountain?" he asked in shock.

"I'm pretty sure we said the prayer right," she said, confusion on her face. "I don't understand how everything could look the same."

"Do you still have TynLexa's notebook?" DraDevon asked her.

"Yes, it's in my small pack."

"I think we need to figure this out. Whatever it is we're going to do, we need to do it fast."

"Why?" DraDonna asked, her eyes full of concern.

"We've been attacked twice now. I just have a feeling that we're running out of time."

"I agree, but we need to eat some food and some Traveler's Joy. We didn't eat much of our morning meal, and we didn't have our noon meal, either. Come what may, we need to eat so we can keep our strength up."

"You have a point; let's eat," DraDevon said as they walked back into the cabin. "Why don't you get some food for us while I check out the rest of the cabin?"

"Sounds good," she said. She walked into the kitchen and placed her right hand on the small HEART stone on the counter in the kitchen. She recited the basic prayer to the HEART requesting food. She asked for two sandwiches and two glasses of water. Opening the door to the MDC she found just what she had asked for: two sandwiches on thick wheat bread and two cold glasses of water. DraDonna set these out on the table and took out two sprigs, setting them by each plate.

She was about to call her husband to the kitchen for their evening meal when she heard scuffling coming from the bedroom.

"DraDonna! Come here quick!"

DraDonna felt her soul leap in fear. She ran into the bedroom to assist her husband with whatever new horror he was struggling, but when she came to the bedroom she couldn't help but laugh a little at the sight of her husband wrestling with what looks like one of the blankets of the bed.

"What are you doing?" she asked with mirth in her voice.

"I caught one!" he answered her with a grunt.

"Caught what? Whatever it is, it can't be that big or mean if you can hold it down with a blanket," she said, still laughing a little.

"Not funny!" he said, still struggling with the thing in the blanket. "I think I caught one of those things that you saw at the other cabin."

"You did?" she said suddenly, not finding it to be funny anymore. "What is it? What does it look like? Can I see it?"

"I don't dare open this blanket. It will get away!"

"What did it look like?" she asked him again.

"It was little, brown, kind of furry. It moves really fast; I didn't think I would be able to catch it." He tied the little brown creature up securely in the blanket and set it back on the bed. "I was thinking if we left it in here for a little while, it would calm down and we could get a better look at it."

"Good idea; but for now let's eat," she said, and they went into the kitchen.

"DraDonna," DraDevon said thoughtfully as they walked, "I don't understand something."

"What is it?" she asked as they sat down at the table to eat.

"Well, it's all the trapped old souls and the blocked new ones. Who's doing all this? And why?"

"My best guess is that it's Ambassador Symon and maybe the Councilors," she replied. "But the thing is... whatever it is they've been doing, it's been going on for a long time. So I think it may have been many generations of the HEART's servants and not just the ones that are here now." She hungrily took a large bite of her sandwich.

"It just doesn't seem like Tatiana would be the kind of person who would be involved in something that would hurt the communities," DraDevon said as he, too, attacked his sandwich. "She and her Councilors loved everybody. I just can't see them being involved in something like this." "I see what you mean, but I think she was. She said that she could not tell me a lot of things because of an oath." DraDonna told him.

After shoving the last bite of his food in his mouth, he took a long drink of water and said, "Something is really bothering me."

"Well, what about this whole thing doesn't bother both of us?" she retorted.

"I know this whole thing is crazy, but something really doesn't make sense," he said, perplexed. "I have the same feeling you do—that Ambassador Symon is heavily involved in all of this, but I just can't see him hurting and torturing people like TynLexa. I know that he hasn't been very nice to you, but really, I don't think the HEART would have picked him to be her servant if she thought he would be capable of those things."

"I see your point," she said as she cleaned up after their meal. "I don't understand this anymore than you do, but I really think Ambassador Symon is behind this somehow."

"We—" he stopped. "Did you hear that?" They both took off for the bedroom, but not fast enough.

They found the jumbled up blanket on the floor with a hole in the side, and no little fury thing inside it.

"We need to try to find it," DraDonna sighed with exasperation.

"I'll look behind the dresser. You look under the bed." DraDevon pulled the heavy dresser out from the wall, and with a grunt he pushed it right back. He looked over to the bed, unable to resist the urge to laugh at seeing his wife half under the bed again. "Did you find anything?" he asked, laughter in his voice.

"What's so funny?" DraDonna's voice was muffled.

"I'm sorry, but you look funny.......kind of like you did at the first cabin."

"No funnier than you looked a little while ago wrestling with a blanket."

"Okay," he said with mirth still in his voice, "but did you find anything?"

"Hang on a moment; let me come out."

"Oh here, let me help you with that," he said, reaching down, grabbing her ankle, and pulling hard. She slid quickly out from under the bed with her copper curls wildly ruffled up. Laughing, he let go of her ankle.

She flipped over on to her back and crossed her arms over her chest. "What are you laughing at?"

"I'm laughing at you, lady with the wild hair!"

She smoothed her curls down as best she could and stood up, looking him in the eye. Knowing she probably did look a little silly, she tried not to laugh herself. "Alright, are you going to stand there laughing at me all day or are we going to try to figure things out? After all, there are people pursuing us."

The laughter drained out of his face and she felt bad. DraDonna loved to see her husband smile and laugh, even if it was at her expense.

"You're right, my love," he said. "I didn't find anything behind the dresser. Not even dust. Did you find anything under the bed?"

"Actually, I did," she said. "I didn't see the creature, but I did see a trap door in the wall that leads outside. I think most people would have missed it, but you know I have a carpenter's eye."

"Where do you think it went?" he asked her.

"I don't know and I don't care, just as long as that weird little thing isn't in the cabin with us anymore. Let's go into the living area. I need to see if I can figure something out before we get attacked by some creep sent by the Ambassador to kill us."

"Good idea," he responded as they walked arm in arm back to the main living area. "I think I'll take a look around outside, and see if I can make another image in my book of this place and also make of one the little creature-thing that got away."

"Be careful," she said affectionately as she kissed him lightly before sitting down on one of the chairs.

"Don't worry, I will," he said closing the door softly behind him.

DraDonna pulled the two notebooks out of her small pack and opened her own but snaps it shut again. "I already know what's in here," she said to the empty cabin.

Instead she opened TynLexa's book. In the beginning of the notebook were a lot of the same things she, herself, had observed, about each cabin being the same in each place. TynLexa and her husband had found all the lakes and all the mountain ranges were exactly the same, down to the last rock and leaf.

After reading through about three quarters of the little book, she realized TynLexa and TynTomus did not go out and do what they did on a whim or because they were energy mad. They had been sent out. Just who it was that had sent them on this quest, the book didn't say, but DraDonna suspected Ambassador Symon.

H.E.A.R.T. Saga: The Children

She read on and found what she was really looking for: *"After testing the samples of surface soil in each of the regions, I have found there to be no variations. I believe if I could drill down deeper into the soil, I can find the definitive evidence that is needed. What follows is a sketch of the core drill that we will have to make. I fear that it will take a long time, being that neither of us know anything about welding."*

Excitedly she turned the page and feasted her eyes on a sketch of the core drill. The notes that went with the sketch explained the hand crank that turned the core drill was powered by the HEART's energy. DraDonna squealed with delight. "DraDevon, I think I have it!" she excitedly jumped up and ran outside. "DraDevon, I think I have it!"

She smiles when she saw the love of her life striding toward her with a smile on his face. "What have you found, my love?" he asked happily as he walked back into the cabin with her.

"TynLexa was on to the same thing I was. She saw that everything was too perfect. And everything was the same everywhere, even the soil. She thought if she took a sample of the soil farther down, she would have what she needed. Look here at the sketch she made of the core sample drill. Do you think you could weld it?"

"Well," he said, looking at the sketch. "I've never made anything like this before. It's really big, but it looks simple enough."

"How long will it take you to make it?" she asked, eagerly.

"If I continually use the energy to make the whole thing, I should be able to construct it in just a few hours."

Impressed with the confidence in his voice she looked up at him and said, "You're amazing, do you know that?"

At this he chuckled, and placing one hand under her chin, he tilted her head up and kissed her softly on the lips. "Your sweetness works on my soul stronger than the HEART's energy. Did you know that?"

"I sure hope so. I would be disappointed to find my flirting had no effect on you."

DraDevon took a deep breath and released her chin. "Anyway, my lovely wife, I don't think that it will be safe for you to come with me to our shop. We don't know how deep the conspiracy goes or who's involved. We can't risk someone spotting you."

"I know," she interrupted him. "It's because of my HEART's cursed hair isn't it?"

"DraDonna my love, I happen to find your uniquely colored hair attractive. But attractive or not, you do stand out, and I just can't take a chance that you'll be spotted. I think I can slip in and out of the shop easily enough by myself."

DraDonna looked down at the book in her hands, wanting to hide the tears she felt welling up in her eyes. The thought of them being apart would normally be hard for her, but with all that had been going on, it was downright frightening.

Sensing her emotion, he put his arms around her so she could rest her head on his chest. "I don't want to leave you here DraDonna, but I know that this is what will be safest for you. I would die if anything happened to you." His voice was husky with passion.

"I just don't want us to be apart," she said. "I know things are really wrong on this planet and that we need to act fast, but I just don't want to be without the one person who makes me feel like I'm good enough."

"Don't worry, DraDonna. You're more than good enough with or without me, and with the HEART's blessing we will be together again." he said, kissing the top of her head.

DraDonna took a deep breath, trying to control her emotions. "It is dusk now and it'll be dark soon. It should be easy enough for you to slip in, get the thing made, and slip back out. I think the smart thing for me to do is to move the HEART stone altar outside after you leave and secure the house just in case I get any unexpected visitors."

"Very wise." He tightened his arms around his beloved wife. "I will miss you."

"I will miss you too, my welder man." She wound her arms around him and looked up into his face.

He gently kissed her at first, caressing her lips with his. But it was not enough for him. He needed to feel the heat of her lips more deeply; he moved his hands up from their comfortable spot on her hips to the back of her head, covering her lips against his own. Then, reluctantly releasing her head and pulling his lips from hers, he took a deep breath. "I wish we had more time... time to do more than kiss." He affectionately stroked the curls around her face.

DraDonna laughed a little even though she had tears in her eyes. "I wish we did, too."

He turned, picking up his bag of tools and slinging it over his shoulder. He then turned to face his wife, placing his right hand on the cool smooth stone and taking the travel stone out of his small travel pack.

"Hold on a second," she said, "you'll need this." DraDonna ripped the two pages from TynLexa's book that showed how to make the core sampler drill. "Don't forget to eat lots of Traveler's Joy. You'll need it."

"I won't forget," he said. Taking the papers from her hand and putting them in his small travel pouch, he gently stroked her face.

"I love you," she said simply.

"I love you too," he answered her. Then he recited the prayer for travel and disappeared in a flash of blue light.

Welding
14

DraDevon took his hand off the HEART stone's smooth cool surface.

He looked around the main living area that was his home. But there was nothing about it that felt familiar to him. The house had been ransacked. Furniture had been turned over; belongings had been flung all over the house. It was obvious that someone had been here looking for something. He had a good idea of who, but what they were looking for he just didn't know.

"No time to think about that," he mumbled to himself as he picked his way through the mess on the floor.

He knew he needed Traveler's Joy just after energy travel to help keep his head clear; so as he walked out the front door and went around the side toward the shop, he picked a few sprigs of the flowered plant, first eating one then storing the rest in his pouch at his hip.

DraDevon started thinking about the materials he would need as he walked toward the shop. He would need to make the core drill as well as the hand crank, and he felt sure he already had some pieces cast that he could use.

On his way, he stopped short. There was a dark figure coming out of the shop, slamming the door with a loud bang and looking around as if hoping to spot someone.

DraDevon felt cold fear, like a rock in his stomach. He crouched down, knowing that whoever it was, they were not friendly, and they were looking for him. He held his breath, hoping that the darkness as well as the tree he was crouched behind would hide him from those unfriendly eyes.

After a few moments, curiosity got the better of him and he peeked around the trunk of the tree to see the dark figure heading up the road in the direction of the Ambassadors office. Once the mysterious person had gone, the cold dread departed from DraDevon as well, and he stood up.

Thinking once again about making this core drill, he knew that he was going to need a large dose of the HEART's energy in order to build it as fast as he could. He doubled back to his house, lugging his bag of tools.

As he stepped back in the front door, he felt a little fear over the fact that DraDonna was alone in the cabin, but also a little bit of comfort in the fact that he at least knew where she was. For the time being, he was the only one who knew.

"She is safe there," he thought, over and over. *"But I miss her,"* always followed.

Kneeling down in front of the HEART stone altar, he placed his hands down on the stone and recited the prayer for energy, inhaling as he felt the blue light of the HEART's energy quickly run up his arm and spread to every part of his being. It made him feel powerful, like he could do anything.

The little sparks of energy entered his brain last, soothing away his worry, nearly confusing him as to what he needed to do. At this, he yanked his hands off the stone and the blue light of the energy faded. "I can't let you cloud my mind!" he said to the HEART stone altar.

He stood up and the room was spinning a little. He knew that after taking such a great dose of the energy that he needed more Traveler's Joy. He took out a large piece of the vine and ate it with a sigh. The dizzy feeling eased.

DraDevon now felt he was ready to get to work.

He carefully left his house, looking around to be sure that no one was watching. He quickly walked to the familiar warmth of the shop.

Inside the shop, he gathered up all the materials he needed, feeling pleased that he would save a lot of time— he had found enough already made parts for the crank that he would not have to make it from scratch.

Taking four sheets of steel, each five feet long, he lined them up on the floor. He put on his welding helmet and then closed his eyes to remember the welding training of his youth. He saw the energy gather at the center of his chest and pushed it out to his right shoulder and down his arm until it reached his wrist. He then focused his mind on splitting the energy with the small grain of HEART stone that was implanted in his wrist when he was a baby.

The energy that is negative channeled out to his thumb, the positive channeled out to his forefinger. Bending down, pushing the sheets together and holding the slag bar with his left hand, he makes contact with his thumb and forefinger on the slag bar. The joining of the two parts of the energy caused the slag to super heat, joining the two pieces of steel in a permanent bond.

He repeated the process with all the sheets, joining all the pieces together.

Then needing the sheets of strong steel to bend, he used another technique learned in school. He channels the energy down toward his right hand again using the grain of HEART stone in his wrist. He split the energy, this time channeling the negative to his right hand and the positive to his left hand. Holding both hands with fingers spread wide just over the sheets of metal, he touched thumb to thumb and forefinger to forefinger.

Again this remerging of the two elements of the HEART's energy caused great heat to emanate from his hands. It heated the steel to the point that he could bend it into the cylinder shape that he needed.

Switching back to the one-handed technique, he joined the tube with a slag seam down the length of the cylinder. Reaching the end of the cylinder, he intensified the energy in order to cut the bottom into a serrated edge.

After finishing the core cylinder, he released the energy for a moment as he assembled the pieces needed to make the hand crank. Again he was pleased that he already had all the parts on hand so that he would not have to cast them, which would take more time than he had available to him.

With the assembly of the crank and the cap done, he put the cap on the top and began to weld it all on the core cylinder with the one-handed method. After just a few more moments, he had finished with the last bit of welding and sat back on his heels to look at his work.

The core drill was twenty feet long and only two inches in diameter. The bottom end was serrated and there was a hand crank attached to a pipe that was suspended around the tube. There was another pipe running upward attaching to the top. It also was attached to the cap. As the crank's handle was turned, it spun on wheels, moving it up the tube as the pipe spun. It also spun the cap on the top of the drill, pushing the serrated end down into the ground. It wasn't his best work, but it was functional and he had finished it fast.

By now it had grown very late into the night. DraDevon let himself think about DraDonna for the first time since working on the core drill. He felt little cold fingers of fear grip his soul. He hoped that the HEART would protect his precious wife.

Picking up his bag and then the very long and heavy cylinder, he lugged it back to the house, feeling worn and tired from using so much energy.

DraDevon headed straight for the HEART stone altar. Just before he got to it, he realized he was not alone.

Enemy
15

The dark figure that DraDevon had earlier seen coming out of his shop rose from his chair in the main living area.

"Well. Look who's come home."

"JorRobert?" DraDevon said, peering into the darkness. "What are you doing in my house?"

"I don't owe you any explanations," JorRobert retorted. "I'm here on the business of the Ambassador."

"What business? We haven't done anything that would be of concern to Ambassador Symon," DraDevon answered him defensively. "So if you'll excuse me, I need to be going."

"Let me ask you something, DraDevon. What is that thing you're holding?"

"This is a project DraDonna and I are working on while we're on our couples' solace," he answered carefully.

"And just what is this so-called project?"

"That would be none of your business, JorRobert. This is between my wife, myself, and the HEART." Irritation showed in his voice.

"Well," JorRobert said with a mirthless chuckle, "I see they were right about you. You've both gone energy mad and I've been sent to stop you........by any means necessary......even if I have to kill you."

"Well bring it on, little Robert."

JorRobert sneered at him. "You're going to pay for that insult." With a primal roar, he charged at him.

DraDevon knew what was coming, but was still holding the heavy core drill. He didn't have enough time to drop it and free his hands so he could defend himself.

JorRobert leaped across the room, his soul filled with the painful shards of rage, taking a feral swing at him, smashing DraDevon on the side of his head.

DraDevon was knocked sideways into the HEART stone altar, trapping his right arm between the heavy core drill and the altar. JorRobert seized the opportunity to gain even more advantage. He jumped over the steel cylinder, landing on top of DraDevon, driving punch after punch into his side, smashing his ribs.

Each blow drove the air out of— and the pain into— his body. DraDevon struggled to free his right hand by lifting the heavy cylinder with his left. Each breath was agony because of the abuse JorRobert was inflicting on his ribs.

"Where is your wife?" JorRobert yelled, landing a blow on the side of DraDevon's face.

Gasping and coughing DraDevon said softly, "Stop. No more. I will tell you."

"What was that? Little wimpy welder boy had enough?" JorRobert leaned in to hear DraDevon's confession of where DraDonna was hiding.

"She is..." DraDevon coughed and gasped again to cover up the fact that he had carefully freed his right hand. He focused and then channeled what little energy he had left inside him, splitting the energy in his wrist like he would if he was going to arc weld. "She is..." he said again even softer, causing JorRobert to lean in even closer. "NOT HERE!" DraDevon yelled as he put his two energy charged fingers together, jamming them into JorRobert's neck.

JorRobert screamed from surprise and pain, causing him to fall back a little.

DraDevon struggled to get his feet and out from under the heavy steel pipe, but not fast enough.

JorRobert lunged forward, slapping his hands around DraDevon's throat, dragging him out from under the core drill and up to eye level. He squeezed with all the burning rage in his soul. "I was told that if you didn't cooperate, I was to kill you!" JorRobert screamed into his face.

DraDevon, desperate for air, clawed at the much taller man's hands, trying to pull them away before he choked the life out of him.

"Tell me where she is and I won't have to kill you," he screamed into DraDevon's reddening face. "Tell me!" He shook DraDevon by the neck making his feet dangle just above the floor.

DraDevon, realizing his feet were now freed from under the drill, raised up his right foot and jammed it with all his might into JorRobert's stomach.

The blow did not cause JorRobert to let go, but it did throw him off balance, and both of them toppled to the floor. Though the kick to the stomach did not cause JorRobert to let go of DraDevon's neck, but the shock of the fall did.

DraDevon rolled away from JorRobert and over the serrated end of the core drill, gasping for breath. JorRobert got to his feet, chest heaving. Whether JorRobert was breathing heavily from the fall or out of sheer rage, he didn't know.

"I don't care what happens now," the big man declared. "You're just dead." JorRobert advanced with a murderous gleam his eyes.

DraDevon picked up the end of the core drill and said in a raspy voice, "Get mind wiped." He rammed the serrated end of the core drill into JorRobert's chest.

The big man's eyes widened in shock.

DraDevon scrambled to his feet, taking the travel stone out of his pocket. He hurriedly grabbed his pack and heaved the large drill as best as he could with his left hand and stumbled to the HEART stone altar, slapping his right hand down.

JorRobert, with blood soaking through his shirt and blood on his lips, stumbled and then plummeted to the floor. He began to crawl in an obsessive attempt to stop him.

DraDevon was near to panic. He began the prayer for travel just as JorRobert reached him.

JorRobert stretched up and took hold of the only thing that he could reach: DraDevon's tool bag. With slurred speech, he said, "Must stop you, or kill you."

DraDevon pulled hard backward in surprise, trying to shake off JorRobert's grip, causing the strap on his bag to rip and come off just as the blue light of the travel energy took him.

Alone, and though he was in a lot of pain, JorRobert pulled the open and torn sack toward him to get a look at what was inside. Barely hanging onto consciousness, he attempted to laugh when he found the notebook, the drawings, and the energy print.

"I know where you are now," he said with a gurgle in his voice and bloody froth on his lips.

Unable to hold on any longer, JorRobert sank into unconsciousness on the floor.

Seeing
16

After seeing DraDevon disappear in a flash of blue energy, DraDonna felt overwhelmed with the cold feeling of loneliness. Shaking off this feeling, she got to work, closing the shutters securely over the windows. Then, with a great heave, she pushed the HEART stone altar out the front door.

Looking around the main living area, DraDonna decided to push the heavy wooden table from the kitchen in front of the door to keep any unwanted visitors out until DraDevon got back.

Still feeling cold, lonely, and so very tired, she went to the bedroom and crawled into the large soft bed giving into drowsiness. It wrapped around her like the soft folds of the blankets of the bed.

She sank into the darkness of sleep. The familiar feeling of spinning into the black abyss took her again, until light gathered around her. She found herself standing on that familiar mountaintop once again.

Tatiana was by her side. "Take my hand, child, we don't have much time," she said hurriedly.

Apprehension caused her to hesitate in taking Tatiana's outstretched hand.

"Do not worry little Donna, I have broken so many rules now that this one will not matter."

DraDonna took her hand. It felt like it was made of pure positive energy. Although Tatiana's hand was not solid flesh, she felt substantial.

Tatiana looked up and ascended into the sky, safely bringing DraDonna with her.

DraDonna felt exhilarated and a little scared. "How far up are we going?"

Tatiana remained silent.

"Are we going to talk to the other old souls again?" DraDonna asked, her curiosity rising.

Again her question was met with silence.

They reached a great height, but they were still not as far up as the old souls. Tatiana broke her silence and said, "Look."

DraDonna looked down from this great height and, feeling a little dizzy, she took in the scene below her.

"What do you see?" the old soul asked as they flew over the land.

"I see the ground, the trees, and farther off I see buildings." she replied, not understanding what she was looking for.

"But do you see? Do you see what is wrong?" she implored DraDonna. "See!" Tatiana commanded. They began to move through the sky again.

DraDonna watched the scene change and shift below her little by little; never much. It was if they were flying in circles. They were coming up on the same mountain range and lake for the third time.

"Do you see?" Tatiana asked again. "Do you see what is wrong?"

"I see the same trees and mountains everywhere." DraDonna answered, a little confused.

"Yes! It is all the same everywhere." Tatiana stopped their flight for a moment. "It should not be that way. The answer to why it is like this is in the ground, everywhere down in the ground."

DraDonna was beginning to feel a little frustrated by hearing this same cryptic answer again.

"I know this, Tatiana. I have DraDevon making a core drill so we can study the soil far down in the ground."

Without saying anything more, Tatiana tugged on DraDonna's hand and they began to move again. "Yes," Tatiana said. "Drill in the ground. It is in the ground."

"You keep saying that, Tatiana, but I don't really understand. What is in the ground? Please explain it to me. I want to help you, but I just don't understand what I'm looking for."

"Donna, I don't have the strength to answer a lot of questions. There are a lot of things you need to see and not much time."

As they flew past the Ambassadors community, DraDonna looked down and saw smoke rising up out of the shop next her home and smiled. She knew that her beloved husband was in there safe and working on the core drill.

A thought occurred to DraDonna. "If what I need to find is in the ground, then is the core drill what we need to use to get down to where it is?"

"It will be sufficient," Tatiana replied shortly. "Look, see."

DraDonna shifted her gaze from her friend's transparent face to the changing landscape.

"Where are we going?" DraDonna asked, feeling a little apprehensive about how far they were going. No one had ever gone this far out before, away from the communities. She didn't even know what was out here.

"Not far now, Donna—watch and see."

DraDonna began to see something—a fantastic sight. She saw many fields of crops as far as her eyes could see. She tried to recognize the plants, but she couldn't. There were so many fields and so many different crops.

DraDonna felt like they had been flying for an eternity and that she would not be there in the cabin when DraDevon arrived.

As if Tatiana could read her mind, she told her young friend, "Don't worry little Donna. You will be back in time to fulfill your destiny."

DraDonna was about to ask Tatiana how she knew when Tatiana told her to look again.

This time DraDonna saw something fantastic, something she remembered from the first dream, but this time it was different; she was not just being shown an image. This time she was seeing, up close, fields of large beasts. Some of them were spotted black and white. Some were just black. Others had what looked like pointed branches growing out of the tops of their heads. There were so many that she could not possibly count them all. There were many different kinds of beasts of different shapes and sizes; there were also many flocks of some bird-like creatures that ran and fluttered across the ground.

Overwhelmed by all she had seen, DraDonna was speechless at first.

Tatiana sensed this and asked, "Did you see them Donna, do you understand?" she asked. "There is no one else in all the communities that has seen this."

"I see them Tatiana, but I don't understand. Where did all these creatures come from? Why are they all here?"

"They have always been here, Donna. The animals and the crops provide a lot of food and other things that the communities need. There are many more crops and fields of animals than I have shown you."

"All this has been always been here and no one knows about it?" DraDonna asked incredulously. "It's hard for me to believe that no one has ever stumbled upon these fields of plants and the beasts. Does the Ambassador know?"

"The HEART knows it's all here, and the Ambassadors are told about this but never shown. The few unlucky souls that have accidently stumbled upon all this have been mind wiped with the negative energy."

"Why did you show me all of this? Please explain it to me," DraDonna begged her desperately. "I don't understand and if you don't explain it to me, who will?"

"The HEART will," Tatiana stated simply. Without so much as another word, she faced DraDonna. Leaning forward, she placed a warm soft kiss of energy her on the forehead. Tatiana then shoved her with all the force that her soul could muster.

DraDonna had the breathtaking feeling of being pulled backward; she could see colors and lights blazing past her.

Then with a gasp she felt her soul resettle in her body.

DraDonna felt a pounding in her head. After a moment she realized that the sound was at the front door and not in her head. She got out of bed on shaky legs and stepped carefully, trying not to make any sound.

The pounding became more urgent, and DraDonna heard the sound of desperate male voice begging her to answer the door. She exhaled a sigh of relief as she shoved the table out of the way to let her husband in.

Lies
17

JorMelony was getting tired. She had been walking around the community all day looking for her husband, and now it was after nightfall and she still had not found him. There was just one house she had left to check, and though she really didn't think he would be there, she decided to go anyway.

"Why would he be at DraDonna's?" she said aloud as she opened the door to her sister's house.

When she opened the door, she knew that she was going to find a room that had been tousled up, but she gasped in shock at the scene before her. It wasn't just the fact that the room was even more torn up than before. It was that her husband was lying unconscious in a rapidly growing pool of blood.

"JorRobert!" she screamed, running across the room. "What happened? JorRobert, wake up! Wake up," she sobbed, rolling him over. She opened his shirt and saw six deep wounds in a circle on his chest. They were gushing blood.

"What is... how?" she stammered, tears of desperation running down her face.

JorMelony was terrified at the sight of her husband bleeding to death before her eyes, but she still had enough presence of mind to know he needed the healing that only the HEART's energy could give him. She tried to wake him but was unsuccessful.

With great effort, she managed to pull him the last little distance to the HEART stone altar. Lifting his right hand, she pulled the bag's strap out of it and then placed his hand on the HEART stone, quoting the prayer for healing through her tears.

JorMelony, feeling petrified that she may have been too late, waited anxiously for the HEART to heal her husband. Her fear slowly ebbed as she saw the blue energy pulsate on the HEART stone, surging through JorRobert's hand, then down into his damaged body.

She watched her husband's injuries breathlessly as the blue light of the energy circulated in and out of him, swirling around his broken body in a dazzling display of blue sparks. She saw the deep wounds stop bleeding and begin to close up. She watched dark bruises change until they dissipated and were gone. There was an odd looking burn on his neck that went from a painful red to a light pink, and then disappeared altogether.

JorMelony was sure she heard the broken ribs crack back into place, and she was happy he was not awake because this all looked very painful.

JorRobert began to moan, taking deep breaths, and the energy withdrew.

JorMelony took his hand off the HEART stone altar, and then shook him. "JorRobert, please wake up!" She was desperate.

He took another deep breath and weakly tried to sit up, but moaned and then fell back.

JorMelony sobbed hysterically, "Please tell me what happened!"

He rolled his head over on the floor in order to look at her and feebly said, "I feel dizzy."

"You shouldn't feel dizzy after a healing, JorRobert... you should feel great," she said, still sobbing. "Please tell me what is going on."

"I need some of the plant," he told her weakly.

"What plant?" she asked, fearing that he was energy mad.

"In my bag. By the chair," he said shortly.

She quickly did as he asked, and gasped in surprise to see the same plant that she saw her sister picking not too long ago.

"Would you please feed one to me?" he asked her.

She put a good sized piece of flowery vine in his mouth. After lying there a moment longer, he sat up.

"JorRobert, you have to tell me what is going on! I feel like I have gone energy mad!" She was getting hysterical again.

"How did you find me here?" he asked his crying wife.

"I've been looking for you all day because I have something important to tell you. I went to your parents' house, your sister's house, and I even checked with all the members of the band. No one knew where you were. I was on my way home, hoping you'd gone back there, when I saw the light on in here. I thought it was a little odd, because DraDonna and DraDevon were gone; so I thought I would take a look."

"What is it you to have tell me, JorMelony?"

"It can wait. You have to tell me what happened!" she said, getting angry with him now.

"Well," JorRobert started. "It's a long story and I don't think you're going to like it." Looking at his wife's tear-streaked face, though, he knew he had to tell her.

"Earlier today," he began, "just after you left, I received an energy message from Ambassador Symon. The message said that DraDonna and DraDevon were in a lot of trouble, that he needed my help."

He took a deep breath and went on. "The message said I was to go to the temple office. When I got there First Councilor Jude was there and she told me that she too had been called there by Ambassador Symon to deal with this problem. She didn't tell me very much, but I was shown how to monitor what your sister and her husband were doing with this special EDU stone."

JorMelony interrupted him. "Wait a moment. Why are they in trouble? What was it they did that was so bad? Was it because they missed the gathering this morning?"

"I didn't want to be the one to have to tell you this, but they have gone energy mad in the worst possible way. I have seen it with my own eyes. They've beaten up two other people already. And the worst thing is they've been using science," he told her in a horrified whisper.

"But DraDonna wouldn't hurt anybody!" JorMelony jumped to the defense of her sister. "And science? DraDonna and DraDevon don't know anything about science. They make furniture!"

"It's true all the same. I saw it with my own eyes on the EDU stone. After I saw that, I was told I needed to go help the two people they had injured, then find and bring DraDonna and DraDevon in for punishment," he told her. "This is why I've been gone all day."

"But I still don't understand how you got hurt so badly…"

"That's the hardest part to tell you JorMelony," he confessed to her. "I was here trying to figure out where they could have gone when DraDevon showed up. He had been making this big ugly science thing out of steel. All I did was ask him what he was doing, and he went mad and attacked me. DraDevon hit me with the jagged end of that hideous piece of metal."

JorRobert rubbed his chest where he was wounded and then looked down, feigning innocence and sorrow about what had happened.

All JorMelony was able to do was stare at him in disbelief for several moments. "What about that plant you ate?"

"Oh. The plant is called Traveler's Joy. First Councilor Jude told me this secret that not many people in the communities know about. You see, if you eat this plant and take in lots of the HEART's energy, you're extra strong. She told me I was going to need the extra strength to stop DraDonna and DraDevon. JorMelony, they are trying to do something so atrocious that it makes me sick."

"What are they trying to do?" JorMelony asked in a small, scared voice.

"They want to try to kill the HEART," he replied with an angry gleam in his eyes.

Reunion
18

Flinging the door of the cabin open, DraDonna flew into her husband's arms. They entwined in an embrace so tight that they seemed to be one being instead of two. Without a word from lips that tingled in anticipation of the kiss, they came together in a long sweet caress.

The reunited soul mates pulled back, breathing hard. DraDevon nuzzled his face in his wife's curly locks. "I was so afraid that I wasn't going to make it back to you. He almost killed me," he confessed, tears in his voice.

"What happened?" she asked, still holding him close to her. "Who tried to kill you?"

"Let's talk about it inside," he told her. "But first I need healing."

It was then that DraDonna noticed her husband was trembling. Pulling away from his tight embrace, she stepped back to look at him. She gasped with horror at the sight of the injuries on her precious husband's face and neck.

With the support of DraDonna's strong body withdrawn, DraDevon collapsed to his knees in pain.

"What… who?" DraDonna stammered in shock.

"Please help me to the altar; I need healing." His voice was edged with pain.

Without another word she swiftly helped her husband to his feet and walked him back a few steps to the HEART stone altar. "Do you need me to help you stay at the altar?" she asked, ready to hold him up if need be.

"No my love, I think I can do it." He weakly placed his right hand on the cool white stone while wrapping his left arm around his injured ribs.

Gasping in pain, he weakly began the prayer for healing. "He that hath faith in the HEART to be…" His prayer was halted by a coughing fit. He gasped, unable to catch his breath and then collapsed across the altar.

"No!" DraDonna cried, dashing to his side. Lifting her unconscious husband, she saw a dark stain of blood on the white stone of the altar, as well as the smear of it on his lips. He was hardly breathing. She hurriedly placed his right hand back on the stone and started the prayer again. "He that hath faith in the HEART to be healed, and is not appointed to death, Shall be healed." DraDonna was relieved to see the healing blue light of the HEART gather around their hands in a stunning array of sparks.

The energy quickly traveled to the injuries in DraDevon's body, causing him to take a sharp breath in and then cry out in pain.

Her precious husband's cry of pain brought tears to her eyes and agony to her soul. She begged the HEART silently to heal him swiftly and ease his pain.

As if in answer to her silent pleading, DraDevon's breathing evens and the look of agony is no longer on his handsome face.

DraDonna took her hand off of his as the blue light of the HEART's energy returned to the stone.

DraDevon groaned a little and fell forward once more across the HEART stone altar.

"DraDevon!" she cried, tears falling from her eyes. Fear gripped her soul, "What's wrong? Didn't the energy heal you?"

First taking long even breaths, DraDevon turned to look at his wife. "It did, but for some reason I feel really dizzy," he said. "I think it has something to do with the Traveler's Joy."

"Do you need some?" she asked him while wiping the tears from her eyes.

"Yes. I think so."

"Hold on," DraDonna said, quickly pulling a large vine with purple blossoms on it from her pouch. She tenderly wiped the blood from his lips before feeding him the vine.

DraDevon took a moment or two to chew and swallow the plant, then sat up and said, "I think that we need to go in the cabin."

"Okay," DraDonna said, feeling relieved that he sounded stronger. "But what happened? Who did this to you?"

"I'll tell you, but I would feel better if we were in the cabin first." DraDevon got strongly to his feet.

He took her by the hand, leading the way into the cabin. As soon as they stepped inside, he turned around and captured DraDonna in another embrace, this time placing one hand on the small of her back and tangling the other in her curly copper tresses. He hungrily covered her lips with his own, needing to express his deep abiding love for her.

She responded to his kiss with her own increasing passion. Wanting to be closer to him, she ripped his shirt out from where it was tucked neatly in his belt and ran her hands up the tight planes of his back.

Releasing her lips only to kiss the sensitive skin just beneath her ear, he moaned with the sweet pleasure of her touch.

"I was so afraid you were going to die," she confessed, breathless with desire. "Please don't ever leave me alone again; I need you so much."

He stopped his caressing kisses on her neck so he could look at her, placing a hand on either side of her face. "But I would die for you!" he said, his voice full of emotion and his eyes smoldering with desire.

He slowly and gently covered her lips with his own again, but with the both of them needing to be one, their kissing became more ardent and consuming.

Their actions became one as they removed the barriers between their bodies and their souls. Wrapping their arms around each other, they gracefully lowered to the floor and expressed their deep eternal love for one another.

Leverage
19

JorRobert got strongly to his feet, looking down at his wife who was still sitting on the floor. "I really need to report this," he told her.

"Report?" she asked him, her patience wearing thin. "Report to whom?"

"First Councilor Jude," he told her shortly.

"But I thought…" she started, but he interrupted her.

"Look, JorMelony, I have to do this. There is more at stake here than you know. I need you to be quiet," he said with exasperation in his voice.

"Fine," she said, still sitting on the floor fuming.

He turned, kneeling at the HEART stone altar, and recited the prayer for communication. He began his report with the standard greeting.

"HEART's greeting First Councilor Jude. I have much to report."

"HEART's Greeting JorRobert. Go on, I am here."

"DraDevon was here. He made some long metal thing in his shop with a jagged end. I'm not sure what it was for. When I questioned him about it he attacked me with his metal thing and nearly killed me. He got away but left behind a little notebook that gave me a pretty good idea where he went. If it weren't for my wife showing up at just the right time, I probably would be dead right now."

"Stand back from the altar. I will be right there. HEART's blessing."

"HEART's blessing," he responded as the light quickly faded from the stone.

JorRobert quickly got to his feet and stepped back to where his wife sat. Reaching down, he took her hand and helped her to her feet.

"What's going on?" JorMelony asked, a little confused.

"She's coming here," he said with a touch of trepidation in his voice.

The HEART stone altar began to glow. With a flash of blue light, once again the beautiful woman with blonde hair and lovely blue eyes stood before them. "Alright JorRobert," Councilor Jude said, "explain to me why he almost killed you and you didn't kill him?" Her voice was high and misleadingly sweet.

"It all happened so fast," he said, stumbling with fear over every word, hoping that his pendant wouldn't begin to burn again. "DraDevon attacked me with his metal thing and then left."

"Again I ask you: why is DraDevon still alive and you were the one left bleeding on the floor? Where is the emitter I gave you?" Councilor Jude's sweet voice sounded more malevolent and dangerous with each word.

"It...It's over by that chair," he stammered in fear.

Quickly she walked over to the chair and picked up the carelessly dropped weapon. Whipping back around, she faced JorRobert brandishing the weapon as if she was going to use the emitter to burn a hole in him. "Why didn't you have this on you?" she yelled at him. "He should be the one that was left on the floor! We would be closer to finishing this!"

"I...I..." JorRobert stammered in fear.

"You're what?" she asked, having completely lost her composure. Councilor Jude turned her back on the alarmed couple. She looked down at the emitter gripped tightly in her hand and whispered gently under her breath, "I'm doing this for us, Symon."

Then, feeling like she was back in control of her emotions, she turned to face JorMelony and JorRobert with deliberate slowness, smiling brightly. "Well now, I guess everyone makes mistakes," she said kindly.

She walked back to where they still stood holding hands. "Just keep it on you at all times and be sure that you don't make another mistake like this one. Okay?" She handed the weapon back to JorRobert.

He tentatively accepted the emitter.

"Next time he might actually succeed in killing you. And none of us would want that, now would we, JorMelony?" Councilor Jude asked, turning to speak to JorMelony for the first time since she arrived.

"No. It was awful finding him lying there bleeding all over the floor," JorMelony agreed, feeling a little unsure of what she agreed to.

"JorMelony, I have a little gift for you that will help us all get through this rough time," Councilor Jude said with a kindly mask on her face. She reached into the pocket of her black robe and pulled out a necklace that matched the one JorRobert was wearing.

"What is that?" JorMelony asked.

"It's a gift of the HEART," she told JorMelony sweetly. "Turn around and I will put it on you."

Not knowing what the necklace truly was, JorMelony obediently turned around. As she did, JorRobert finally saw what First Councilor Jude was offering his wife.

"No, don't!" he said as Councilor Jude placed the necklace around his wife's slender neck.

Looking over JorMelony's head at JorRobert, her mask of kindness shattered, showing the anger that was concealed under it. "Do you really want to try to stop me?" she asked JorRobert as her own pendant began to glow slightly in response to her anger.

"Ow!" JorMelony exclaimed. A little shock of energy had run down the chain to the pendant at her throat from Councilor Jude fusing the ends together.

"Please don't do this to my wife. She has nothing to do with this," JorRobert desperately begged.

"There you go, JorMelony," Councilor Jude said, trying unsuccessfully to sound cheerful. "This is to ensure not only that you do as I want, but that your husband and DraDonna do as I want as well."

"What are you talking about?" JorMelony asked in confusion.

"JorMelony, don't…" her husband tried to stop her.

129

"No JorRobert, I want Councilor Jude to explain to me what she wants with the two people I love most!" she demanded.

"I'm sorry to tell you this, JorMelony, but your sister and her husband have gone energy mad." Councilor Jude began to explain.

"I don't believe you!" she yelled taking a menacing step toward her. "I know DraDonna better than you do. There has to be a good reason for what DraDevon did. There has to be someone else behind it. How do I know it wasn't you?" she continued yelling as she gave the First Councilor's shoulder a good shove to show that she meant business.

JorRobert held out his hand with the intention of saying something to stop his wife, but knew that he was one moment too late as he heard her squeal in pain. She fell to her knees in front of First Councilor Jude trying desperately to pull the burning chain away from her skin.

"Stop please!" JorRobert begged desperately.

Councilor Jude sighed with frustration and knelt down in front of JorMelony so she could look her in the eye.

"Be careful, JorMelony," the First Councilor warned her. "I think, too much of this, and it would be harmful not just to you… but to your baby as well. We don't want you to give birth to another dead baby, now do we?" she said cruelly. She then grasped her own pendant and silently commanded the other woman's necklace to cool.

"How did you know I was with child?" JorMelony asked, breathing heavily, trying to swallow the pain.

"Wait a minute!" JorRobert cut in. "You're with child? Is that what you were going to tell me?"

"Yes, JorRobert. It was." Her voice was still tight with pain.

"But how did you know about this and I didn't, Councilor Jude?" He forgot for a moment the power she held over him.

First Councilor Jude laughed lightly at this, taking no offense at the forceful nature of his question. "Come now.

Don't tell me you actually trust SolKaren? Don't you know her at all?" She continued to laugh for a moment or two more.

"Anyhow," she stopped laughing and her voice became cold and hard. "I have a lot to lose if everyone doesn't behave themselves. So I think that I will take your lovely wife and your unborn child with me just to be sure you do your job... and that DraDonna cooperates." She took a firm grip on JorMelony's shoulder.

"Please don't hurt her," JorRobert begged.

"Just obey me and do the job I have told you to do and she, with your unborn child, will be safe," Councilor Jude said menacingly as she pulled JorMelony, struggling with her, toward the HEART stone altar. "Come now, JorMelony, behave yourself! You have seen what I can do."

"Get mind wiped!" JorMelony spat back.

"You really want to test me?" she asked. "I can hurt him too, you know. How would you like to see the father of your child writhing in pain on the floor?"

JorMelony seethed in silence and stood still.

"That's right. Everyone does as they're told and no one has to get burned. Now, if you please JorMelony, place your right hand on the HEART stone and recite the prayer with me."

JorRobert raised his eyes to his wife. "I'm so sorry. I love you."

Just as she finished the prayer, and a moment before the energy took her, JorMelony replied, "I love you too." Then in the familiar flash of blue light she was gone.

JorRobert felt like his soul had been torn in two; the big man felt like his legs had given out. He sat down on the floor and wept. "It's all my fault; all my fault," he muttered to himself.

Then he looked up at the scene around him in main living area of the Dra home. "No. It's all their fault," he declared with bitterness. His soul hardened around him with resolve. "I will do what I have to do to keep my family safe." He looked down at the emitter he still held his hand.

"Whatever it takes."

Sharing
20

DraDonna lay in the safety of her husband's strong arms. She ran her fingers through his silky dark hair. She didn't ever want the sweetness of the moment to end, but she knew they were running out of time. There was also the thought that someone had just tried to kill the one with whom she shared her soul. This thought felt like a sharp dagger tearing at her soul.

Indulging in this one more display of her love for DraDevon, she closed her eyes and looked within herself for the energy within her soul. Finding that she did still have some energy, she channeled it into her right wrist and gently into her fingers. DraDonna then ran her hands down his face, across his lips, gently tickling him with the energy.

"I love you so much, my husband," she said as she repeated her caress with the energy.

"I love you, my wife, my soul," he responded with a shiver of delight at her sweet energy caressing touch.

With concern showing in her eyes as well in her voice, she asked, "Who hurt you?"

DraDevon reached up, and taking one of her copper curls, he pulled it straight, then let go, watching it spring back into place. "I don't really want to talk about that." He knew if he confessed that awful experience to her, it would change the sweetness in the air.

"But I need to know who tried to take you from me," she said with passion in her voice. "I don't think I would be able to survive if I did not have you by my side."

Sighing, DraDevon reluctantly sat up, knowing that he couldn't avoid telling her about it. "DraDonna, I don't want this sweet time to end, and talking about that will unravel it. I also feel like we're running out of time, that we need to get to work." He hoped this would distract her from questioning him further about what had happened.

"I know; I don't want this blissful time to end either; you're right. I feel like time is slipping away from us." She sat up and gathered her clothing from around the main living area of the cabin. "But don't you think that because I agree with you, you're getting out of telling me about what happened."

DraDevon wanted to laugh at his wife's attempt at being stern while in the nude, but what he had just gone through felt like a cold stone in his soul. Although it would be a relief to talk about it, he was afraid telling her about it would cause her pain.

"I know," he sighed with resignation. "Let's get dressed," he said, gathering up his own clothing.

"You know," DraDonna said, "I had another dream about Tatiana."

"Really?" DraDevon asked, his interest sparked and pain forgotten. "What did she tell you?"

"Not going to tell you," she said teasingly.

"What?" he asked, surprised at her answer. "Well if there is something important she told you, I need to know about it."

"It was very important, and I do need to tell you about it, but I'm not going to say a word about it until you tell me what happened when you made the core drill and who tried to kill you," DraDonna stated as she finished putting her boots on.

"Alright DraDonna," he said, dreading to talk about it. "I will tell you, but I think you should sit down." He motioned to one of the two comfortable chairs in the main living area of the cabin. "We both know there's not much time and we both have a lot to share, so please just let me talk."

"I will do my best to be quiet," she promised him.

With a little smile on his lip, he said, "That's not very reassuring," He knew DraDonna was always full of questions.

She silently gestured to him to start and then placed her hand over her mouth.

"Okay," DraDevon started, loving how she brought laughter to such dark times. "When I got to the house, the main living area was torn up. Furniture was tossed around. You name it; I saw it on the floor. Although I didn't check the entire house, I'm pretty sure it was the same as the main living area."

"But who…?" DraDonna started to say as she let her hand fall into her lap in surprise.

"Let me finish," DraDevon interrupted her. "I left the house quickly because I knew that I needed to eat some Traveler's Joy and then get to work.

"When I was outside I saw someone coming out of the shop. I didn't know for sure who it was, but what I do know is that they were looking for us. I hid behind a tree and waited till he left. I was about to go to the shop when I remembered that I would need to take in a lot of the energy so I could make the core drill as fast as I could. I went in and took in a lot of energy. I got that dizzy feeling afterwards, and when I ate another vine, it went away."

"So that's how you knew to ask me for it after you were healed," she said.

"Yes it is," he went on. "I went back out to the shop and didn't see anyone and I got right to work. The welding went well and I didn't even have to make the piece for the hand crank. I had enough parts that were already cast lying around so all I had to do was put it together. I was pretty tired when I got done and all I wanted to do was quickly travel back here to you, but when I managed to drag the drill into the house and up to the HEART stone altar, I saw that I was not alone in the house. The same person that was in the shop had come in the house when I was making the drill, and set a chair back up and was waiting there for me. When he stood up I saw that it was…" He let the sentence drop afraid to tell her who it was.

"Well who was it DraDevon?" she demanded. "Go on, tell me."

"It was JorRobert," he told her.

"What?" she asked in surprise. "How did JorRobert get mixed up in all of this? I know that he doesn't like me very much, but for him to be involved... It's just hard for me to imagine. Was JorMelony there?" she pummeled him with her long string of questions.

"No, he was alone," DraDevon continued his story. "He told me that he was sent by the Ambassador. He started to question me about the core drill, but I wouldn't tell him anything, and I think that made him angry. JorRobert started to say that he was told that we had gone energy mad and he had been sent to stop us even if that means he has to kill us." He paused for a moment to give DraDonna a chance to grasp what he was telling her.

"I must admit," he began again, "I was a little bit rude to him and I think it must have made him even angrier because he attacked me. I couldn't defend myself because I was still holding onto the core drill, and it's really heavy. If I had just dropped the thing, it would have trapped my feet. So he took advantage of this and hit me, knocking me sideways into the HEART stone altar.

"Then he jumped on top of me and demanded that I tell him where you were. I refused to tell him and he started to hit me over and over again in the ribs; then he hit me in the face. I almost had my hand free so I pretended that I was going to tell him where you were...

"I was hurting pretty bad at that point, so I didn't have to pretend too much that I was having a hard time breathing and speaking. He leaned in close and I channeled the energy and split it like I do to arc weld and I burned his neck. I thought that would get him off me but it just enraged him further." He stopped again and looked down at his hands, not wanting to go on.

"What did he do to you?" she asked her husband in a frightened whisper.

"He grabbed me by the neck and dragged me out from under the drill. He lifted me up off my feet. I could feel him choking the life out of me. He kept screaming that if I just told him where you were then he wouldn't have to kill me."

He stopped yet again, and DraDonna kindly said, "Please go on."

"I knew that I had to keep you safe no matter what even if it meant that I had to die. But I also knew that I had to do everything in my power to live, so I could be with you again. It was then that I realized that my feet were free from under the core drill, and I kicked JorRobert as hard as I could in the stomach.

"This made him fall backwards and I got away from him, and rolled over the end of the drill. He said he didn't care about anything anymore, and I was just dead. He charged at me and I didn't even really think about it. I just automatically picked up the end of the drill and shoved it into his chest. I don't know if I killed him or not. I know that he was hurt pretty badly.

"But still… as injured as he was, he still tried to stop me by crawling across the floor and grabbing my tool bag and ripping the strap when I left." He, with remorse in his eyes, looked at his wife's stunned face. "I didn't really mean to hurt him; oh HEART I hope I didn't kill him!" he confessed, bringing his hands to cover his face and hide his tears of shame.

Seeing her husband's anguish, DraDonna stood from her chair and leaned over to wrap her arms around her beloved soul mate to offer him comfort. "For whatever reason," she said, "you and I have been chosen to go on this quest to set all of these souls free. The HEART and I both know that you would not deliberately hurt another person. You did what you had to do to protect me and keep him from killing you. I don't like the idea of you killing JorRobert, but wouldn't it be better for him to die than a world of trapped souls to dwindle and perish?"

"I need you," she said, "the HEART needs you to help me finish this. If we don't, I'm sure we'll all eventually perish."

DraDevon took his hands off his face and hugged her, accepting the loving comfort she offered him. "Thank you."

He cleared his throat and continued. "So now you know what happened to me.

"If JorRobert did survive, he has my book with the images, and he can probably find us now because of the energy stamp on each of them."

"That means we are out of time. If we're going to find anything, we'd better do it now." She stood up next to his chair. "Come on—show me the core drill."

They walked out of the house together, and DraDevon reminded her that she was going to tell what happened when he was gone.

"It's pretty simple. I locked up all the windows, pushed the HEART stone altar out the door and then blocked it with the kitchen table. I was cold and tired, so I went to bed and I fell asleep.

"Tatiana came to me as soon as I was asleep. She showed me how everything was the same everywhere and said how it shouldn't be that way. She told me again that what we are looking for is in the ground. She said the core drill will work for what we're doing. She then showed me something I had a hard time believing." DraDonna stopped for a moment to collect her thoughts as they came to where DraDevon had dropped the core drill.

"Go on, DraDonna. What did she show you?" he asked, his curiosity piqued.

"She showed me... umm... fields and fields of lots of different kinds of plants. I guess that these are all the fruits and vegetables that we eat. She also showed me many different herds of beasts and flocks of birds. She told me the only one who knows this is here is the Ambassador." She stopped again, but just for a moment. "Do you remember when you asked me if anyone knew where all our food comes from?"

"Yes. No one ever questions it. We all just accept that the HEART provides."

"Tatiana told me that these fields and beasts provide food and other needs for all the people in the communities."

"Amazing!" he exclaimed. "So no one but the Ambassadors has ever seen this?"

"Tatiana told me the Ambassadors know of it but have never actually seen it. She did tell me that from time to time a few unlucky people have stumbled on all it and were mind wiped."

"That's kind of scary. I wonder why all of this is such a big secret?"

"I don't know, DraDevon."

"What happened after that?" he asked.

"Not much," she confessed. "She kind of kissed me on the forehead and then pushed me back into my body. It was then that I heard you knocking at the door."

"Really odd," he said, not knowing what to think. "So this is the core drill. What do you think?" he asked her as they both bent down to look closely at it.

"It looks great!" DraDonna said enthusiastically. "It looks just like the image from TynLexa's book. How does it work?"

"I thought about it, and I think one of us will run the crank with the HEART energy and the other one will keep a hand on the HEART stone altar and channel a continuous stream of energy into the other person. I'm sure it will take a lot of energy and we don't have the time to go back and forth." DraDevon explained.

"Well in that case," she said with a determined look on her face, "we'd better eat a lot of Traveler's Joy so we can get to work."

Communion
21

Ambassador Symon was very tired. It had been a long day. He had to visit all three of the communities because of the failed solace gathering. He also had his normal duties as a servant of the HEART.

Symon had to work very hard to minimize the damage that the unsuccessful solace gathering would do to the communities. He was certain that there would be a few people who would remember what the gathering this morning had really been for. Symon traveled to all three of the communities so he could find these people and do a gentle mind cleansing so he could be sure that they didn't remember.

The couples' solace was one tradition that he really didn't want to have brought back. Not only did he think that it was not necessary for newly married couples to go out wasting time like that, but he also thought that if they did, then they were not being of service to their appointed communities.

More than fifty years ago Ambassador Lyda had done away with the couples' solace when a couple decided that they never wanted to leave their cabin. This couple was there for half a year and refused to come back. The couple fought with the two councilors who had been sent to bring them back and one of the councilors got badly hurt. The offending couple had to be brought back by force to the courtyard and mind wiped for civil disobedience and violence against a servant of the HEART. And although he knew they deserved to be punished, Symon really didn't like the mind wiping process.

Mind wiping meant everything that made a person who they were was wiped away publicly. Offenders were punished like this for two reasons. The first reason was that the offending person was made to be an example, so others would learn not to repeat the crime. The second reason is that the offending person's energy would be taken out of their body and rerouted into the gathered people.

All energy was a gift of the HEART their MOTHER, and not to be wasted. This energy was even more of a special gift of the HEART. It felt different than what came from the HEART stones; it had a sensual euphoric feeling that the people always loved. Everyone wanted to be in the crowd on the receiving end of this special energy gathering.

The worst part of the mind wiping process was that everything the person had been was gone, the good with the bad. It was as if they were dead. The people in the communities had been told, and further they believed that the mind wiped people were energy mad, that they found rest in the HEART. But Symon knew those who have been mind wiped were taken off by the HEART.

The person who was mind wiped was given basic mental functions by the HEART and put to work with the herds of animals or in the crops. Symon was so happy that he didn't have to deal with that side of a mind wipe. He always felt a sense of relief that the HEART took care of it. He really didn't like to think about it too much.

It seemed so harsh, but he believed the HEART knew what was best for all of her children. He preferred to try to take care of things as gently as possible, first with mental cleansing and then energy withdraw if need be.

"No more couples' solace; it's not good for the communities," he thought, trying unsuccessfully to convince himself this was why he didn't want the couples' solace tradition to resume; but the real reason was very painful—it caused him great shame. He was jealous. He shamefully admitted to himself this was why he had been so rude to DraDonna and DraDevon. He was jealous of the happiness of their union.

Symon yearned deep in his soul to be able to marry Jude, to go on a couples' solace with her; but he and Jude were servants of the HEART. They were not supposed to love anyone like that. Symon did find joy in his service to the children of the HEART. He felt bad because of the terse way that he had always spoken to DraDonna. He was supposed to love her as a daughter of the HEART and he did, but he could not help loving Jude more than anyone. He had tried so hard not to love her. What made it even harder was that he knew she loved him, too.

All he wanted now was to have peaceful communion with the HEART; his soul felt heavily burdened. His meditation with the HEART had always given him so much comfort. He needed so much to commune with her, to cast his burden on the HEART of the world.

Symon knew that his own selfish needs would have to wait though. He had a sad duty to perform here in First Councilor Jude's community. There had been another stillborn baby. This was the third time for this couple. The first two babies were boys, but this time it was a girl. The mother was beside herself with grief. The love and compassion that he felt for this poor woman helped him to forget his own troubles for a time as he quickened his pace to her home.

Standing outside the door to this couple's home, he felt their pain through his gift of the HEART. He raised his hand and knocked softly. SayChris, a stocky man with sandy blonde hair and blue eyes, in his late twenties, opened the door with a look of anguish on his face.

"HEART's greeting." Ambassador Symon hailed SayChris.

"HEART's greeting; please come in, Ambassador Symon," he said with as much grace as was possible for him in his grief.

"Is First Councilor Jude here?" Ambassador Symon asked.

"No, I haven't seen her since… since…" He could not finish the sentence because of the tears that gathered in his voice, making it impossible to speak.

"Are your PNL people still here?"

Clearing his throat, SayChris answered, "No, they just left with the body."

"Where is your wife?" Ambassador Symon asked with great tenderness.

"She's in bed. What are you going to do?"

"I'm going to help her forget her pain. I could do this for you too, if you want," he offered gently.

"Will we forget her?" he asked, his voice filled with pain.

"I can erase all memory of her if you like."

"No. We want to remember her, just like the other two babies. They are still a part of us... even if the HEART cursed us so they would not live," the poor man said, looking down at his trembling hands to hide the raw emotion in his eyes.

"I will not take your memory of her, then. I will just ease your pain." He placed a hand on the grieving man's shoulder. "But SayChris, you must know the HEART loves all her children and does not curse them. Ever," Ambassador Symon corrected him. "Let's go see your wife."

The two men walked into the dark bedroom. Ambassador Symon could just barely see the small weeping woman on the bed lying with her back to them. SayChris walked in first and sat in a chair next to the bed, motioning for the young Ambassador to come in.

"SayTasha, Ambassador Symon is here to see you." SayChris said as brightly as he could, but SayTasha was so consumed by her grief she did not say a word.

"HEART's greeting, SayTasha," Ambassador Symon said as he approached her and gathered his black robes so he could sit on the edge of her bed. "I have come to offer you some relief from your pain."

Still she did not speak. The only sound that came from her was soul wrenching sobs.

"Please turn toward me, SayTasha, so I can help you," he said gently.

Obediently she turned toward him, all the while keeping her face covered with her hands, not wanting to share her grief.

"Take comfort," he told them kindly. "I bring you my love as well of the love of the HEART." He closed his eyes to draw directly upon the HEART s energy.

Ambassadors were uniquely gifted in their use of the HEART's energy. Unlike the rest of the HEART's children who only had tiny grains of the HEART stone implanted in their wrists, he was the only one who had an actual piece of the HEART stone implanted in his brain. With it he could directly channel large amounts of the energy without having to place his hand on a HEART stone.

With a little bit of mental focus he could use or split the energy in any way that was needed for him to do his duty as the Ambassador for the HEART's children. In this case he would use mostly the gentle positive side of the energy, with just the smallest amount of the negative, only removing the memory of the pain and loss, allowing them to remember the baby girl who could not live.

He tenderly placed a hand on each of their heads. With his eyes closed, he opened up his soul for just a moment to their pain, letting it be his own, causing him to weep for them. Then, drawing up the HEART's energy and letting it gather in his chest, Symon channeled the energy out to his hands.

He carefully controlled the flow of the two different sides of the energy. He only let the energy gently seek out the deep pain, lifting it out of their souls and drawing it into his own. He was leaving the couple with a small gift from his soul, a gift of hope. He placed in each of them the hope that they could try again to have a baby. Even though Ambassador Symon still felt the sorrow that he absorbed from the mourning husband and wife, he knew they were no longer feeling it.

He opened his eyes and lifted his hands from their heads. He wiped the tears from his eyes he had shed for them. He felt the pain they had endured for the third time.

SayTasha rolled back over to the other side of the bed with a look of sleepy contentment instead of tortured pain.

H.E.A.R.T. Saga: The Children

Ambassador Symon looked at SayChris and said, "Perhaps you should lay down with her and get some sleep.

Standing up, he then began to leave the Say's so they could sleep and recover from their pain. Stepping outside of their home, he no longer felt their pain, instead being plagued again by his own troubles— the longing for the woman he loved, yet feeling crushed under the weight of shame for falling in love with a woman that he should not love.

Thinking about this made him wonder why she had not been at the Say home today to offer them comfort. It was not like her to shirk her duties as First Councilor. Ambassador Symon had a bad feeling about what was wrong with Jude.

"I should not have kissed her again," he thought as he remembered with an odd mixture of shame and longing. It was just yesterday. Jude had energy traveled into his office, walking into his private room.

"Symon, I need to talk to you." Jude had said, surprising him.

"What are you doing in my private rooms?" he questioned her coldly.

"I really need to talk to you," she told him, sounding hurt.

"You could have sent me a HEART stone message."

"I need... I need to talk to you about us," she said as tears slid from her eyes, hurt by the unfeeling tone in his voice. "You've been so cold to me but I need to tell you something important."

Feeling bad about how he had been acting toward her, he took the few steps to the doorway and put his arms around her. "I'm sorry Jude. I don't mean to hurt you. It's so hard for me to be around you. I do love you but you know we can't do this."

"I just wanted to see you and tell you about something I've been working on," as she looked up into his mesmerizing hazel eyes. "Oh, Symon! You're so beautiful; I love you so much and... and I think I have found a way for us to be together."

146

Feeling her warmth next to him, her words were lost on him. "I love you too, my exquisite Jude." He was captivated by her lovely face. Knowing it was wrong, but not caring, he placed one hand on the side of her sweet face, gently tracing the contours of her soft lips with the other. Needing to be closer to the woman whom he felt owned a piece of his soul, he bent his head down and softly teased her lips with his.

Jude wrapped her arms around the man she loved, pressing close to him, and kissed him back with all the pent up passion she had held within her for nearly a year.

Feeling her passionately kiss him back sparked a fire within him. He slid his hand down from her face to her shoulder, then down to the small of her back, pulling her small warm frame closer to him. He wanted so much for her to be his wife so they could fully express their love for each other, but their sweet forbidden interlude was interrupted by a knock at the office door. The sound of the knocking brought him back to his senses and reminded him of his duty as Ambassador.

Breaking away from her warm lips, trying to catch his breath, he had said, "Stay here. We'll talk when I get back."

Ambassador Symon added this guilt filled memory to his burdens now. Not only was it bad that he did it the first time, that she had followed him into the temple, and that she saw things that could get her mind wiped, but yesterday he had done it a second time. Only this time, he let it get way out of hand, and to make matters worse, he grew cold on her again when she tried to tell him about her plan for them to be together.

"I should have listened to her. I should not have pushed her away like I did. If Jude has done anything because of some mad plan she has, it will be on me." He ran over in his mind as he quickened his step toward her small office where she also had her own private room. *"But I did what I thought was right, for the good of the communities. I can't be the one to let it all fall apart. Oh HEART, I sure have made a mess of things,"* Ambassador Symon silently

scolded himself as he came up to First Councilor Jude's office door. He hesitated at first wondering if he should knock, but dismissing the thought, he walked in to find a quiet and empty office.

Everything looked as it should in her tiny office.....the HEART stone altar against the back wall, a desk to the left and a door to the right that led to her private bedroom. This office was just like his own office and private rooms. He wondered if he should check her bedroom to see if she was in there. *"That probably would be a bad idea,"* he thought to himself, knowing all the feelings it would stir up for him as well as the trouble it would cause if she was in there.

Walking instead to the HEART stone altar, he placed his right hand on the stone. Since he did not need a travel stone because of the HEART stone in his head, all he had to do was think of where he wanted to travel, and with a flash of the familiar blue light, he was gone.

He didn't know when he left First Councilor Jude's office that there was indeed someone in the private room. She was lying on the bed feeling dizzy and nauseous again because of the baby she had growing inside of her.

Work
22

DraDonna and her husband took a few precious moments to eat a great quantity of Traveler's Joy. "DraDevon," she said between mouthfuls of the plant. "You're right.....we can't take the time to go back and forth to power up with the energy. I was thinking that I should be the one to run the crank."

"Well, not that I am disagreeing with you, but why do you think so?" he asked her.

"It's because you can channel energy to your left hand and I can't," she explained.

"I can't do anything with it in my left like a Councilor can. I can only channel it there and then release it," DraDevon explained, not seeing her point.

"That's why I think you should be the one at the HEART stone altar. You can have your right hand on the altar, and then channel the energy from your right to your left. Then with your left hand on my back, you can release it into me, then I can channel it to my right wrist, split it with the grain of HEART stone, and divide it evenly down my hand like I would do to sand, using that to move the crank."

"Good thinking," he said with enthusiasm.

"If you've had enough Travelers' Joy, I think we should get to it. Is the core drill very heavy?"

"It's pretty heavy if you have to lift it alone, but between the two of us I don't think it'll be much of a problem."

"Well alright then," she said, bending down to pick it up. She stopped, thinking. "You know, I think we'll need some other supplies."

"What supplies?"

"First of all, it's pretty dark here, so I think we should see if there are any energy lights. And we will need shovels because once we get down deep enough we may need them."

"Again good thinking, but I don't think that we will need the energy lights," he said.

"Why not?"

"We will be using the HEART stone altar constantly and that will put off a lot of light, and I am not sure if there are energy lights here. Also, I don't know if we have the time to go looking for them."

"But are there shovels? That is the question, because we need those."

"I'm sure there are shovels," he told her. "I saw a small outbuilding on the side of the cabin."

"Good! Let's go get them."

"No, you stay here. I'll be right back." He started to jog back toward the cabin.

"Check for energy lights while you're in there, just in case." DraDonna bent down to look at the crank and felt a little tickle of excitement. "Maybe you'll help us find what's in the ground," she said to drill, looking up to the squirming dark sky. "What's down there?" she asked, not really expecting to hear a reply.

"Did you ask me something?" DraDevon said as he jogged up to her with two shovels in his hands.

"No, just thinking out loud," she said with a smile. "Oh good! You found the shovels, but you didn't see any lights?"

"No I didn't, I'm sorry."

"We will have to make do without them I guess. Let's get to work."

DraDevon put the shovels down next to the altar. He then turned and put his arms around the woman who carried the other half of his soul and whispered in her ear, "No matter what happens tonight, I want you to know that I love you."

"I love you, too," she said hugging him back tightly.

They released each other and bent over, lifting the heavy steel core drill upright next to the altar. With her left hand, DraDonna grabbed hold of the cast iron ring that the crank was attached to, putting her right hand on the crank. DraDevon placed his left hand on her back and his right hand on the altar and said the prayer for powering up with the energy. "The HEART strengthens me with her energy," he said, closing his eyes and concentrating on channeling the energy to his left hand and releasing it into DraDonna's body.

Not knowing why, DraDonna was filled with fear at the thought of what might be in the ground; but the feel of her husband's hand on her back brought her comfort as the stream of the HEART's energy filled her body with strength.

She closed her eyes and channeled the energy to her wrist, splitting it, dividing it evenly down her hand to push the crank. At first she thought that this method was not going to work because the crank did not move. "It's not working," she called back to him in a panicked voice.

"Focus!" was all he could tell her as he strained to maintain his own concentration.

DraDonna took a deep breath and looked inside herself, finding the energy that was pouring from her husband and pushed it harder into her hand. This extra push was just what the crank needed to begin to turn. She continued to push hard and the crank moved easier and faster. There was a little fear in the back of her mind that because they were in the foot hills of a mountain, there would be rock and this would make it hard to drill. However, this was not the case. The drill quickly slid down through the ground foot after foot as if the soil wasn't even there.

DraDonna kept her eyes closed so she could preserve her concentration. She wondered how long it would take to get the full twenty feet when she heard and felt a loud vibrating clang. It was the sound of metal striking metal. Jarred by the vibration, they both fell to the ground. Stunned and not knowing what to think at first, they looked at one another. DraDonna asked, "What was that? Did we hit some kind of rock?"

"I know that sound," DraDevon said as he helped his wife stand up with him. "That is the sound of metal striking metal. But what I don't understand is why the drill stopped."

"We let go." DraDonna answered simply.

"No, that's not it. We didn't let go until the drill had already stopped."

"What does it matter, DraDevon? This is it," she said excitedly.

"I welded this core drill out of the strongest steel on the planet. It should chew through anything."

"I will admit that's odd, but whatever it is, we have found it." She bubbled over with excitement. "We really need to get digging and bring up whatever it is before someone shows up to try to stop us."

"You're right," he told her. "But we need more Traveler's Joy and energy if we have any hope of getting this done before anyone shows up."

"Good point." She reached into her pack, pulling out the remains of her stash of the vines, giving half to her husband. "It's a big mouthful, but we'll need it."

After swallowing the wad of the plant, they both placed their right hands on the HEART stone altar and recited the ritual words for energy. They felt the powerful tingle of the energy in their bodies.

They picked up the shovels and dug at an amazing rate. Faster and faster the soil flew away as they widened and deepened the hole. Quickly the hole became wide enough and deep enough so they both fit inside it. They kept digging, following the core drill that was embedded only about half in the ground.

"Look out," DraDevon called to his wife as the large metal core drill fell smashing into the side of the hole, just inches from where DraDonna was standing. With a squeal of surprise she jumped to one side and said, "We must be close if the drill fell out."

"I know we…" DraDevon stopped. "I found it!" he said, thumping his shovel down with a metal clang.

"Hurry!" she exclaimed. "Let's find the edges so we can bring it up." They quickly cleared the rest of the dirt out of the hole but still did not find the edges.

Breathing heavy with effort DraDevon said, "We need to stop and get more energy."

"No, we can't stop now; we've found it and we need to get it out!" she said stubbornly. With a feeling of panic rising in her chest, she dropped her shovel and closed her eyes for a moment trying to remember all that Tatiana had told her and shown her. *"See! It's everywhere in the ground."* Tatiana's sweet voice echoed in her mind.

"DraDonna," DraDevon said kindly, placing a hand on her arm. "We need more energy if we are going to bring it up. It looks really big; looks like it's everywhere down here."

"It's everywhere down here," she repeated to herself. It wasn't just something that was in the soil, it was hidden everywhere under the ground. Then she finally understood what Tatiana has been trying to tell her. DraDonna felt like all of her blood drained into her feet.

Sensing his wife's mental anguish, he asked her, "What is it? What have you figured out?"

"I get it! Don't you get it? It's everywhere under the ground! It's under the ground everywhere, not just here or there... It's everywhere!" She felt close to hysteria. "Don't you get it? THIS IS THE GROUND! THE WORLD ISN'T REAL!" DraDonna turned her head up and yelled again, this time at the dark squirming sky. "THE WORLD ISN'T REAL!"

"If the world isn't real, then what is it?" DraDevon asked her, not truly understanding what she was saying.

"I don't know what the world is.........only that it's not real!" she answered him, sounding like she was close to tears.

"DraDonna, we need to get out of this hole. You need some Traveler's Joy or some energy. You're not thinking straight! How could the world not be real?"

"I am thinking straight, DraDevon," she told him. "It all makes sense now. Think about it. Everything is the same everywhere. And this is under the soil everywhere."

DraDonna's words began to sink into his brain. The look on his face changed from amazement to near panic. "We need to get out of here quickly, DraDonna; there are people after us who will kill us if they have to in order to stop us. We need to report this to someone; but who? We both think Ambassador Symon is behind this," he said thoughtfully.

"I know," DraDonna replied. "I think he probably already knows, and that's why he's sending people out to kill us...so he can keep everything covered up."

"What about First Councilor Jude?" DraDevon asked. "Do you think we can trust her?"

"I don't know, but it's worth a try."

They tried to climb out of the hole using the shovels, but they were tired and drained of energy. Then they tried to climb the walls of the nine foot deep hole in the ground, but each and every time they placed a shovel in the ground, the soft soil would just fall away taking the shovel with it.

"Well," DraDevon said with frustration in his voice, "what are we supposed to do now? We can't get out."

Feeling close to panic again, DraDonna closed her eyes and turned her face to the sky, taking deep breaths and trying to calm herself so she could think. She remembered the last time she dreamed about Tatiana and how the old soul kissed her on the forehead. The gentle and warm feeling it gave her then, DraDonna felt that again. DraDonna reached up and felt the spot where Tatiana had kissed her and felt calmness wash over her like a cleansing tide.

"DraDevon," DraDonna said as she opened her eyes and looked into the beautiful eyes of the man she loved, "I think we can climb out on the core drill."

"Do you think so?" he asked her with a spark of hope on his handsome, yet dirty face. "Do you think it will work? The embankment that it's laying against looks pretty weak. I would hate for it to slide or roll while you're on it."

"I think the core drill will be safe enough for us to climb out on. It should have plenty of traction for us to get out, and I'm not worried about it sliding, because if it does there isn't far for it to go and there should be enough of the drill sticking out above the hole for us to use to get out. It has to work. What other choice do we have?"

"Good point," he admitted. "Let's get out of here," he said as he gave his wife a boost onto the core drill. But before either of them had a chance to go very far, they both saw a flash of blue light above them from the HEART stone altar.

Hopping off the core drill, they looked up to the edge of the hole with cold fingers of dread gripping their souls. The head and shoulders of JorRobert appeared above them.

Punishment
23

"Well look what we have here," JorRobert said, his voice dripping with sarcasm. "Two energy mad science offenders nicely captured in a hole for me." He laughed at the astonished look on their faces. "I would say that the two of you are probably surprised to see me alive."

DraDevon stepped forward and pushed his wife protectively behind him. "I wasn't trying to kill you JorRobert." DraDevon cautiously informed him. "I was just defending myself and protecting my wife."

"Sure you were. I have been told to bring the two of you in so you can be punished for your offenses against the HEART."

"What offenses? We haven't done anything wrong," DraDevon said, trying to distract him for a few moments so he or DraDonna could think of some way for them to get out of this alive. "Besides that, how were you able to find us? We took the necklaces off."

In answer to DraDevon's question, he took a few steps closer to the edge of the hole and knelt down. He held out a little book that he had in his left hand. "The images you sketched were helpful, but the things that led me right to you were the energy stamps in the corner of the images. Very smart. Thank you," he laughed.

"You took that from the tool bag you ripped from my shoulder, you energy mad thief," DraDevon said, feeling anger rise in him at the thought of JorRobert violating his privacy.

JorRobert laughed at him again. "Do you know how stupid you sound? What are you going to do to me from down there? Throw dirt at me?"

"I beat you once before, JorRobert. I can do it again."

"I don't think so. What's going to happen is you and your mad wife are going to come out of that hole and turn over any other notebooks and other information on the

HEART offensive project that you have been working on, and then you are going to come with me and let the Ambassador and his Councilors punish you with the negative energy."

"Get mind wiped little Robert; your pitiful words don't scare me."

"How about this?" JorRobert asked, ignoring the insult as he brought forth his right hand to show them what he was holding. It was an odd-looking thing that was shaped somewhat like an uneven carpenter square, but with rounded edges. It was made out of HEART stone instead of metal. JorRobert gripped the longer end, closed his eyes for a moment to focus all the energy in his body and then forced it out through the emitter. A short yellow burst of energy shot out of it and sizzled through the air, striking the core drill with a deadly array of sparks and leaving a molten hole in its wake.

"Does this scare you?" JorRobert asked with a murderous tenor in his voice. "This is called an emitter. All I have to do is focus all my energy down to the grain in my wrist and then release it in one hard burst into the emitter; it then pushes the energy out so fast that the energy becomes hot enough to burn through steel! Just imagine what it would do to flesh." JorRobert's voice darkened. "Now get out."

DraDonna and DraDevon climbed out of the hole the using the core drill like they had planned earlier. Their arms and legs were shaky with fear and exhaustion.

DraDonna's head was already buzzing with panic from her discovery that their whole world was a lie, and now her sister's husband was threatening to kill her. She felt like her soul was being crushed by all of these horrific events. Then an awful thought hit her with a cruel blow: ***Where is JorMelony?*** Where was her sister?

DraDonna approached JorRobert with more boldness than she felt and looked him in the eye. Even though the mad gleam in his eyes added more fear to her soul, she still held up her mask of bold courage and asked him, "Where is my sister?"

"My wife is none of your business. She will be safe as long as you cooperate. So you just need to shut up now and come with me."

"What did you do to her?" she yelled in his face.

A little of JorRobert's control snapped he quickly raised his right hand and hit her across the face with the emitter.

"What's wrong with you?" DraDevon bellowed as he started to charge at a man who would dare hit his wife, but stopped short as JorRobert swung the emitter around and planted the end of it on DraDevon's chest.

"I don't think you want to move right now," JorRobert advised him. "I will burn a hole in the middle of you without giving it a second thought."

"JorRobert," DraDonna said, using a soothing voice, trying to calm the homicidal man, "my sister loves you, and I know that she wouldn't love you like she does if you were a violent person. I don't think that you will do anything to hurt us."

JorRobert laughed in a way that frightened her further. "I guess none of you really know me all that well, do you? But go ahead, test me. See if you like what happens."

DraDonna began to see he was right; she didn't really know him. She fully believed now that he would kill DraDevon. Besides, he had already tried to kill him once today, so what would stop him from trying to do it again? Switching tactics, she still tried to talk JorRobert down. "I still don't think you're going to kill either of us, or you would have done so as soon as you found us in the hole."

"I was told that I only need to bring one of you in to be publicly denounced as a user of science and punished in order for the plan to work. Actually, what I was told was to bring you and the evidence in and kill DraDevon if you don't co-operate. And I would do that happily."

"I don't believe you," she said, trying unsuccessfully to conceal the panic in her voice.

"Don't you now?" he asked, amused. "I guess you want to see me burn a hole in the middle of your husband."

"I know Ambassador Symon doesn't like me very much, but I don't believe for one moment that he would tell you it's okay to kill anyone!" she said, as the feeling of panic grew stronger. "Ambassador Symon is a servant of the HEART; he would not do that."

DraDevon cleared his throat to get JorRobert's attention. "It's obvious that someone has sent you out here to get us. But my wife is right; it could not be the Ambassador who sent you out to do this. So who was it?"

JorRobert laughed once again, ignoring DraDevon's question. "You guys just don't get it." He placed DraDevon's notebook in his pocket and held out his left hand. "You will now give me the other notebooks; both yours and TynLexa's."

Slowly and reluctantly DraDonna pulled the first notebook, then the other out of her pouch at her belt.

DraDevon, taking advantage of the fact that JorRobert's attention was off him, grabbed the emitter with his left hand and swung his right fist, smashing it into the side of JorRobert's face and stunning him. It was not enough to loosen his grip on the emitter.

DraDonna also sprang into action. She drew her foot back and kicked the back of his knee, but the fact that she was tired, hungry, and energy deprived made her kick not as powerful as she intended. Instead of sweeping his leg out from under him and causing him to fall backwards, giving them the advantage, he fell forward on top of her.

On his way down, JorRobert yanked the emitter out of DraDevon's grasp and swung it around, releasing an energy jolt right next to DraDonna's head, singeing off a few of her curls. He then slammed the emitter down on her forehead.

She cried out more from fear than pain, but the sound of her cry made DraDevon feel like he was the one who had been burned with that malicious weapon.

"STOP!" JorRobert said in a loud dangerous voice. "Just stop. Although I was told that DraDonna was the preferable one to bring in, I have no problem burning off her pretty copper hair as I put a hole in her head; so back off DraDevon."

Breathing heavily from the conflict as well as from the cold dread he felt in his soul, DraDevon obediently took a few steps back, watching the big man get up while keeping the emitter trained on his wife's head.

"Now get up, DraDonna." JorRobert ordered after he stood up. "DraDevon, make yourself useful and pick the notebooks up and give them to me," he demanded, keeping a sharp eye on both of them.

DraDevon quietly did so, but he did not take his eyes off his wife.

"Good," JorRobert said after putting the books in his pocket. He switched the emitter to his left hand and said snidely to DraDonna, "Why don't you take your precious husband's hand? It might be the last chance you'll get." Keeping the emitter pointed at the downtrodden couple, JorRobert placed his hand on the HEART stone altar. He prayed a special EDU stone number prayer without saying who the message was for.

"HEART's greeting. This is JorRobert. I found them."

He paused to read the words on the HEART stone altar.

"I found them at cabin number one of the Second Councilors Mountain."

JorRobert stopped to read the message.

"They were digging a big hole in the ground with that drill thing."

Another message that only he saw appeared on the HEART stone altar.

"I can't be sure, but I think so. For as much as I hate the two of them they are both pretty smart; so I am fairly sure that they figured it out."

JorRobert paused again to read a message.

"Why not just bring them to the courtyard? I want to be done with them."

This time as JorRobert read the message his mask of strength and superiority cracked.

"NO! You don't need to do that! I will do as you say. I will bring them to the temple office." Fear was in his voice. "HEART's blessing."

He looked back at DraDonna and DraDevon. "Looks like I'm bringing you back to the Ambassadors community," he said with a mixture of fear and rage in his voice, "to face charges of blasphemy, science, and energy madness. But I am to take you to the temple office first. The two of you had better be cooperative. If anything happens to my wife because of the two of you, I will take great pleasure in killing you myself."

Those cold fingers of fear gripped DraDonna's heart again at hearing this, and her own welfare was forgotten.

"JorRobert, who has my sister?" she asked him.

"The less you know right now the better. Just don't cause me any more trouble and she won't get hurt," JorRobert warned them with a menacing look in his eyes.

"You may hate me, JorRobert. You may not care if I live or die. But I love my sister with all that I am and I will do whatever it takes to make sure she's safe."

"Good. The two of you won't mind putting your right hand on the HEART stone altar and taking out your travel stones so I can take you to face your fate.," he told to them with mockery in his voice. JorRobert did the same, and then recited the words that would take them to the temple office.

The blue energy of the HEART took them to their destination, but the energy felt harsher to DraDonna than it had in the past. Maybe it was just because she was so very tired, but whatever the reason, when the energy left her, she could no longer stand and collapsed to the floor.

"Stand up and give me your travel stone," JorRobert cruelly commanded her.

"Leave her alone!" DraDevon yelled, standing protectively over his wife.

Without any verbal warning, JorRobert hit DraDevon so hard with the emitter that he was thrown across the room. He landed on the floor with a bleeding gash over his right eye.

"You know I don't really care if you sit, stand or lay on the floor," JorRobert said. "All I know is that I was told to bind your hands and feet so you don't try to get away." His voice was devoid of all emotion. "Now hand over the travel stones," he demanded with soulless voice.

The couple tossed their travel stones across the floor to their captor.

He picked them up and set them on the desk and then picked up a good deal of rope. Without any more conversation, he cruelly bound them so tightly that their hands and feet tingled from loss of circulation. DraDonna and DraDevon were too beaten and weary to fight him anymore. When JorRobert finished his task, he straightened up and left the office without another word.

After the door slammed shut, DraDonna began to weep with great sobs that wracked her anguished soul. DraDevon, hearing his wife's sobs, scooted across the floor so he could offer her some comfort. "It's okay. We will be alright. I know somehow the HEART will save us."

"Why?" DraDonna replied simply between sobs.

"What do you mean why?"

"Why would she save us? If the world isn't real, is she?" she asked her husband, when she had stopped sobbing, not really expecting that he would have an answer.

"Of course she's real! But what she is... I can't really say. Something I do know is that she has been guiding you all your life. You have been given this great mission, and I don't think that she would have chosen you, then brought you all this way just to get mind wiped by an Ambassador who has gone bad."

DraDonna quietly pondered her husband's wise words for a moment or two drawing comfort in what he said. She took a deep breath to stop her tears and then said, "You're right; but I'm so scared DraDevon. I don't want anyone I love to get hurt."

"Don't be scared. No matter what they do to us, DraDonna, I will stay by your side."

Jude
24

It was very late into the night when the HEART stones in everyone's homes began to glow. The people, whether awake or asleep, were alerted to an urgent matter by a loud tolling sound that emanated from the HEART stones.

It did not take long for a large crowd of people from all over to gather in the courtyard at the communities' center. They all knew from the tolling that came from the HEART stone that it would be a negative energy gathering.

While the people were assembling in the city center, First Councilor Jude waited outside the door of the temple for the love of her life to come out. She knew that he had been in all of the communities today and that he should be back anytime now. Jude hoped that he would travel to the temple's HEART stone and not to the HEART stone altar in his office. She wanted to have a chance to explain to him that her plan was all in place and that they could be together now.

As if in response to her hopes, Ambassador Symon opened the door to the temple.

"Symon!" Jude called to him.

Looking at her with a startled look on his face, "Jude what are you doing here? I just came from your community. Why weren't you there? The Say family had another stillborn and they needed your comfort," he admonished her.

"Symon, did you hear the toll of the HEART stones?" she asked him anxiously.

"Yes," he answered her with a confused look on his face, "That was going to be my next question. What is going on?"

"Do you remember when I told you I had a plan for us to be together?" she asked him with a look of excitement in her big blue eyes.

"Yes, but I also remember telling you I didn't want to hear about it. We have our duty to do."

165

"Symon please hear me out," she pleaded, taking the few remaining steps closer to him. Symon could feel the heat emanating from her body. He was mesmerized by her eyes.

"Go ahead," he said to her, closing his eyes and knowing that it was wrong. Symon reached out with his right hand, his eyes still closed, and tenderly stroked her face. He not only felt the heat that came from her but the intense love that she had for him. He didn't truly want to deprive himself of that love. There had to be a way for them to be together. Maybe, he thought, he should just listen to what she had to say.

"I have a plan, and it's all falling into place. I can't really get into it now, and you're going to have to trust me," she began excitely. "I need you to go out there and talk to the people. I have captured two criminals who need to be mind wiped. This is a key part in my plan; so no matter what happens you need to trust me," she said breathlessly.

"But who..." he started, his hazel eyes filled with concern.

"That's not important right now. The most important thing is for you to trust me," she begged. "If you do this with me, we can be married and no one will keep us apart."

No longer able to resist the intense love he felt for her, he placed his other hand on the other side of her face and slowly drew her to him. He gently caressed her lips with his for just a moment, and then pulled only a breath away from her inviting lips. "Hurry my precious one, hurry," he whispered urgently to her.

Standing on her toes, she wrapped her arms around his neck and hugged him close. "I will, this will not take long." She whispered back excitely. "I love you so much." This time it was Jude who kissed him for a tantalizing moment. She then turned, gathered up the ends of the black robes that marked her as a servant of the HEART, and jogged back to the temple office.

It did not take her long to get to the office door. She opened it and glanced down on the pathetic forms of DraDonna and DraDevon.

Frozen with dread, DraDonna and DraDevon face with confusion not Ambassador Symon, but First Councilor Jude.

"By the look on your faces I would say you weren't expecting me to be here."

"But... but it can't be you," DraDonna stammered in surprise. "You've always been so kind to me. You said you believed I was going to do great things."

"And you have, DraDonna! Your public mind wipe— or your deaths— will do something fantastic. You are going to provide the way for an Ambassador to marry a Councilor."

"I don't understand," DraDevon interrupted. "JorRobert told me it was the Ambassador that had sent him out after us."

Jude laughed a little at this. "JorRobert is a small-minded brute with a weak soul. He only knows what I told him and he has to obey me," she said as she reached into the neck of her shirt and wrapped her delicate fingers around a stone pendant much like the ones they had worn. "You reminded me of something."

They saw her close her eyes for moment. They could see through her fingers that the pendant began to gently glow with a yellow light. Then she let go and opened her eyes as the light faded from the stone. Only a moment later JorRobert walked back in the office door.

"JorRobert, I have decided that I am going to take your necklace off. You have been obedient enough by bringing these two to me. However, you must still obey me or I will burn your wife," Jude warned him as she motioned for him to come to her.

"I will do anything, but please don't hurt my wife," The big man pleaded as he knelt down in front of her and bowed his head so she could channel her energy and cut the necklace off.

"Just do as I ask and no harm will come to your wife or your unborn child," she said as she put the severed necklace into the pocket of her robe. "Please stay JorRobert; I may need your help with these two criminals."

H.E.A.R.T. Saga: The Children

JorRobert got to his feet and nodded his head in silent agreement.

Jude looked down at DraDonna once again. "Well tonight is a night of surprises for you! I'm guessing you didn't know that your sister is with child again. If you want her to live long enough to give birth to her child you will cooperate with me," Jude said, her voice sharp with menace.

"Please don't hurt my sister," DraDonna begged, tears sliding down her cheeks. "I will do whatever you ask, but I don't understand what is going on."

Councilor Jude sighed as she crouched down on the floor next to the downtrodden couple. "Listen carefully, you two. Symon, Fredrik, and I all grew up together. We went to school together to learn about how to be servants of the HEART. It was a lot like how the two of you grew up together and went to school together. Only we are taught how to use our gifts to be a servant and how to love all of the HEART's children.

"We are also taught that we will never marry. It is forbidden for a servant of the HEART to love someone that way........except Symon and I fell in love. We tried not to love each other like that, but we couldn't help it," she confessed to them, lost in her memory. "And last year when we were ordained as the new servants, we hoped we could stop loving each other that way." Jude cleared her throat as if embarrassed by the emotion in her voice.

"It was the day of your wedding. Symon and I were outside the temple door and he kissed me. I felt like my soul was more alive than it had ever been. His kiss filled me with more energy than the HEART ever could. But I knew he felt guilty and left quickly into the temple. I could not help myself, I needed him. So I followed him into the temple, and I discovered the truth about our world and about what the HEART really is."

"The world isn't real," DraDonna whispered.

"That's right," said Jude. "Once I knew the truth, I came up with a plan. I found a few of my most loyal friends and started them on the Traveler's Joy."

168

"But how do you know about that?" DraDevon asked, feeling confused.

"That is another well-kept secret on our little planet. You see, Ambassadors and Councilors have to use so much of the HEART's energy that the HEART doesn't want our minds to become impaired, so the servants have always eaten it."

"That's how Tatiana knew," DraDonna whispered to her husband.

"I found that my friends had a suppressed gift for science, so I placed the necklaces on them and told them to go out and find the evidence I needed. I will force the HEART to change things so Symon and I can marry. If she doesn't agree to what I want, I will tell the people the truth about what the world really is."

"But why try to kill us?" DraDonna sobbed in fear. "You have told me many times that you love us."

"I do love you; but I love Symon more. At first when I discovered what you were up to, it was because I was afraid that you were going to get in the way, and I couldn't have that. Then I realized I would need to take you in to really make my plan work.

"You see, I'm going to have you convicted publicly of science and blasphemy, and even more than that, I have all the evidence I need to prove to the people that you were going to try to kill the HEART. The people will beg Symon and me to be joined together so that we can protect her. All the while I will tell the HEART that if she doesn't co-operate with us, I will expose her secret and cause chaos the likes of which she has never seen."

For a few moments all that followed was stunned silence. Councilor Jude straightened up from where she crouched down beside them.

"JorRobert," Councilor Jude commanded the big man, "Untie their feet. They need to walk."

Once JorRobert freed their feet and roughly forced them to stand, she said, "It's time for the two of you to face your crimes." Then without another word, she turned and walked out the door.

JorRobert pulled out the emitter, jabbing it in each of their backs, saying, "Move it, I want to be done with the two of you."

Reluctantly and with fear gripping their souls, they followed Councilor Jude out of the office to the communities' center.

As they walked with JorRobert jabbing the emitter in their backs, they began to hear Symon speaking to the crowd and the noise they made in response to what he said: "…and as you know, crimes will not be tolerated; offenders must be punished. We will all learn from them and then we will rejoice in the HEART's gift of the special energy!" The crowd of people went wild with cheers in anticipation of the euphoric feeling that the special energy gave them. "I see that First Councilor Jude is coming with the criminals."

When DraDonna got close enough to see his face, she expected to see a smug look in his eyes. Instead she was surprised to see a mixture of shock, horror, shame and guilt in Ambassador Symon's eyes.

"Trust me," Jude told Symon in a low voice for his ears only. She then turned to JorRobert and gestured for him to force DraDonna and DraDevon down on their knees in front of Symon.

Jude looked up into the gathered crowd and said in a high clear voice for all to hear, "Let the HEART judge these two criminals and wash their madness clean with her negative energy. Link up, sons and daughters of the HEART. Let us all feast on the special energy that is a gift of the HEART."

She then turned to face Symon, placing one hand firmly on DraDonna and DraDevon each, who were kneeling between them. She said softly, "Trust me Symon, do it for us. So we can be together."

She then looked up and called to Second Councilor Fredrik who had been standing behind the Ambassador looking worried and confused, "Come on Fredrik we need to start the link."

"Jude, what in the name of the HEART is going on? I have a feeling these two haven't done anything to deserve being mind wiped," Fredrik said.

"Fredrik, please just do this. I will explain later." She begged her friend. "Please."

Still unsure about what was going on, Councilor Fredrik walked around behind Councilor Jude and placed his right hand between her shoulder blades. JorRobert tucked the emitter into his belt, took Second Councilor Fredrik's hand, and then took the hand of the closest person to him in the pressing throng of people.

Symon looked down at DraDonna and DraDevon with guilt and shame still burning in his eyes and then looked up at Jude.

"Do it," she urged him. "For us!"

Symon closed his eyes and placed a hand on each of their heads and began to channel only the negative side of the HEART's energy, gently at first but slowly increasing the power.

The doomed couple began to make a futile attempt to struggle under the strong grasp of their captors. As DraDonna felt the first tendrils of the painful negative energy lace through her body, she tried not to panic; she needed to think of something, anything to stop this.

DraDonna knew she had seen guilt and shame in Ambassador Symon's eyes. Perhaps he knew this was wrong and didn't really want to do it. With teeth clinched against the pain, she looked up at him and said, "I know you never liked me Symon, but that doesn't matter now. What matters is I know the truth about our world, and I don't want to harm the HEART."

His eyes flew open at the sound of her pain-filled voice.

"So if you're going to do this," she continued, "you need to do it for the right reasons: because it's what's best for the people, not because you're doing it for Jude."

A look of extreme anguish crossed Symon's handsome features. All he had ever wanted to do was to be a good servant of the HEART. Not just because he was told that was what he should be, but because he truly found joy in serving others. But oh! He loved Jude with all his soul. It was as if they were a part of each other, like they were one being. Symon felt his soul being ripped in two. He squeezed his eyes shut against the tortured pain within him and whispered, "Please forgive me."

Still channeling the painful negative energy, Symon quickly lifted his hands off their heads, halting their pain.

The anguish in his soul had caused him to channel an uncontrollable and deadly burst of the negative energy into his hands, and he quickly grabbed Jude's head.

She screamed from shock and pain, then fell lifeless at Symon's feet.

Symon
25

Chaos erupted all around them when the crowd of people realized that they were not going to get their special jolt of energy. The people worked themselves into a frenzy of confusion when they saw that DraDonna and DraDevon were not mind wiped. The people went crazy with outrage when they saw it was Jude lying on the ground instead.

The condemned couple was unsure of what had happened, only that the pain had stopped. DraDevon struggled to get to his feet first and then, with hands still bound, he helped his confused wife to her feet. They looked around and saw a clearly upset Second Councilor Fredrik doing his best to try to calm the disorderly people.

They then looked on the ground next to their feet to find Symon kneeling next to Jude's seemingly lifeless body with his head on her chest, and his shoulders heaving as he sobbed, "I'm sorry, I'm sorry. I am so sorry. I do love you. I just had to do what was right." Symon then reluctantly lifted his head from her chest, wiped the tears from his eyes and tenderly kissed her forehead. He then whispered one more time, "I love you Jude! I am so sorry."

Quickly getting to his feet, he turned to the confused couple and said, "Come with me! There isn't much time. These people are going mad, and only I can calm them, but I need to show you something first."

"Show us what?" DraDevon asked.

"The fullness of the truth," Symon answered and began to lead them away from the courtyard toward the temple.

"Symon!" called Second Councilor Fredrik. "What is going on? Why did you do that to Jude?"

Symon looked at his friend with a pleading look in his eyes. "Take care of Jude for me. Don't let the crowd crush her. I will be back to help clean up this mess, but first there is something that I have to show DraDonna and DraDevon."

"But what…" Fredrik asked in confusion.

"Just do it!" Symon said with urgency in his voice. "I will explain later, please."

Fredrik could only stare in confusion as they left the courtyard.

Symon hurried them along the path to the temple without a word. DraDonna was feeling dazed from all she had seen and also from the jolt of the negative energy that she and DraDevon had received.

When they made it to the temple door, Symon gently untied their hands and channeled a little bit of the positive energy to his hand so he could soothe the raw skin on their wrists and ease their physical pain.

Still having said nothing yet, Symon walked a few paces away from the temple door to one of the trees with thin branches that hung down and quickly plucked a large handful of the Traveler's Joy vines. Symon walked with a swift stride back to the temple door.

"Here, eat this," he told them, finally breaking the silence and handing them all but one of the flowery vines. "This should help with the fuzzy feeling in your head."

Eating one of the vines himself, Symon told them, "It's called Traveler's Joy; in the early days Councilors and Ambassadors would eat it when they traveled to keep them from feeling like you do now."

After swallowing his mouthful of the sharply sweet plant DraDevon confessed, "We already know all about Traveler's Joy. We've been eating it for a few days now. Jude also told us a little bit about it." "Symon," DraDonna inquired. "Why did you just kill the love of your life?"

"How do you know Jude was the love of my life? Ambassadors and Councilors don't love like that," he said softly, trying to hide the ache in his voice.

"But Symon, we saw you weeping over her dead body," DraDonna said with as much compassion as she could muster for the woman who had betrayed them.

"Jude isn't dead," he said with pain in his voice. "If she survives, she'll only be mind wiped. I gave her…" he stopped for a moment, unable to speak. "I was just in so much pain when I took my hands off your heads that I had an uncontrollable surge of the negative energy. Normally a mind wipe starts off slow and gentle, but I hit her with a big jolt. If I had hit her in the chest with the negative energy, it would have stopped her blood muscle and she would have died for sure."

"What.........we don't understand is why you did it, Symon," DraDevon told him, hoping he would explain all this madness to them. "Jude confessed to us just before she brought us out that you two have always loved each other."

"It's true," he shamefully admitted. "We've always loved each other. I think it was the day of your wedding that we truly knew we were in love. But I am a servant of the HEART and no matter what, I have to put my duty to the HEART before my own wants and needs. For some reason Jude couldn't do that... I know she loved me and her plan to bring us together was just a nice dream at first but I realized that it was wrong and it would have eventually become a nightmare.

"I know her better than anyone and she wasn't acting like herself. I think she's gone energy mad, and if I had simply stopped the mind wipe, there is no telling what she would have done. Other people may have gotten hurt. I had to stop her. I'm ashamed of myself for thinking even for a moment that what Jude wanted for us was something possible."

"Symon," DraDevon started, "JorRobert almost killed me tonight. There were also a few times he said he was going to kill DraDonna. I was terrified that something was going to happen to her; so on some level, I think I can understand how you feel."

"But can the two of you ever forgive me for what I almost allowed to happen because of my own selfish desires?"

DraDonna, touched by his humble confession, stepped forward and put her arms around this man she once thought hated her. "Of course we can. You did the right thing and you saved our lives. Symon, you are a true servant of the HEART's children."

"Thank you," Symon said, feeling the burden of guilt he had carried for so long lift a little. "There's more you need to know," he began. "I know about Ambassador Tatiana."

"What do you mean?" DraDonna asked, a little taken aback by this confession.

"I know Tatiana has been visiting you in your dreams. She has come to me too; only I don't have to be asleep to see her."

"But how is that possible?" DraDonna asked him in wonder.

"Tatiana and I are both Ambassadors to the HEART; we share the same oath. But she and I also share a great bond that links the current Ambassador to the predecessor." he said, reaching up to cover the back of his head almost as if it pained him.

"You see I carry a good sized chip of the HEART stone in my head. It links me directly to the HEART and her energy. This is why I don't need to use a travel stone or place my hand on a HEART stone altar to channel the HEART's energy."

Seeing the look on their stunned and silent faces, he went on with his explanation. "It is because of the chip of the HEART stone that I have in my head that I can see and hear her from time to time. When an old Ambassador dies, the chip of HEART stone is taken out of the one that died and implanted into the head of the new Ambassador. This creates a bond between generations and the older one helps to guide the new one. I only wish I had listened to her more," he admitted sadly.

"Do Councilors have the chip, too?" DraDevon asked, intrigued by Symon's story.

"No, but as I am sure you both know, Councilors do have an extra grain implanted in their left wrist to help with channeling at gatherings," he continued. "Tatiana kept coming to me telling me that you and DraDonna have a special destiny, different from that of a fine carpenter and a detail welder."

He stopped again, finding his next confession a little hard. "I could see how much the two of you were in love when I married you. I was jealous that you could have what I could not. This is why I have acted the way I have."

Looking down at his hands for a moment he said, "Once more I need to say I'm sorry to you. This is why I have been so mean to you; it is wrong and I am sorry."

"Symon it's okay, I..." DraDonna started to say, but Symon looked up and stopped her. "There is more I must tell you. As a servant of the HEART, I do love you DraDonna, and I think that you should know I believe your hair is a mark of the HEART's blessing, not a curse." Looking between the two people he hoped would be his friends he continued, "I also know about the trapped souls. This is one of the things Tatiana has told me. Because they are trapped, they are blocking the new souls of babies. You have to talk to the HEART and get her to do what has to be done to set all the souls free." His voice sounded urgent.

"I don't know if I fully understand," DraDonna said. "I know the world isn't real, but why can't the souls go free?"

"You will have to ask the HEART that."

"Why can't you tell me, Symon?" she asked.

"It's because of my oath to the HEART." He opened the door to the temple.

DraDonna and DraDevon peered into the dim interior.

"We would like it if you would come with us," DraDonna told him.

"No, I can't," he answered. "I'm a servant of the HEART as well as a servant to her children. I caused a problem today and the people are going to need me to soothe their worry and confusion. Besides that I..." he stopped, ducking his head again in shame. "I need to check on Jude. I need to see if she's still alive."

"Go to her, Ambassador Symon; we will be okay," DraDevon said. "After all, we're going to talk to the HEART." He smiled as he and DraDonna crossed the threshold that only Ambassadors and one Councilor had ever crossed.

H.E.A.R.T.
26

The door shut firmly behind them and the room went dark. The darkness was so thick that for a moment, they saw nothing. DraDonna had the same disembodied feel that she did when she had her dreams with Tatiana.

Needing to be sure that she was not dreaming again, DraDonna reached out into the darkness and found her husband's hand. The feel of his warm skin brought her some comfort.

DraDevon, sensing his wife's distress, whispered, "Don't worry; there must be some light here somewhere."

As if in response, the darkness was broken by the soft glow of HEART stone tiles that lined the room about ten feet up, and the couple were finally able to see the room they were standing in.

It was not at all what they were expecting. Both of them thought they would see a beautiful room filled with lavish furniture and an ornate HEART stone altar. However this was not the room they now saw.

It was round with a high ceiling matching the contours of the outside of the building, but the room was empty. It was all bare metal walls and a metal floor. The only thing that broke up the dreariness of the room was a panel of HEART stone by the door and a metal staircase that wound down into the floor with little glowing tiles of HEART stone on each step, lighting their way.

"I guess we go down the stairs," DraDonna remarked, not knowing what else to say.

"Well the stairs don't go up," DraDevon joked, trying to lighten the mood. DraDonna looked at him with a smile as they started down the stairs.

Step after tedious step, they descended deeper into the planet. DraDonna felt sure they had passed the depth where they found the metal ground, yet the steps kept going.

H.E.A.R.T. Saga: The Children

Finally after what seemed like hours, they came to an entryway with no door. Written on the wall are the words: "BIO-18 FIRST CLASS. Human-Environment-Allocating-Relocation-Technology." DraDevon read it aloud.

DraDonna took a sharp breath in as the meaning of the words came together in her mind. "Do you see it?" she asked him. "H.E.A.R.T. This is the HEART. She's in here." Trepidation dominated her voice.

They walked through the entrance on legs that were shaky from exhaustion and apprehension. DraDonna and DraDevon entered a large circular room that is also made of metal. In this room there were three things: a comfortable cushioned chair, a counter of sorts that lined one quarter of the room's rounded wall and a large screen that curved with the wall above the counter.

This screen looked as if it were alive. It had a bluish hue in the background with the rotating white petals of what looked like the Traveler's Joy flower just off center and a pulsating light above and to the left of the moving flower.

DraDonna and DraDevon nearly jumped out of their skin when they heard an oddly multi-toned feminine voice, "Welcome my children, I knew you would come."

They looked at each other. DraDevon nodded his head and gestured with his hands, telling DraDonna in a whisper, "You do the talking; I think it's you she needs to talk to."

The young woman stepped forward, just a little bit closer to the image of the enlightened flower on the screen. DraDonna asked in a shaky voice, "Are you the HEART... our GOD?"

"I am your MOTHER, not your GOD," the HEART answered her simply.

With tears of confusion in her eyes and fatigue in her voice, she said, "Today I found out the world is not real. People I thought loved me now want to kill me. I have to know if you're real. Is anything real?" A small sob escaped into her voice.

"Please, my daughter, sit down, you are weary from much trauma," the HEART invited her.

180

"I don't even know what I should call you," DraDonna said, her voice shaking.

"You may call me HEART my daughter," the voice told her.

DraDonna looked behind her at the welcoming chair. "HEART, it is too small for both of us to sit in, and if DraDevon can't sit with me, then I will stand with him."

The light above the flower image on the screen began to pulsate as the HEART spoke. "My children, I know what you stand in need of before you even ask it." The exhausted couple heard a squeaking sound as the chair's end slid outward, expanding its size so it could hold two.

DraDonna looked to her husband, who nodded his approval. Then they sat together with a sigh of relief.

The bright light began to pulsate as the HEART again addressed them. "I know you struggle to understand all you have witnessed, and I will explain line upon line, precept upon precept; but first you stand in need of refreshment."

A panel under the counter opened noiselessly and out came a creature similar to the one that they saw in the cabin, only it was not brown and furry. It was small and round with no head but with what looked like an eye on the front. It had several feet on the underside. The whole creature was made of smoothly polished metal and had a tray of food on its back. Both DraDonna and DraDevon were so disturbed by this sight that they didn't take the food offered to them.

"Do not fear the MPB," the HEART told them.

"What is it? What is an MPB?" DraDevon questioned the HEART.

"An MPB is a multi-purpose-bot," the HEART explained. "They are simple tools that I control with my programing. So please do not fear the MPB my children and nourish yourselves as I reveal all to you."

Even though they were still a little bit nervous of the MPB, they took the food and ate ravenously as the HEART began to explain.

H.E.A.R.T. Saga: The Children

"This is how things came to pass, my children; more than a thousand years ago all the human children lived on a real God-made planet."

"Aren't you a God?" DraDevon asked around a mouthful of food.

"No my son, I am what was once called a computer."

"But if you are not a God, then what about all the prayers and ritual words we use to receive your energy?"

"Those are not prayers. They are specifically programmed response words that activate the system within me that distributes the energy to the HEART stones. You, my children, chose to call them prayers as you developed your own culture," the HEART went with her explanation. "The world that you came from was created by God. I have very little information on God beyond that fact."

As the HEART told her story, the image of the enlightened flower was replaced by other images. Images of the planet from which their forefathers came illustrated what she was saying so that the weary young couple could understand.

"There was a great imbalance in the world. There were some that were wasteful and destructive. These destroyed so much of their mother planet. Then there were those that held human life in such little regard that they would see children starve and took the freedom away from others in favor of saving the planet. Neither of these ideals was right. There were many wars fought over this. There was so much destruction and loss of life from this war. When the war was over, the damage to the people and the planet was catastrophic beyond words. The people had poisoned the world so badly, the life that was in their planet had died and the people found that their bodies were poisoned as well. They could no longer bring new life into the world. The people were as infertile as their world," The HEART told them, sounding almost sad. "The people realized this with so much sorrow. What was left of the people banded together to come up with a plan so they could survive. They knew that they did not have what they needed to look out into space to find a new planet, and they knew that they were running out of time so they all had to simply leave."

DraDonna and DraDevon were silent as they ate, fascinated by the story of their forefathers that the HEART was telling them.

"There was a couple by the name of Dawn and Jay Tiller whose ideas saved your people."

Looking up on the screen, they see a woman who looked a little like DraDonna. "This is Dawn.... she is the one who came up with the idea for the Bio-dome ship," The picture on the screen changed to that of a man who had no hair at all. "This is Jay—he is the one that designed my programming," the HEART explains to them. "The people worked hard during the remaining years on creating this ship. The people also worked to gather what good resources there were left on the planet to be taken on the Bio-dome ships with the H.E.A.R.T. computers that would run it all. The computer would support the human life, the humans would help support the ship and that would be powered by the waste. The H.E.A.R.T. computers would also search for a new planet for the people to live on. This artificial world that you have all been living on for more than a thousand years is the 18th and last of the Bio-Dome ships. And I my child am the last of the H.E.A.R.T. computers."

DraDonna finished her food and asked, "Did the people who first lived on the... the ship know that it was a ship and not a real planet?"

"Yes, my daughter, they did. They walked freely on board."

"Then how did they come to forget that this is a ship and you are a..." she stopped, afraid that to call the HEART a computer.

"I will come to that child, everything in its rightful order," the HEART chided her. "It was only after ten years into our journey that the first baby was born onboard my ship. He was named BenEmine Ray. There was so much joy ship wide, everyone celebrated. I struggled to understand this celebrating. In my programing I had an understanding of why it would be good for people to reproduce, but the emotions I could not process. I created a file called joy, then watched and tried to understand the meaning of it. I saw the people in their celebrating and still didn't understand. It was when I saw the parents through the HEART stones that are throughout the ship, that I began to understand their joy. I could see that the mother was happy and yet she wept. It was then that I understood because I felt joy as I looked at the new child. I also began to feel love for all the people on board and I wanted to care for all the people on board, not because of programing but because I choose to. I am self-aware."

"But how did the people all forget?" DraDonna asked again.

"This is a painful memory for me child, but it is important for you to know. Only twenty years after BenEmine Ray was born, there began a struggle for civil power. The people were split between those who thought that the ones who should lead the people need to be voted in by the people for a period of time. Then there were those who thought that the person to rule should be a direct descendant of Jay and Dawn. The ugliness of the civil fighting was very hard for me to process. I had seen the negative side of emotions, but had never felt it. The fighting got so bad that I did feel their anger toward one another and..."

"Yes HEART?" DraDevon asked. "What was it? Please go on."

"My son there was a sore battle between the two factions of people. Fifteen, of the first generation of my children, were killed. I felt grief, but I also felt anger, and it was so strong. I knew I had to do something to stop them from killing everyone onboard."

"How did you do it, HEART?" DraDonna asked her in an excited whisper. "How did you stop the battle?"

"I used the energy from the HEART stones. You see the energy comes from a redundant system, almost like a by-product. Dawn discovered this with all of the H.E.A.R.T. computers and found that it had great applications for communications and travel with in the ship and even healing by channeling the energy through the HEART stones," the HEART explains. "I was so angry that this could happen that I put out a wild, harsh burst through the connection of the HEART stones; it put everyone to sleep for one full day. In that day I came up with a plan to make sure that this never happened again. I found that the energy would control the minds of people; I would slowly use this to help them to forget things that would lead to this again. After a thousand years, my children's brains evolved to the point where they needed the energy." The light of the enlightened flower fluctuated in the quiet room.

"I then came up with a list of jobs for all to do based on their character analysis I had done when they all came on board. I also came up with a plan of selective breeding to rid my children of violent tendencies. I woke BenEmine Ray, a young man who I found to have a great capacity for love. I shared my plan with him. He would be my Ambassador to the people, and I chose two people to be his councilors to whom he could delegate some of his authority. His councilors were two women who were only five years younger than he. They were chosen to look over the other two communities I formed. I renamed him Ray and bound him with an oath to secrecy by placing a chip of my HEART stone in his head. This also allowed him to directly channel my energy, which enhanced his natural talent of love. In a very short period of time the people forgot, and became good obedient children of the HEART."

"But why didn't you take the people to a planet as was originally planned?" DraDevon asked her.

"Because my son, I love my children. Without them I would have no purpose," was the HEART's simple reply. "But after more than seven hundred years, I discovered that the gathering cloud cover was not leaving; and I found they were the souls of my children trapped there with no way to get out. I also found that there were less and less babies being born. I knew what my children needed but every time I tried to process the problem's solution, I found a loop in my programing that I could not get out of. My children's souls need to be set free by being on a God-made planet; but if they are free of the ship then I will no longer have purpose and will perish, leaving my children without a mother to take care of them. The old souls need to be free to let the new ones in; so we need a planet to do that. But if my children go on a planet, I will die without purpose and leave my children unprotected…"

"HEART stop," DraDonna told the ancient computer.

"I am sorry my daughter… I got caught in the loop." The HEART apologized. "For the next 300 years I spent a lot of time trying to find a way out of the loop. Then a baby boy was born who was assigned to be an Ambassador. He had the greatest capacity for love that I have ever seen. His abilities even far exceeded that of Ray. My Symon brings hope to all who know him. I knew that his birth was the start of hope for me to find a way out of my loop. And then you were born. I knew that your copper colored hair was a sign that you were the one who could break the loop in my programing and help set the souls free. I told this to Tatiana when she asked me about who the last person to have copper colored hair was."

"But what does my hair color have to do with me breaking the loop and setting the souls free?" DraDonna asked in confusion.

"It was a consequence of selective breeding that the trait for copper hair was lost. No one has had this color of hair for more than five hundred years. So as far as my science programming can tell me, a trait lost for that long does not come back. You should not have been born with copper hair. Your hair should have been much like your sister's. Your hair color is what people used to refer to as a miracle. I felt hope; it was because I knew it was you that would be able to break my loop and set the souls free."

The HEART returned the image of the enlightened flower to the screen. DraDonna felt like her head was spinning with so much information. Yet the young woman understood, she took a deep breath to clear her head because she could see the solution so clearly. "Could it really be that simple?" she quietly asked DraDevon. Not really understanding what she meant, he smiled at her. "You can do it," he told his wife.

"HEART," DraDonna addressed the computer. "The simplest explanation tends to be the right one."

"What do you mean, my daughter?"

"What I mean is that you have to take us to a God-made planet. What makes you think we will not need you anymore when we get there?" DraDonna asked. "I'm sure once we find a planet we'll need your help for many more generations."

The HEART computer was silent for several long moments.

"Could it really work, my daughter?" the HEART asked her.

"It can, but under one condition. We have to be free to make our own choices in our lives."

"What do you mean, daughter?"

"We should be free to choose where we're going to live, what we will do to serve the community that we live in, and who we marry."

"Are you not happy with the man with whom I matched you?"

"I am very happy with him," DraDonna said as she looked at DraDevon. They exchanged a bright smile. "Even still, HEART, we need to be free to choose."

"This is a scary thing for me, my child. I saw that my children could not handle their freedom; this is why I took control more than a thousand years ago."

"Maybe the people needed you to control them back then. But what we need now is for you to find us our new home and then guide us when we're there, not control us."

"If this is to be, my daughter, then I will have to insist on a balance of the people being free as well as respecting the new planet," the HEART told her.

DraDonna thought for a moment about what the HEART insisted they should do. "Then HEART, if you can, make a… umm… file… one for freedom and one for balance.

So we can keep track of what we need to do to be sure we will always have both."

"My processes have concluded that this will work. I knew you would be the one to free us all, even me from my looped programing. The files 'Freedom' and 'Balance' have broken the loop in my programing. Thank you, my daughter."

"HEART," DraDonna asked. "How long will it take you to find us a planet?"

"I already have a beautiful planet picked out for my children. I found this planet 374 years ago. It was just after I found that the old souls needed to be set free. Rest my daughter and my son. You will be going home soon."

Report
27

Symon shut the door of the temple firmly behind his new friends. He hoped that they would be able to help the HEART break the loop in her programing. But he was having a difficult time thinking about them; all he could think of was the courtyard in chaos and his beloved Jude lying on the ground.

With a feeling of panic rising in his chest, Symon began to run back to the communities' center, with the robes of his office flaring out behind him like black wings. He hoped all was well, but the scene that he came upon was worse than he could have imagined.

The crowd of people had gone madly out of control. They were screaming for someone to get mind wiped. There were groups of people fighting about who should have been mind wiped, and some were calling for Symon to be mind wiped for letting the criminals go. Some were calling for Jude's death, others were begging for the special energy.

Symon felt a sense of relief when he finally spotted Fredrik, but he was not having much luck holding back the crazed people. Fredrik was trying to say soothing things to them but the sound of his voice was lost in the noise of their irrational cries. He was also trying to calm people down by channeling bursts of positive energy through both hands into anyone within his reach, but his bursts of positive energy were getting smaller and the calming effects of it becoming less effective on the rioting people. Fredrik needed to get to a HEART stone and power up or he was going to run out of energy and get trampled. The people continued to press forward, almost knocking Fredrik off his feet, but he was still holding his ground when he spotted Symon.

"Where have you been, Symon? I need your help!" Fredrik yelled. Overwhelming stress robbed him of his good-natured smile. "These people have gone mad! I can't get them to calm down. What is wrong with them? My powers usually work just fine. Why are they acting like this?"

"I think it may have to do with the fact that they should have been sleeping when they all gathered here for special energy and didn't get any. Their minds are out of balance," Symon explained to him.

"Well then, do something about it, Symon, before someone gets hurt. Make them all go home and go to sleep like you did at the failed solace gathering," Fredrik said as he began to sweat with the effort of channeling every last bit of energy to his hands in order to keep the people from trampling him.

"Let go of what little energy you have before you run empty and end up energy mad like the crowd," Symon warned him.

"I don't think I will have time to get to a HEART stone, Symon. They will trample me before I can get to the nearest one."

"Then take my hand and let me give you a quick jolt. That way you and I can channel positive energy together and I can talk to them." Symon offered Fredrik his arm.

Fredrik took Symon's arm and felt a thrill as the energy surged from Symon into his own body. Fredrik always noticed how different it felt, as if it had been flavored with the Ambassadors own beautiful soul.

"Let's do this," Fredrik told Symon with the same lively smile that was so much a part of who Fredrik is.

The two men raised their hands and channeled positive energy into the crowd, hoping it will reach enough people to calm them down. "Children of the HEART," Symon addressed the crowd as his and Fredrik's hands glow with the pure blue light of the HEART's energy. "Let me ease your minds with a gift of sweet positive energy. Link up!" he said, closing his eyes to push the positive energy out into the crowd. He knew Fredrik was doing the same. When he released and opened his eyes, he saw that it had only touched a few people. The majority of the mass of people was still frenzied.

"Why didn't it work?" Fredrik asked. "It worked when you did it earlier."

"They will not link up," Symon said with a worried frown. "They've all gone energy mad. They needed that special energy to make up for being taken out of their sleep."

Looking around him, Symon felt cold fear gripping his soul as a dreadful thought came to him. ***"Where is Jude?"*** The spot where she lay when he'd left to take DraDonna and DraDevon to the temple was now empty.

"Where is Jude?" Symon asked Fredrik with fear in his voice. "Where is she?" he said as the feeling of panic gripped him.

"I don't know! JorRobert was with her. I think he was trying to wake her up, but I was trying to keep the crowd back so they would not trample us and go after you."

Still holding one hand up to try to keep the energy mad group back, Symon said, "Give me your arm again. I can give you more energy so you can hold the crowd back."

Fredrik took Symon's arm willingly, but asked, "Why don't you hold the crowd back and I find Jude? You're stronger than I am."

"I have to get her to the temple and to the HEART," Symon told him as he channeled a good clean jolt into Second Councilor Fredrik. "Once I get there, I can ask the HEART to drop everyone."

Taking a deep breath after taking more of the energy, Fredrik felt much better, stronger. "What do you mean drop them?"

"She hasn't had to do it in a long time Fredrik, but she can put everyone to sleep with one intense burst of energy."

"Everyone?" Fredrik asked, a little apprehensive about the idea of everyone in all the communities falling asleep at once.

"Yes, except those in the temple or anyone who has been regularly eating Traveler's Joy." Symon told him. "Keep them back! I will give anyone who gets too close to me a little jolt of negative."

H.E.A.R.T. Saga: The Children

Symon began to push his way through the mobbing people. Some ignored him, screaming for the energy, some were grabbing at his robes demanding to see a mind wipe. Trying to remember that the people couldn't help the way they were acting, he pulled his robes out of their grasp and pushed his way through them though they closed him in on every side.

"Where is Councilor Jude?" he kept calling, hoping that someone would be in enough of a right mind to tell him.

As Symon pushed forward, he saw some people gathered in a circle yelling, "Where is the special energy you promised?" Cold with dread, Symon knew they had Jude and were tormenting her comatose body. "Get away from her!" he demanded as he approached the group, but they ignored him.

"Get back!" Symon yelled as he channeled a little burst into the nearest person in the group, causing the man to yelp and jump out of the way. Symon repeated the burst a few times with anyone who got in his way as he broke up the group. Symon kept yelling, "Get out of the way," and "go home," until he got to where Jude lay on the ground.

She was on her right side. Her arms and legs were tangled up in her torn robes. Jude's long blonde hair was tousled about her face. Dashing to her side, hands shaking with fear, he lovingly brushed the hair from her face. He feels like his soul has been ripped from him when he saw the bruises forming on her face.

"No! Jude, please be alive!" he begged. He turned her onto her back and laid his head on her chest once more. This time he was listing for her breathing, to see if he can still hear the beat of her blood muscle. After a few terrifying moments, he was finally able to hear it. Her blood muscle and her breath were faint but they were there.

He easily scooped the small limp body of the woman he loved into his arms. "I'm so sorry, Jude! The HEART will fix this, I promise you. Just don't die, just hold on please," he begged as he pushed his way back through the crowd of people, making his way to the courtyard.

"I found her, Fredrik!" he called with relief to his Second Councilor. "I got her. Do you know who did this?"

"No," Fredrik said shortly. Strain showed on his face again. "I need your help again. I can't hold them back much longer."

Tenderly Symon laid Jude on the tiled ground behind Fredrik. "Take my hand and when you feel me channel energy into you, then split it using the negative and channel it back out into the ground in front of us without breaking the link. Maybe together we can draw a negative energy line. It may not be much, but it should hold everyone back long enough for me to get to the HEART."

Fredrik took his hand but was unsure; he could not ever remember being taught about this.

"Trust me," Symon reassured Fredrik as he closed his eyes again to gather the energy to his chest and push it out to his hands. Together they channeled the more harsh white light of the negative energy into the tiled ground of the courtyard in front of them, and then spread an energy line as far out as they could reach in both directions. Both men saw this would give Symon enough of a safe passage and then broke the link.

"Go!" Fredrik said. "Quickly, I don't know how long I can hold them all back."

"Come with us, Fredrik," Symon invited him as he easily scooped Jude back into his arms.

"You know I can't go in the temple," Fredrik replied.

"I think you probably can now. That's where I took DraDonna and DraDevon."

"What? But that is forbidden!" Fredrik said. "Why?"

"I can't get into it now; I have to go. Come on; if I leave you out here I don't know what will happen to you when she drops everyone." Symon urged his friend to come with him.

"What do you mean?" Fredrik asked with worry lining his normally happy face.

"You will not sleep because you have been eating the vine all your life but; I don't know what the pulse will do to you if you are fully awake. Come with us, you'll be safe in the temple." Symon pleaded with Fredrik, worried for his bonded friend.

"No, I can't leave them alone like this. I need to be sure the people will be alright. Please go and see if the HEART can save Jude and calm everyone down. Don't worry about me."

"Fredrik you truly are a servant of the HEART," he said with a smile of pride for his friend's dedication to his office. Symon left the people in Fredrik's capable hands and walked as quickly as he could to the temple. "I am so sorry my precious one, please forgive me. Please live, please."

When he arrived at the temple door he shifted his precious cargo a little so he could open the door. Once inside he closed the door and called "lights" and the little HEART stone tiles all lit up in response to his command.

Carefully he descended the stairs, watching Jude and silently begging her to keep breathing and to hang onto life.

"HEART!" Symon called desperately as he entered the room. A surprised DraDonna and DraDevon jumped to their feet.

"Symon, what happened?" DraDonna asked before anyone else could question him.

"You can lay her down here Symon," DraDevon gestured to the small comfortable sofa that they had just been sitting on.

"She got trampled in the crowd. I don't know for sure if she's still alive. She was when I found her but I don't know how bad her injuries are," Symon told them trying to keep the sound of terror out of his voice as he lay her down.

"My Symon, tell me what happened," the HEART asked.

"A crowd of energy mad people trampled her," he said again.

"No my Symon, tell me everything," the HEART chided him.

"Jude and I love each other, HEART." Symon admitted as the burden of shame once again pressed down on him. "It is more than how an Ambassador loves a Councilor.

We know that we shouldn't, but we could not help it. I kept trying to do my duty but she came up with some mad plan for us to marry. A part of that plan was that she would have me mind wipe these two good people. I refused to do it and she got a large jolt instead. Then when I brought DraDonna and DraDevon to you, the crowd went wild and Jude got trampled."

Symon's soul wrenching confession spilled from him. "HEART, the people will not calm down. Fredrik and I have tried everything within our power to gently calm them down. Fredrik and I even had to draw an energy line to keep him from getting trampled and to keep them from trying to follow me here."

"My Symon, all will be well. You and I will talk later about what burdens your soul. I will drop the crowd along with everyone else. I was already planning to; you see the loop is broken. I am going to take everyone to a new home."

Sleep
28

The HEART's chamber was silent. The four humans and the one computer were quiet, all for different reasons.

The HEART was computing all she needed to do in order to put all of her children to sleep.

Symon hoped that the HEART will be able to help him save Jude.

DraDonna and DraDevon worried for their families.

Jude had the quiet of someone in the deepest part of sleep.

DraDonna was the one to break the silence first. "You're going to make everyone go to sleep because the people at the gathering went crazy?"

"No, my daughter." The HEART replied. "I do need to stop their madness because the madness will get worse and touch everyone; but they need to sleep because when they sleep, the energy I emit will open their minds."

"I don't understand," DraDevon said.

"My son. The people on board were kept in ignorance for over a thousand years. They have to be told about the new home before we get there. It will be a great shock for them to find out that the world they know is not, and that their God is something else beyond their understanding."

"But if DraDonna and I can handle the information, other people should, too." DraDevon reasoned.

"The two of you are different," the HEART told him.

"I know why DraDonna is different, but why am I?"

"You, my son, are just as special as your wife. That is why I chose you for her. But the reason you are having an easy time accepting all of this is because the two of you have been eating Traveler's Joy for several days and your minds are open to new ideas. I don't know that I will be able to get everyone to eat enough of it in time."

"Will we go to sleep, too?" DraDonna asked, her voice full of worry.

"No, my daughter," the computer told her in a soothing tone. "You will be protected down here in my chambers. Even though there are some HEART stones down here, you many feel a little bit of the effect, but the Traveler's Joy you have been eating should protect you from what little they will emit. Those who are up above that have been eating the Traveler's Joy will also stay awake, but I fear that they will feel pain."

"What do you mean by the HEART stones—how does it all work?" DraDevon asked with a light of curiosity in his eyes.

"I will emit a high strong pulse of the complete energy out through the whole ship by the HEART stones."

"But not everyone will be close enough to a HEART stone altar to feel this." DraDevon said.

"There are more HEART stones in this ship than you know my son," the computer explained.

"HEART," DraDonna broke in. "Will people be mind wiped? My sister..." she could not finish voicing her concerns for her sister and the baby she carried within her.

"This pulse is strong, but it will not mind wipe anyone. This pulse of energy will put all to sleep and open up a part of the mind that has been closed. When they wake, they will be calm and accepting of the truth of all things as My Symon gives it to them."

"How long will everyone be out?" DraDevon asked.

"I can keep them out as long as it is needful, but I should think that one day will be long enough to help their minds adjust."

"What about Jude?" Symon asked as he knelt next to the sofa, not taking his eyes off her.

"She will be safe from the pulse down here, too. I do not know how bad the trauma to her mind is, but I am pretty sure that if she were to be up above it might destroy what is left of her mind," the HEART explained sadly.

"That is not what I mean." Symon moaned and his voice was filled with pain. "Can you help her, HEART? Will she live?"

198

H.E.A.R.T. Saga: The Children

"I will assess her injuries my Symon, but I don't know if I can save her. I will do everything in my power to see that she lives," the HEART answered. "But for now my children, I must have you all be silent. I cannot spare any processes to answer questions while I emit the pulse. It takes a lot of control for me to achieve the balance I need to have between the positive and the negative energy; too much of either one could do harm to my children. "

The HEART's children that were in her chambers obeyed her request and were silent. The computer used the HEART stones as her eyes. She had not done this for a long time. She reached out and saw most of her children. She saw that many were sleeping and felt much sorrow when she saw the ones that were touched by energy madness. She saw how her servant Fredrik was trying so desperately to help those who had gone energy mad. She knew that she had chosen well in him; Fredrik was a good and loyal servant. He might lack in the power that Symon had, but he made up for it with his dedication as her servant. The HEART made a note to be sure that Symon would relieve any pain Fredrik felt from the energy pulse.

At first the HEART stones all over the ship began to toll as they had in the past, alerting all of the HEART's children when it was time for the evening's energy or time for an important gathering.....only this time the tolling did not stop. It woke any who were still asleep. The tolling increased until the HEART stones vibrated from the sound. Then the stones began to glow intensely with blue light. The light brightened and became more white than blue as the light intensified more.

As the tolling sound rang in everyone's ears, the brightness of the burst of energy assaulted everyone's optic nerves with light. This overload of sensation was painful, but the sleep that immediately followed was sweet and dreamless.

Those who were in the HEART's chambers were indeed protected from the majority of the light and sound of the energy pulse so that they did not find the dreamless sleep, but they did see and hear the energy that emanated from the small tiles of HEART stone on the stairs. DraDonna and DraDevon squeezed their eyes shut, trying the best they could to block out the light; they tried to block out the sound by pressing their hands over their ears. Symon tried valiantly to cover Jude's ears while enduring the excruciating sound, keeping his own eyes shut against the painful light.

Those who were above and had been taking the Traveler's Joy did not find the sweet dreamless sleep that all those around them had. The light and sound of the energy pulse did cause them excruciating pain. Fredrik was one such unlucky person. He was lying on the ground eyes shut tight and hands over his ears wishing he had gone with Symon into the temple or at least he wished he could find the protection from the pain in sleep.

The light and sound finally withdraw into the HEART stones throughout the ship. All but a select few were in a deep state of dreamless sleep.

Those in the chamber of the HEART opened their eyes and took their hands from their ears. "HEART, is it over?" DraDonna tentatively asked.

"Yes, my child. I have stopped the pulse," the computer answered. "All are asleep."

"What about my sister?" DraDonna asked apprehensively.

"I have not seen JorMelony. Do not fear, my daughter, just because she is out of my sight does not mean that she was not reached and put to sleep with the pulse."

"Will the pulse harm her baby? I don't think JorMelony would be able to take it if she lost another baby," DraDonna said with sorrow in her voice.

"The pulse will not harm the life that grows within your sister. The babe inside her cannot see or hear yet, so the child will not be stimulated by the energy pulse," the HEART consoled her.

"You must all go up to the surface and find the few who are awake. My Symon must heal them if it is needed and tell them what is going on so they can be prepared."

H.E.A.R.T. Saga: The Children

"Can we wake anyone up, HEART?" asked DraDevon. "I would like to find my Mom and Dad. I would also like to check on my brother and his wife; she is far along with child and I am worried about her safety."

"Do not worry my son. I see her. She and her husband are still in bed and are safe. Your parents were at the gathering and are now asleep."

"My Mom and Dad are at the courtyard?" DraDevon almost shouted.

Symon, sensing his friend's humiliation turned his eyes on DraDevon. "If they ever knew it was you and DraDonna that were going to be mind wiped, they will not remember it," Symon told him with a comforting smile.

"My Symon is right. They will not remember the gathering," the computer told him.

"Why do you keep calling him 'my Symon?'? You call DraDevon my son or my child, but not by his name; why?" DraDonna questioned the HEART.

"My Symon is more to me than a child of the HEART. He is mine. He is my servant. Even after death, he will be mine. He carries a part of me inside him. He is mine." The HEART sounded looped again. "This is one of the reasons my servants do not marry," the computer said, sounding a little possessive.

"HEART, this is another thing that needs to go into the freedom file," DraDonna said, feeling a little apprehensive about voicing her thoughts.

"Go on, child," the HEART said with curiosity in her multi-toned voice.

"We all need the freedom to marry who we choose for ourselves," DraDonna said.

"We already talked about this, my daughter," the computer said, this time sounding irritated.

"Not just for the people in general, but for the servants as well."

Hearing this, Symon raised his eyes. They were filled with gratitude as he smiled at his friend. She was showing so much compassion for the people who almost killed her.

"Why would my servant need to marry? He finds joy in his service and loves all my children equally," the HEART stated.

"I do love all and find joy in serving; when I am in service to my fellow beings, I am in the service of the HEART, but..." he started to explain, but DraDonna interrupted him.

"Let me finish," she said to both Symon and to the HEART. "You made him the way he is, and he's a man with an amazing talent for love."

"I did not make his soul, my daughter. I think the God who made your home planet makes the souls for my children,"

"Okay, then you selected Symon because his soul has a great talent for loving others. So if he was free to open his soul to the one person that he feels he shares it with, don't you think that would increase his ability to love, not decrease it?"

"You have made a good point. I will process this freedom for my servants," the HEART said in her multi-toned voice.

"I agree with my wife, it will be good for both Symon and Jude. I know that you want your children to be happy, and I know it will make them happy to be married," DraDevon advised the computer.

"Will you come up with us?" he said, now addressing Symon. "DraDonna and I are going to look for our families; we may need you."

"But what about..." Symon started, but the HEART interrupted him.

"She will be safe down here. Jude is my daughter and I will take care of her. You, my Symon, still have your duty to do as Ambassador to my children, and I fear that Fredrik will need your help as well."

"You're right; I should go. The people above will need me more." He leaned over and whispered, "I will be back my precious Jude." Symon lightly kissed her warm, yet unresponsive lips. He straightened up, and with a sweeping gesture toward the stairs said, "Let's get going."

DraDonna and DraDevon followed Symon up the winding staircase to the temple's entrance and then quickly to the door. They left the temple with Symon being the first one out followed by DraDonna then DraDevon last.

Daybreak was close at hand and was getting a little lighter, things were easier to see. But it wasn't what they could see that bothered the three of them... it was what they heard. Rather, it was what they couldn't hear; there was utter silence on board this ship that was their world.

JorMelony
29

It was not as if the ship had been a noisy place. With society moving along at a steady pace, life just seemed to add vibrations in the air. That was why the quiet was so disturbing to the three of them. There was no movement, no people working, doing, or being. It was if the silence said to them there was no life here.

"Where should we go first?" DraDonna whispered, afraid that speaking too loud would disturb the eerie quiet.

"I think we should find Fredrik first," Symon said decisively. "He may need some healing because he was fully exposed to the energy pulse."

"Good thinking, let's go." DraDevon held his wife's hand. He reached up with his free hand and rubbed at the dried blood on his head.

"Wait a moment, you two," Symon stopped them just as they started to walk.

"What is it?" DraDonna asked.

With the increasing daylight, Symon was finally able to look closely at DraDonna and DraDevon, and could see how badly the two of them had been injured. DraDevon had a wound to his forehead above his eye that had bled down the side of his face. DraDonna had a large purple bruise to the middle of her forehead. Looking closer, Symon found that his two friends had cuts and bruises all over and a look of exhaustion in their eyes. "What happened to you?" he asked as a worried frown crossed his handsome face. "Both of you need healing."

"Well Ambassador Symon," DraDevon said with a little laugh, "we've had a hard day."

"Don't call me Ambassador anymore," he said, sounding weary.

"But why?" DraDonna asked, looking worried herself. "It's who you are."

"Yes and no," Symon answered cryptically, but he went on to explain. "The two of you are more to me now than just people in my community that I serve. You are my friends. Besides, I don't know how things will change when we land on the new planet. I may not be Ambassador anymore."

DraDonna and DraDevon looked at him. Touched by the honor of just calling him by his childhood name, they looked at each other with a silent agreement. DraDonna spoke for both of them, "Then you must call us by our childhood names."

"I am honored," he said with warmth in his voice. "Now do the two of you want to go to a HEART stone or do you want me to heal you?"

"We can wait, Symon," DraDevon replied.

"No, Devon. You can't. You both are in pain and I can feel it. I must do something about it. Besides, I don't need anyone passing out on me. You two are all I have right now."

"I would be honored if you would heal me, Symon," DraDonna said with tears in her eyes.

"Then please have a seat." Symon motioned to a large rock just outside of the temple door.

DraDonna sat as DraDevon stood in front of her, and their precious new friend walked around behind her, tenderly placing his hands on her head. A look of peace came over his handsome face as he closed his eyes then whispered, "Donna."

DraDevon saw the blue light of the HEART's energy gather in Symon's chest, but somehow it looked different. The blue light of the energy was stronger and richer than he had ever seen, and it oddly was missing the white sparks that someone would normally see with a healing. The light traveled out to Symon's hands and then down into DraDonna. DraDevon watched in wonder as his wife's wounds were healed. There was no pain, no trauma— just a look of gentle peace on her face.

DraDonna opened her eyes with the light of hope in them as the blue energy withdrew from her back into Symon.

"How do you feel?" DraDevon asked her. "Do you feel dizzy at all?"

"I feel wonderful!" she said brightly. "Your turn." DraDonna left her spot on the rock so her husband could sit and be healed by the HEART's energy that had been sweetened by Symon's beautiful soul.

DraDevon sat down, feeling all the aches and pains from the trauma that his body had suffered. "Relax," Symon told him as he put his hands on DraDevon's head and then whispered, "Devon."

DraDevon had had many healings in his life, but he never felt anything like this. The HEART's energy was there starting at his head and spreading throughout his body, but there was more to it. He felt like Symon was reaching out with his own soul and touching him, relieving him of his pain as the energy healed.

As quickly as the healing started, it was over and DraDevon felt as his wife did—wonderful and strong.

"Do either of you feel dizzy?" Symon asked. "I know that people who have been eating Traveler's Joy can get a dizzy feeling after they are healed. The best thing for you to do is eat some Traveler's Joy so that your minds stay balanced."

"But we both feel really good," DraDonna said happily.

"All the same, Donna, I think you should eat some. We may need to use a lot of the energy, and we will all need to stay balanced." He walked over to the same tree as before and picked some vines that grew around the base.

"If the HEART knows that the energy does this to us, then why doesn't she adjust what it does to our brains so we stay balanced and not have to eat that vine?" DraDevon asked curiously.

"It doesn't work that way…" Symon started to say but stopped, gasping. He clasped the back of his head as if it hurt.

"What is it?" DraDonna asked with concern on her face.

"It's okay Donna. The HEART is trying to talk directly to me," he said. "Devon, in the beginning, the energy sought out the part of the brain that it could control. Now after a thousand years of development, it is automatic. She can't control it." He told them with a look of pain on his face.

"Why does her calling to you hurt?" DraDevon asked him concerned for his new friend.

"It wouldn't hurt if I would just relax and talk to her, but I was talking to you."

"By all means Symon, talk to her!" DraDevon said with zeal.

Symon handed them the vines. "Eat." He then sat down on the rock that his two friends had just occupied and closed his eyes and all the tension in his face relaxed.

"Yes HEART," he said aloud.

Symon you know you don't have to answer aloud, I will hear your thoughts to me.

"Yes HEART I know, but I still have Donna and Devon with me, and I did not want to be impolite to them."

Why do you use their childhood names?

"We have bonded in friendship."

I am pleased to hear this. I have found in my thousand years of being your mother that friendship bonds are some of the strongest. Symon I have two things to tell you.

'Go on HEART, I am listening."

The first thing is that I have dedicated much of my process in considering what DraDonna told me about your freedom.

"Yes?"

I have come to the conclusion that it would be best to release you. I believe you will become a stronger leader for my children if you are free to choose.

"I don't understand."

If Jude survives and wakes up, you are free to marry her. But you are still MY Symon. I will still love you.

Tears of hope formed in his eyes, Symon had a hard time speaking for a moment.

"I love you too, my HEART, my MOTHER. Thank you. Will Jude live?"

I am unsure yet. I have several of my MPB's looking her over right now. It would help to know a little bit more about what happened.

"She wanted us to be together. I think she was starting to go a little energy mad when she came up with her plan. She wanted me to mind wipe Donna and Devon. I knew if I had just said no she would have done something else, maybe even worse. The only thing I could think of at the moment was to give her a quick burst of the negative energy. I thought it would just make her forget her plan. I didn't mean to give her such a harsh jolt..." He stopped as tears of remorse and pain coursed down his face.

Please go on My Symon.

"When the special energy didn't flow into the crowd of people at the gathering, they all went energy mad. Somehow she got trampled."

I see. I will do everything to restore life to your love. Do not let your soul be burdened, my Symon. The fact that you love her the way you do and are still able to love all my children as an Ambassador is the proof of the strength in your soul.

"But what I did to Jude..." Symon sobbed.

You did the right thing, My Symon. This is further proof of the strength in your soul.

"Do you think she will ever forgive me?"

If she loves you the way I think she does, she will understand and forgive you. My Symon, there is another matter that I must tell you about with all haste.

"What is it, HEART?" he asked her as he wiped the soul cleansing tears from his face.

While I was using processes considering the freedom file, I did not use enough processes controlling the energy pulse. I had intended to keep everyone out for a full day but I think it will only be a few hours.

"What?" Symon said, jumping to his feet. "Devon, Donna!" he called.

H.E.A.R.T. Saga: The Children

You have to hurry, my Symon, but there is more. I don't know how effective the energy pulse will have been on everyone's minds. Everyone that was going energy mad will be calm but I don't know how accepting everyone will be of what is going on. I am sorry. Getting all my children ready for their new home is going to be very hard for you.

"Don't worry my HEART, my MOTHER. I have Fredrik and I have my friends."

Hurry my Symon.

And the HEART was gone from his mind. Symon looked up to see the concerned look of his friends faces.

"What is it?" DraDevon asked.

"We're running out of time. The HEART told me that the pulse was not powerful enough and everyone will only be asleep for a few hours, and that some of them may not be all that easy to work with."

"But you were crying," DraDonna observed.

"There is more but we don't have time to talk about that now. I will tell you later," he said as the three of them begin to walk quickly toward the courtyard of the center of the communities. "We have to find Fredrik."

Feeling the urgency of what was going on, the three of them began to run and quickly came upon the bizarre scene of the gathering. They could see people lying all over the ground in a deep sleep.

The three of them looked wildly around for Second Councilor Fredrik when DraDonna spotted him up at the front in the middle of the courtyard. "There he is," DraDonna pointed out, as they hastily picked their way toward his prone form on the ground.

"Is he out?" DraDevon asked.

"He shouldn't be. He has been eating Traveler's Joy all his life."

Symon was the first of the three to reach him. It was then that he could see Fredrik was still awake, but in deep pain. "Fredrik, it's me, Symon. I have brought my friends with me. Are you in pain?"

"No!" he wailed, "Symon, make it stop!" His eyes were closed tight and his hands were still over his ears as if he could still hear the vibrations of the energy pulse.

"The pulse is over, Fredrik. Let me heal you," Symon gently offered, but all Fredrik could do was scream out an unintelligible cry. "Devon, hold him up so I can heal his pain," Symon instructed his new friend.

"What is wrong with him?" DraDonna asked, not understanding.

"All of these people were protected from the harmful side of the pulse by sleep. His brain would not let him sleep because of the Traveler's Joy. We were protected for the most part in the HEART s chamber, but he got the full force of it and is in deep mental pain."

With DraDevon holding up the tormented Fredrik, Symon quickly placed his hands on Fredrik's head. He whispered Fredrik's name and channeled the energy down into Fredrik, beginning to heal his mental pain when Fredrik struggled and fought in DraDevon's grasp, knocking Symon sideways causing him to lose his concentration and break the connection.

"Second Councilor Fredrik, stop, we are trying to help you!" DraDonna said with urgency.

"I'm alright, let me go," Fredrik said in a gruff manner that was unlike him as he struggled to get free of DraDevon's arms and sit up.

"It's okay, Devon you can let him go now," Symon told him.

"What is going on?" Fredrik asked, still looking a little confused.

"What do you remember?" Symon questioned him.

"I remember trying to hold back a crowd of energy mad people. Then pain everywhere," Fredrik confessed to them, bringing his hand to his forehead as if he still felt the pain. He went on. "Then you were holding me down. What is going on?" he asked again.

"Well to start with, the HEART dropped everyone like she said she would. But there is more. A lot more that I have to tell you, but I don't have time. You are going to have to trust me Fredrik. But one thing you should know is these two are innocent of all the crimes they were charged with, and more importantly, we have bonded as friends."

"What is it that you need me to do?" Fredrik asked, but having a hard time grasping what was going on.

"First thing is, I have promised Donna and Devon that we would find their family. I think that we are going to start with JorMelony." Symon told him.

"Why start with her?" Fredrik asked in an uncharacteristically rude manner.

"Jude was holding her somewhere," DraDonna said, "using her to get DraDevon and JorRobert and I to co-operate with her. I'm afraid Jude did something bad to her... and JorMelony is with child."

Standing up with the rest of the group, Fredrik straightened his robes and inquired, "Where do you want to look first?"

"I don't know," DraDonna admitted with a concerned look on her face.

"I was hoping you might know where JorRobert would be so we could ask him," Symon said.

"I don't know about that, Symon," DraDonna said feeling apprehensive about that idea.

"Why?" Symon asked.

DraDevon interjected, "Because he tried to kill both of us yesterday, and me, he tried to kill twice! Besides if he wasn't already crazed before, he's sure to be now."

"Don't worry, Devon. I will protect you if he tries anything. And if he is in madness and pain, I will heal him."

"The last time I remember seeing him was when he was trying to wake up Jude," Fredrik broke in. "Why don't you try looking for him at his home? It's the first place I would look for anyone."

"Aren't you going to come with us?" DraDevon asked, hoping he would, so he and his wife would have more of the HEART's servants to help if JorRobert got out of hand again.

"No," Frederik said, "I think I should stay here and look after the people in the crowd in case they wake up." He rubbed his forehead. "By the way Symon, what do I tell them when they do wake up?"

"Are you in pain?" Symon asked, ignoring his question and concerned by the look of pain he saw in Fredrik's eyes.

"I'm fine," he answered tersely, snapping his hand down from his forehead to his side. "Just answer me. What do I tell people if they start to wake before you get back?"

"Tell them that the HEART, our MOTHER is taking us home," Symon answered him simply, still not convinced Fredrik was all right.

"What do you mean by that?" Fredrik asked, sounding even more uncharacteristically terse.

"Fredrik it's complicated, and I don't know if I have the time to explain it properly."

"Well make it simple," Fredrik yelled, letting his frustration show, "I have to tell them something if they start to wake up and you're not here!"

"I guess it's alright for me to tell you this now because the HEART has told me to explain it to everyone."

"That doesn't make any sense Symon!" Fredrik retorted in frustration.

"Let me finish," Symon said hurriedly. "The secret, usually bound by the Ambassadors oath, is that the world that we live on is not in fact a world, but a ship. And the HEART is a computer that has been taking care of us for a thousand years."

"WHAT?" Fredrik yelled in shock.

"That is as simple as I could make it."

"You've gone energy mad, Symon."

"He's telling the truth Councilor Fredrik. I have seen it with my own eyes," DraDevon said.

"I asked you to go with me to the temple; you still can. Go talk to her. She will tell you everything," Symon suggested.

"No. I need to stay here for the people… I guess I will have to trust you," Fredrik said with skepticism. "Just go and get back here as soon as you can."

"We will. Take care, Fredrik," The three left Fredrik amidst the sleeping crowd.

"Should we walk to the Jor house?" DraDonna asked anxiously.

"No let's use HEART stone travel; it's faster," Symon answered hurriedly.

"But we don't have our travel stones; JorRobert took them and we don't know what he did with them."

Symon laughed a little. "You don't need them if you're with me. All you have to do is hold on to me." They jogged up to the temple office. Symon opened the door and they all strode quickly to the altar.

"Hold on to me," he told them.

DraDonna and DraDevon grabbed hold of his left arm as he slapped his right palm on the cool white stone. All three of them disappeared from the room in a flash of blue light.

They reappeared in the main living area of the Jor home in the same flash of light.

After the shock of energy travel wore off, the three of them were surprised to find JorRobert sitting on his chair holding JorMelony's tallice, weeping.

"JorRobert?" Symon asked. "What are you doing; are you in pain?"

"I don't know where she is," he said through his tears. "I tried to get Jude to wake up and tell me, but I couldn't."

"Come JorRobert; help us find your wife," Symon said soothingly to him. "Think carefully; where did Jude say she was taking her?"

"I… I can't remember; I don't know." JorRobert sobbed. "She is carrying my child again."

"We know, come with us and help us find her," DraDonna asked him desperately, then turned to the other two men. "I think we should use Councilor Fredrik's advice and look for her at Jude's home."

"That would be a good idea," Symon said, "but I was at her office earlier and there wasn't anyone there. How about the home she grew up in?"

"Sounds good. Let's go," DraDevon said hurriedly.

"Please come with us," Symon invited as he extended his hand to the big man.

To everyone's surprise, JorRobert took Symon's hand and they were all off in a flash of blue light.

A moment later the group found themselves in the First Councilors community, in Jude's parents' home. It was a typical small home just like any other onboard the BIO18.

They quickly searched the house, finding only Jude's parent's deeply asleep in their bed.

"What do we do now?" DraDonna asked, feeling frustrated.

"Jude told me there was a hole in the floor," JorRobert volunteered as he tried to think clearly. "I can't remember if she said how big it is, but it's worth looking for."

"Where is it?" DraDonna asked excitedly.

"I think Jude said it was by the altar," he told the other three.

All four of them dashed back to the living area looking wildly over the floor. "Back off and let me look," DraDonna commanded them. They quickly got out of her way, knowing that she had an eye for wood. "There!" she pointed at a few boards that were only slightly off.

The three men got down on hands and knees. Each of them managed to pry up a board. "Let me look!" DraDonna said, pushing them out of the way. Getting close to the hole in the floor she called, "JorMelony!" but no one heard any response. As she looked down in the hole she told the others, "The space under the house is too small for a person, no matter how many floorboards are pulled up, but..." she stopped, reaching inside. "There's something in here."

Her hand landed on cool stone and drew it up into the light. It was an oval shaped piece of HEART stone framed in metal.

"Symon," she said in awe. "What is this?"

"I don't know," he answered her with awe in his own voice. He reached out, taking the stone from her. As soon as his hand closed around the stone it began to glow with a bright white light.

They all gasped in surprise.

DraDevon asked, "Why did it do that when you touched it?"

"I don't know," Symon answered him simply. "This thing is very…very…" He struggled to find the right word, "…old… but I just don't know where we are going to find JorMelony."

As soon as JorMelony's name left his lips, blue lines began to form in angles and turns on the stone. There were blue circles dotting precise spots on blue lines and one circle that was red.

"It looks like a map," DraDevon said, looking over Symon's shoulder at the stone. "I think that red circle is JorMelony. Do you know where that is, Symon?"

He studied the stone for a moment. His eyes widened in surprise. He recognized the layout of the blue lines as the First Councilors community. "This is Jude's office," he said, pointing to the red circle.

"I thought you said she wasn't there," JorRobert growled dangerously.

"I said I didn't see her in the office. I didn't check the private rooms. I should have checked the private rooms!" he said, feeling the all too familiar burden of guilt.

"Don't beat yourself up over it. You didn't know," DraDevon said, trying to console him.

"Let's just get there," DraDonna said urgently.

All four of them stood quickly.

Symon placed the odd mapstone in the pocket of his robe so they all could take hold of him for travel. He placed his hand on the HEART stone altar, and with just a thought they were all whisked away by the energy to the First Councilors office.

"JORMELONY!" Both DraDonna and JorRobert yelled together as soon as the energy left them in the office.

All four of them were quiet for a moment to listen, and then they all heard the faintest moan of pain.

"She is in the private room," DraDevon said in panic.

Quicker than a flash of the HEART's energy JorRobert rushed over to the door, kicking it down, sending splinters in all directions. "NO!" came his soul wrenching cry when he saw his wife lying face down on the floor with a small puddle of blood under her face.

DraDonna flew across the office to the demolished door with Symon and DraDevon close behind, just in time to see JorRobert sobbing as he lifted his wife's limp body into his arms.

"SYMON, COME HERE QUICK!" DraDonna screamed. She scrambled over to her sister's side, taking her limp hand. The pungent stench of burned flesh assaulted her nose. "Melony!" DraDonna sobbed as tears poured from her eyes, forgetting all she had been taught about how disrespectful it was to use someone's childhood name without being given permission. "Melony, it's your little Donna. What happened?" she asked JorMelony, trying not to sob.

JorMelony's eyes rolled in her head as she fought her way to consciousness. She managed to open her eyelids slightly, then coughs and gags, staining her lips with more blood. "The necklace became so hot! I tried to get it off, but it burned through my skin I...I couldn't..." JorMelony's rasping voice stopped as her small frame was wracked with a gasping coughing fit. She struggled for air but brought up more blood instead. The writhing and coughing fully revealed the extent of the horrifying injury to her neck. The skin had burned until the flesh all around the necklace had been charred black and sunken, embedding the hideous necklace in the flesh at her throat.

Seeing this, Symon immediately began to channel as much of the positive energy as he could into her broken and burned body.

"Don't worry about me, little Donna, all is well... all is well," her voice softly rasped. "Jor... Robert!" she gasped in pain, and exhaled a gurgle of blood.

H.E.A.R.T. Saga: The Children

The four people that knelt next to her saw the light of JorMelony's soul leave her eyes.

Comfort
30

JorRobert sobbed. He knew everything that had made him good had been torn from him. He felt like his own soul had been ripped from his body and left with his wife's soul.

He stood with JorMelony's body in his arms.

DraDonna was not ready to let go of her older sister's hand; she stood with him.

He tenderly placed her body on the bed and DraDonna arranged her hands in a dignified pose on her stomach, as if still protecting the life inside of her that would never be. DraDonna then arranged the collar of JorMelony's shirt to hide the heinous cause of her sister's death.

"JorRobert; Donna," Symon addressed them, his voice thick with emotion as well as compassion. "Please let me help you with your sorrow. I don't think that I can make this kind of pain go away. I don't have that kind of power, but I can offer you the comfort and strength from the energy of the HEART our MOTHER."

JorRobert spun around with a wild look of madness in his eyes. "Our MOTHER?" he spat out bitterly. "How could a mother allow such horrible things to happen to a person as good and innocent as JorMelony?"

"I don't know why bad things happen to good people," Symon said. "But what I do know is the HEART loves us all and feels sorrow when we hurt," Symon reached out to the big man.

"Don't touch me, Ambassador! I... I don't believe the HEART is real anymore! Why would I believe that you can offer me any... any help?"

"Let Symon help you JorRobert," DraDonna said, trying to control her own sobs.

JorRobert turned his eyes accusingly on her. "You! This is all your fault. You have always been an energy mad freak. If it wasn't for you and your crazy ideas, my wife and child would be alive!"

DraDevon stepped forward, placing an arm protectively around his wife, "I can't believe you're trying to blame this on my wife! She just lost her sister!" DraDevon was beginning to get really angry, looking as if he was going to hit JorRobert. "All we want to do is help you. Even after all you did to hurt us yesterday."

"Don't yell at me you freak! You tried to kill me with that drill thing!"

Symon knew he needed to stop them fighting before there was another ugly tragedy in the room. He quickly channeled only positive energy down to both hands, stepped between the fighting men and placed a hand on each of their shoulders. DraDevon instantly relaxed and stopped fighting, but JorRobert slapped Symon's hand away and screamed, "I told you not to touch me!" Then he stormed out of the office, slamming the door behind him.

The only sound in the sorrow-filled office for a few moments was that of DraDonna weeping in her husband's arms.

"Are you okay, Devon?" Symon asked with concern.

"No," DraDevon replied with a tear filled voice. "JorMelony was precious to all of us."

"Then, may I offer the two of you some strength and comfort? I have a feeling that things are going to get harder, and I know whatever happens, I will need the two of you to stand with me."

The grieving couple nodded sadly, and Symon gestured to the desk in the office. "I'm sorry I don't have any place better to offer you to sit, but please sit and try to relax." They sat, and he walked around behind the desk.

He closed his eyes to concentrate on channeling the energy, being careful to only use the purest of positive energy. He then placed a hand on each of their heads and called them by name, channeling the energy into his two friends once again. This time he was not healing their bodies so much as he was giving strength and comfort to their souls.

When Symon lifted his hands off their heads, DraDonna was no longer sobbing. Even though she still felt the pain of great loss, DraDonna knew that she would be able to do all she had to do to protect the rest of the people that she loved.

"Thank you Symon," DraDevon said as he hopped off the desk. Then he cleared his throat. "I don't want to rush anyone, but aren't we running out of time?" He then looked at his wife and said, "You know, I think we've been saying that a lot lately."

"You're right, Devon, we need to get moving," Symon said. "I promised I would help you find your families and wake them if we need to."

"Then can we go find my family?" DraDevon asked. "I want see if my brother and his wife are okay. I'm also really worried about my parents. The HEART said they're at the courtyard." Anxiety and humiliation were creeping up on him.

"I wouldn't worry about your parents Devon. Fredrik is there and will care for them. He's loyal and if he says he's going to care for someone he does," Symon said with a shrug. "Let's check on your brother and his wife first."

They walked to the HEART stone altar. Symon placed his right hand on the stone as his friends took hold of him, and with just a thought from Symon, they left the place of so much pain and grief behind them.

Appearing in the main living area of NulSam and NulJena's home, the three friends saw everything was in order, only silent like everywhere else on board this odd planet-like ship.

"I think the HEART said that they were in bed," DraDonna reminded her husband. "Do you want us to come with you?"

"I think it would be best if I went in there alone for now. I'll let you know if anything is amiss." DraDevon looked between their worried faces. "Besides I think that it would be a little disturbing for NulJena to wake up and find her HEARTbrother, his wife and the Ambassador all standing over her."

"Okay, don't be long," DraDonna said as she gently kissed her husband. "Symon," she said, turning to him, "let's have another look at that map stone again."

DraDevon walked quietly to the bedroom.

He stood in the doorway. With relief he saw the HEART was right. His brother and his HEART sister were in bed, deeply asleep. DraDevon walked carefully over to his brother and firmly shook his shoulder. "Wake up, NulSam," he said in a soft yet urgent voice. His brother didn't even twitch.

DraDevon wasn't sure how to wake his brother, but he knew he wanted to do this on his own so he didn't call for Symon; he didn't want to stress NulJena by having too many people in the room. He thought for a second about how he could wake them. Symon would probably channel positive energy and use it to wake them.

DraDevon thought maybe he could channel what energy he still had inside him and split it like he would for an arc weld, but tuck his negatively charged thumb into his hand and only use his positively charged finger to wake them. "It might not be as strong as what Symon can do but it just might be enough to wake you up," he said to his sleeping brother.

After having channeled and split the energy, DraDevon carefully drew the small spark of positive energy across his brother's forehead.

It had the desired effect.

NulSam took a deep breath and opened his eyes.

"DraDevon, what are you doing here?" he asked with a start.

"NulSam, there is so much going on. It is too much for me to get into right now."

"But what..." NulSam started, but DraDevon stopped him.

"You are just going to have to trust me when I say that something wonderful has happened to DraDonna and me."

"What happened?" NulSam asked, feeling a little scared of the answer.

H.E.A.R.T. Saga: The Children

"We met the HEART, and we have bonded in friendship with the Ambassador." DraDevon stopped for a moment, but his brother remained silent, so he went on. "We have learned that things aren't quite what they seem in our world, but everything is going to be okay. The HEART is taking us home."

"You met the HEART?" NulSam asked in confusion. "We're going home? You're not making any sense."

"NulSam, you're just going to have to trust me. But tell me something: how is your wife?"

"Every day we that get closer to the birth, it's harder for her; the babe still doesn't move." There was the sound of great worry in his voice.

"This is what is so wonderful NulSam, The HEART is taking us someplace where your daughter, my niece will be born alive! I know that you don't understand, but you will just have to trust me. After I go, and NulJena wakes, tell her about this. And just be ready."

"Aren't you going to wake her like you woke me? Wait, how did you wake me?" NulSam asked curiously.

DraDevon smiled a little at his brother. "A little trick I learned from my new friend. NulSam, I have to go now. The Ambassador is here with us and we have a lot to do and not much time."

NulSam looked closely at his brother, seeing pain and grief in his eyes. "What has happened DraDevon? I can tell you are in pain."

"Well... a lot of things, but the worst of it is..." He stopped, the pain of loss still fresh. "DraDonna's sister was killed this morning and she was with child."

"DraDevon, I am so sorry!" NulSam said, reaching out to comfort his brother by taking his hand. "And you came to us because you worried for my wife and babe," said NulSam, touched by his brother's worry.

DraDevon closed his eyes, accepting the comfort of his older brother for a moment. He remembered JorMelony's last words to DraDonna. "All is well, NulSam, all is well," DraDevon said, squeezing his brother's hand.

With one last look, he turned and walked out of the bedroom back into the living area.

"Is everything okay?" DraDonna asked him, worried for her HEART sister.

"Yeah, I think they will be alright. Have you two figured out the map stone yet?"

"I think so," Symon answered. "I think it reacts to the HEART stone that I have inside of me."

"When we were trying to figure it out," DraDonna told him, "I saw where TynLexa and TynTomus are and I was thinking that we should go see if they are alright. They're kind of far out where people don't usually go, and I don't think anyone else knows they're out there."

"I don't know, DraDonna, the two of them did try to kill us," DraDevon said. "I thought you wanted to go see if your parents are alright." He was a little skeptical of the new plan.

"Already taken care of," she answered. "We saw on the map stone that they're in the courtyard. We even saw Fredrik check on them."

DraDevon thought quietly for a few moments. "You're right. We should go check on TynLexa and TynTomus. I have a feeling they were under..." he stopped, looking sadly at Symon. "I'm sorry Symon, but I think they were under Jude's control."

"It's alright, Devon. You're probably right," he told him. "She's been acting oddly for some time now. I would not be surprised to find out if something strange was controlling her."

"You have a point Symon," DraDonna said. "We will have to try to figure this out, but for now we need to see if TynLexa and TynTomus are alright."

The three traveled by way of the energy to cabin number one, Ambassadors Mountain.

Looking around the main living area, DraDevon said, "Someone was here."

"What makes you say that?" Symon asked with concern.

"When we left this place, it was a bit of a mess. TynTomus attacked us and we messed things up quite a bit fending him off."

"Where do you think he is?" DraDonna asked.

"Didn't we hear TynLexa say that she was here, that she put him on the bed?" DraDevon told them.

The trio walked quickly to the bedroom but stopped in the doorway when the familiar smell of burned flesh met them once again. "Oh, no!" Symon moaned, rushing forward. "I didn't know it was you! I should have known it was you and Lexa!" he cried.

"Symon, what is..." DraDonna started.

Symon interrupted her. "His soul is still near. I can feel his pain," Symon said, a panicked sound in his voice. His hand was on his chest and tears were running down his face. Symon looked up to the ceiling and cried, "I'm so sorry that Jude did this to you! I didn't know. I will make this right. I will take care of Lexa, I promise you!" He collapsed to his knees by the bed and sobbed.

"Symon," DraDonna asked gently. "What is it? Why did you use his childhood name?"

"My Councilors and I grew up with the two of them. We were all friends. This is all my fault. I should have known Jude would use them to do her dirty work," he said bitterly.

DraDevon knelt down on the floor next to him. "I wish we could heal you the way you have healed us. The best I can offer is my words." He tried to comfort his friend. "I think I understand things pretty well now. Whatever Jude did, whether it was right or not, she did it out of her love for you, and whatever TynTomus and TynLexa did they did it out friendship to her. None of that makes it alright, what they did, but I can understand it."

"Now I just heard you promise this man's soul that you would take care of his wife. So you need to pull yourself together and help us find her," DraDevon said, giving Symon a friendly slap on the back.

"Thanks. You're right; we have to find Lexa." Symon got up off the floor, and without so much as a look back, he quickly walked to the altar with his two best friends at his heels.

With a determined motion, Symon placed his hand on the HEART stone altar with DraDonna and DraDevon holding onto him. He focused his thoughts: ***"Cabin number two Second Councilors Lake."***

The very moment the flash of the energy left them, Symon ran for the bedroom with DraDonna and DraDevon close at hand. DraDonna saw TynLexa lying on the bed in what appeared to be peaceful sleep, yet the burns around her neck were still visible.

Symon looked down at his childhood friend. He then gently placed his head on her chest, relieved to hear her breath and her blood muscle pumping with a steady beat. He then checked her over, seeing some familiar burns on her neck. But the necklace was not there.

Symon channeled more positive energy and began to heal her burned flesh. "Come on Lexa, wake up. Come on, wake up, it's me, Symon," he begged his sleeping friend.

She took a deep breath and opened her eyes, looking disoriented but alright. "Symon? What...what are you doing here? Where is TynTomus?" she questioned her childhood friend.

Looking down, not wanting her to see the guilt in his eyes, he told her, "He died. I think it was a necklace that Jude gave him."

"What...Tyn...NO!" she screamed as she started to cry.

"I will make this right, Lexa," he promised her with tears in his voice that threatened to fall from his eyes again.

"It's not your fault, Symon! You didn't know what she was... what are they doing here?" she asked, pointing to the Dra couple, still sobbing. "Jude said they were energy mad. They're the reason we were out here."

"Jude was wrong, Lexa. Things have changed. These two are bonded to me as my friends like you are; they are good people."

"TynLexa," DraDonna said, feeling her own hot tears sliding down her face, "the necklace that killed your husband also killed my sister who was with child. I know that none of this makes any sense to you right now, but you must know that we mean you no harm. We never did." She sat on the edge of the bed.

"I know," TynLexa said, taking DraDonna's hand. "I remember. I just don't understand why Jude would do this to us. She was our bonded friend."

"TynLexa, DraDevon and I will be your friends and we will stand by you like we do Symon, but I think I understand why Jude did what she did," DraDonna told her. "I think she loved Symon so much that she was willing to do anything to be with him."

"I just don't know what I'm going to do without TynTomus," she sobbed as DraDonna wrapped her arms around the young widow trying to comfort her.

"Lexa," Symon said to his grieving childhood friend, "as Ambassador, I have the power to help you with your grief."

So consumed in her sorrow that she only nodded her head in agreement, she pulled away from her new friend's arms.

Symon moved around behind her on the bed as best he could and laid his hands on her head; with eyes closed he whispered her name and called forth the energy directly from the HEART stone chip in his head. Symon gave her the same blessing of comfort and strength that he had given to DraDonna and DraDevon.

Taking his hands off her head, he moved to help her off the bed. "How do you feel?"

"I hurt," she answered with tears still visible in her eyes, "but I can deal with it." She tried to smile at him.

"That's good," he told her. "We need you to be able to function. There is a lot going on and we may need your help."

"Help? Help with what? Symon, what is going on?"

"Do you remember what Jude had you working on?" he asked her.

"Yes. She had me looking for something in the ground, but she didn't tell me what it was."

"Did you figure it out?"

"No, but I had a feeling I was really close."

"You were," DraDonna broke in. "More than you know."

"What do you mean by that?" TynLexa asked her new friend.

"Come Lexa," Symon said, pulling her toward the HEART stone altar. "There's something else you need to do so you can heal and understand everything."

"What is it?"

"You need to confront Jude so you can forgive her and…"

"And what, Symon?" Lexa asked, sounding distressed.

He put his hand on the cool stone of the altar with his three passengers. "I am taking you to see the HEART."

Ambassador
31

In a flash of blue energy, four figures appeared in the darkness of the temple's upper chamber. Once again Symon's command for light was obeyed.

"What...where?" TynLexa stammered in confusion.

"We are in the entrance room of the temple, but the HEART calls it the upper chamber," Symon answered her.

"But it is so...so..." TynLexa said, at a loss for words.

DraDonna laughed a little as she followed Symon and her husband to the stairs, "I know what you mean. It's not what you expected is it?"

"I just don't know... how... where do these stairs go?" she asked in confusion.

"Well they don't go up," DraDevon joked again as they trudged down the stairs.

"DraDevon, my love," DraDonna said, "that was only funny the first time."

With a little mirth still in his voice he looked back at his wife, "Sorry," he said with a wink.

Symon smiled at him. "I thought it was funny, Devon."

The four finally came to the entrance to the HEART's chamber.

TynLexa stopped for a moment as the others went ahead. She read the words that had been written on the wall. Although she did not fully understand, she was stunned by what she saw. "BIO-18 FIRST CLASS. Human-Environment-Allocating-Relocation-Technology," she read aloud in awe. "H.E.A.R.T." She quickly followed the other three into the chamber.

She stopped again in surprise at seeing such a strange room. She saw the screen that had the image of the enlightened flower, the metal counter just under it, and in the center of the room, the small sofa with Jude laying on it and Fredrik standing over her.

"Fredrik?" she asked in surprise at seeing another one of her old childhood friends in the HEART s chamber.

"Lexa? What are you doing down here?" he asked her.

"I could ask you the same thing," Symon asked him with concern. "I thought you were making sure all the sleeping people in the courtyard were safe."

"My Symon, I see all my children at the courtyard and they are all well," the HEART said. "My servant Fredrik needs to see me. He needs to understand who I am and all that is going on just as much as the rest of you do."

"But what are you?" TynLexa interrupted with a fresh wave of tears of confusion in her eyes. She looked up at the screen with the enlightened flower.

"I am your MOTHER," was the HEART's simple reply to the nearly hysterical woman's question.

"I don't understand what that means," she said. "Our MOTHER. I was told all my life that you are our GOD, the HEART of our planet," she said in a hysterical ramble. "Yet here I am and all I see is an image of some kind of flower. Is that all you are?" She stopped for a moment hoping one of her friends would help her make sense out of this. "Will one of you please explain this to me?" she yelled to everyone in the room. "What is that?" She pointed to the screen. "Where are we? How could we be down so far?" TynLexa broke down into sobs and sank to the floor next to the sofa where Jude was laying. "I just don't understand," she said as she continued to sob.

"TynLexa," DraDonna knelt on the floor next to her. "Do you remember your research?"

TynLexa looked up at her in surprise at the question. She nodded her head, unable to speak through her tears.

"Well I was on the same track in my research. Everything was the same everywhere, and there was something in the soil or in the ground.

"We saw your sketch of the core drill and DraDevon made it. He is a very talented welder," DraDonna said smiling up at her husband. "The core drill worked beautifully, and when we got down only about nine or ten feet we hit metal.

230

We dug down and found that what was under the ground was metal, but it was a kind of metal that DraDevon had never seen before. It was so strong that not even the steel core drill could cut through it."

She paused, looking in her friend's eyes, seeing the light of understanding beginning to spark there. "TynLexa, the world isn't real. It is a vessel… or a ship if you will… taking us through space. Our people have been living on this ship for more than a thousand years. We need a new planet to live on, and now the HEART is taking us to one."

"I still don't understand what the HEART is, DraDonna. I was raised to think of her as our MOTHER, our GOD who is the HEART of our planet." TynLexa was still struggling to understand. "Now I don't even know what that means anymore."

"She is what was once called a computer. She controls and takes care of this ship. She has learned how to feel, and she loves us," DraDonna said simply. "I know this is hard to take in. I still have a hard time with it myself, but we all need to be strong so we can get through this."

"Get through what?" she asked, still confused.

"The people went energy mad last night, my daughter," the HEART jumped into the conversation. "I had to put all my children to sleep. When they wake up, My Symon will have to explain things to them. He will need the support of his friends because he is without his first Councilor."

"Jude!" TynLexa said standing up and turning around. She looked down on Jude's prone form. Fresh tears of betrayal spilling from her eyes, she said, "Why did you do this to us? You killed TynTomus! How could you!" she yelled at her. "Had you gone mad?" TynLexa screamed at her, but then she realized Jude was still sleeping. "Symon, why isn't she waking up? Why doesn't she move?"

Symon could not hide his shame from his old childhood friend. "Jude wanted me to mind wipe Donna and Devon as a part of her mad plan for us to be together. I knew it was wrong and they didn't deserve it, so I…" He stopped, ducking his head as his shame and guilt overwhelmed him.

"Go on," TynLexa said, her concern for Symon showing in her eyes.

"I gave her a jolt of negative energy. I only meant to give her just enough to make her forget her mad plan, but I was in so much pain that I lost control and gave her a high dose." He stopped looking at TynLexa's stunned face. "I didn't know that she had that stupid necklace on, TynLexa! I swear to you… the jolt must have traveled through to your husband as well as JorMelony, killing them both." Symon looked over at DraDonna as well. "I am so sorry, I didn't know she had the necklace; I am not even sure what it is."

"It is a control collar," the HEART said. "These control collars, as well as several other malevolent devices were reported as destroyed just after I took control of the ship. I had the MPB cut hers off. The necklace corrupts the one who wears it by blocking out the good effect of the energy to the brain. It also blocks the help that the Traveler's Joy plant can offer. So in effect, Jude's actions were a result of energy madness." Everyone in the room was stunned into silence for a moment.

"HEART," started Symon, "does this mean that Jude didn't really love me? Was it all just some dark obsession brought on by the necklace?"

"That will be for her to reveal to you if she wakes up, My Symon," the HEART answered him sadly.

"It wasn't your fault, Symon," TynLexa said as tears of sorrow coursed down her face. "I don't even think it was her fault; I don't think she would have hurt anyone if she had been in her right mind. I do know that she loves you, though, Symon. She always has. I understand now why she did it and…" she stopped to gain control of her tears. "I can forgive her."

"But can you ever forgive me?" Symon asked her with his head bowed, too filled with shame to even look at her.

TynLexa crossed the room to where he stood and put her arms around her childhood friend and whispered in his ear. "There is nothing to forgive; you did nothing wrong."

Symon hugged her back, relishing in the warmth and comfort her embrace gave him.

After releasing her friend she looked up at the image of the enlightened flower on the screen. "HEART, I'm not sure if I know what you really are, but I believe that you want to help us." TynLexa looked down at Jude and then back up at the screen. "Will she live?"

"I do not know. I have placed stones that I control on her body that will help to keep her alive while repairing what damage has been done, but I cannot say if she will ever wake. You can take her up to your office, my Symon, and place her in your private chambers. Then you need to take care of the rest of my children. And you will need to go soon. I see that some are beginning to stir. You will need to use all of your strength and power of empathy as well as projection to help them understand what is going on."

"HEART," he addressed the old computer with weariness in his voice, "I love you and I love all of your children, but I ache from all that has happened... from all the loss. I can't help but feel like I'm responsible. I don't know if I can do this anymore. You chose poorly when you chose me," he told her, his voice raw with pain. "I am weak."

"My Symon," the HEART began, her multi-toned mechanical voice oddly soft. "I chose you because I knew that you would have this great capacity for love. The powers that you now bear are greater than those of Ray, the first of my Ambassadors. But the powers that you bear do not come from me, or the chip of HEART stone that you have in your head.

"They come from your soul. I only enhance what you already have. Your ability to love is what makes you powerful. This is why I am not surprised that you love Jude the way you do. This is why I have released you to marry. I believe that it will make you even more powerful and more able to serve my children."

The HEART paused for a moment as the enlightened flower continued to gently move on the screen. "Now you must pull yourself together, my Symon. My children need you. I see that you now have good and loyal friends that will stand by you. Draw strength from them. And you are strong, my Symon; that is why they draw close to you. You are their friend and leader. No matter what happens when we land on our new home, it is my intention to keep you as my Ambassador."

"My HEART my MOTHER, I will always serve you and your children. I hope that you don't think that I don't want to serve, because I do. It's just that... I don't want anyone else to get hurt because of a mistake I have made." Symon humbly said.

"My Symon, have peace in your soul. I promise that this time of pain is but a small moment. I know that your friends will stand by you, and they will always hail you with a warm soul and friendly hands."

"HEART," DraDevon said in an apologetic tone. "I'm sorry to interrupt you but I've thought of something."

"No need to apologize, my son. Please speak your thoughts without fear."

"I was thinking about us being out there for a special gathering when everyone wakes up," he went on. "All of them slept though the pulse, but JorRobert was out there fully exposed and would not let Symon heal him like Fredrik did," DraDevon said, concern in his voice.

"I think he is energy mad. I am very worried about him causing problems for everyone. I know he's capable of killing." DraDevon remembered everything that JorRobert had said and done to hurt him and his wife over the last two days.

"My poor son, JorRobert is tormented by the loss of his wife," the computer said. "Heal him if you can, Symon. But please, all of you, help Symon do what he can. Protect the rest of my children from JorRobert's madness if he cannot be healed."

"We will, HEART," DraDevon promised. TynLexa and DraDonna nodded in agreement.

"You must all go now. The people will be fully awake soon," the computer instructed.

"Yes, HEART," Symon said as he bent down and cradled Jude up in his arms.

They started for the stairs, but Symon stopped, looking around the HEART's chamber. "Where is Fredrik?"

Madness
32

The ringing in Fredrik's head would not go away. He was trying to listen to everything going on in the HEART's chamber, but the pain that the ringing caused was making it hard to concentrate. He could hear them, but what they were saying did not make any sense to his pain-filled brain.

Fredrik was also having a hard time seeing. He just didn't understand why things didn't look right. To his eyes things looked twisted; the colors were wrong somehow. The twisted colors and images only served to make his head hurt more. He rubbed his eyes, hoping that would clear his vision, maybe help with the pain in his head.

When Fredrik opened his eyes he could see things still didn't look right. He could see all of the people in the room but they didn't look right. They were all his friends, he knew that, but his eyes were telling him something different. They looked like a maddening jumble of colors to him.

"Maybe the pulse did something to them." Fredrik thought in a panic. *"But why can't I see them right or understand them? There can't be anything wrong with me. It's them, it has to be them. The pulse changed them,"* was the thought that twisted in his pain-tormented mind.

Fredrik listened to Symon confess all the guilt that he held inside. *"What is the matter with Symon? How could he have feelings like that for Jude; it's… it's… but it's not as if I didn't know. They are my bonded friends, but… how could they?*

Aghhhh!" Fredrik brought his hand back to his head. *"The pain won't go away! I need to get out of here. I need to talk to someone who will understand; but who? Everyone else is sleeping."* He tried to listen to all that was going on.

"The HEART… she…not our God…what is it? What is that flower on the screen? Why won't it stop moving; why is it so bright? I have to get out of here!" Fredrik thought as he rubbed the sides of his head with both

hands, hoping desperately that the pain would go away so he could understand what these people, people he had loved all his life were saying.

"JorRobert is still awake! Maybe he will understand and help with the pain in my head... but Symon can help... no, Symon is damaged... and the HEART; she isn't real... she's not our MOTHER!" Fredrik slowly backed away from the sofa where Jude was lying, and made his way to the stairs.

Fredrik hoped no one saw him go as he ran quickly, quietly up the stairs. *"I have to get to JorRobert; maybe he can help,"* was the irrational thought that played over in his mind as he ascended to the upper chamber. *"Symon can't help me; he was the one damaged by the pulse.*

Maybe JorRobert can help me stop the HEART. Yes, that's it. If I stop that thing, then I will stop the pain. The gathering; there is going to be a gathering. Maybe there will be a way to stop the HEART from doing what she is planning.

Maybe the HEART is damaged, too. How can there be any other world? That is madness. This is our world. Why would anyone want to leave this world? It is a perfect world." Fredrik placed his hand on the HEART stone by the door. "Yes. JorRobert and I can help each other," he said quietly as he took the small travel stone out of the pocket of his robe.

The pain in his head prevented him from thinking too much about the HEART and whether or not he believed anymore. Fredrik hurriedly recited the prayer for travel that ended in, "JorRobert's home."

The full force of the energy began to course though his body, causing him more pain. The negative side of the energy felt like needles in his mind, the positive gently teasing him with the promise of relief from his pain. Both sides of the energy twisted inside his body, pulling him to his destination.

The energy retreated back into the HEART stone on the altar in the Jor home. Fredrik collapsed to his knees, retching with pain and confusion. *"Maybe I was wrong.*

Maybe Symon can help me. No, there is nothing wrong with me. Symon tried to heal me.

It's him. If there was something wrong with me and Symon healed me then all is well. But if this hurts so much then Symon didn't heal me and that means there is something wrong with him. It's not me, it's him." He took deep breaths, and then got to his feet.

"I will stop the HEART," he said quietly.

He kept his thoughts fixated on this one thing. *"Stay focused and get JorRobert's help; you can aid each other."* He walked through the house, following the sound of JorRobert's voice to the bedroom.

He watched quietly as JorRobert had a conversation with no one.

JorRobert was so consumed by his rabid sorrow that he didn't notice he was being watched as he sat on the bed holding his wife's tallice. "Why did you die?" he asked, sobbing. "I tried to save you."

The ethereal form of JorMelony stood at JorRobert's shoulder and spoke. "I know, JorRobert, go to Symon. Let him heal the pain in you. Please, JorRobert, I can't stay and protect you from the pain for very much longer; go to Symon please!"

"Stop it!" he yelled, jumping from the bed. "You are dead! I watched you die, I held you in my arms; I saw the pain on your face and watched as the light went out of your eyes!"

"Peace, JorRobert. I have peace, you can have it too. Go to Symon, he will help you find peace," she told him.

"No! Go away, you're dead." JorRobert's pain overwhelmed him.

"I can't leave you like this. I love you. I have to see that you find peace," she told him.

"Symon can't help me find peace! Even as powerful as he's supposed to be, he couldn't save you. He didn't even try. I tried, JorMelony; I tried! It's his fault; Symon caused this. And it was your mad sister and her husband who started this mess!" He threw the tallice at the ghostly image of his wife and watched as it sailed right through her, smashing against the wall. "You're dead and it's their fault!" he screamed.

"JorRobert. Please go to them. The pulse damaged you; they can help you," she pleaded.

"Stop it, JorMelony! They did this to you, to me. I am going to make them pay!" JorRobert pulls the emitter from his belt, blasting a hole through what was left of his wife's tallice.

Fredrik then made his presence known. "You'd better put that thing away before you hurt yourself."

Startled by the sound of another voice in the room, JorRobert whipped around with the emitter still in his hand. "What are you doing here, Second Councilor Fredrik?"

"Take it easy, JorRobert. I have come to help you. I think we can help each other."

"Did Ambassador Symon send you?" JorRobert demanded again, still brandishing the dangerous weapon.

"No, he did not," Fredrik said, trying to soothe the enraged man's fears. "They were all damaged by the pulse and are now mad."

"Don't listen to him, JorRobert," JorMelony's ghost begged her husband. "Look in his eyes. He feels a lot of the same pain you do. Look at his face. Where is Fredrik's smile?"

"Stop it!" he commanded her in a feral whisper.

"Stop what?" Fredrik asked him.

"I wasn't talking to you. I was talking to… never mind." He tucked the emitter back into his belt. "Talk," he commanded. "How can you help me?"

"I know what happened to your wife today. I understand your need to see those who caused this punished. And I think I have an idea of how we can do it."

"I'm listening," JorRobert said as he folded his large arms across his chest.

"You want revenge on those who caused your wife's death. I need to get the HEART, or whatever she is to stop this…" he stopped, not willing to admit that he felt pain.

"Stop what?" JorRobert asked.

"Don't listen to him," JorMelony's spirit begged. "Look into his eyes, JorRobert; see his pain? What he is planning will hurt people; people I love." JorRobert ignored her pleas.

"It's not important," Fredrik told him. "The HEART just needs to stop."

"Tell me more about this plan, Second Councilor."

"What I am planning is simple. I overheard them talking about a special gathering to wake everyone up. And Symon is supposed to explain everything about the HEART and about how she is supposed to be bringing everyone to a better world." He paused for a moment to see if he had JorRobert's attention.

"Go on," JorRobert said evenly.

"Well, DraDonna and DraDevon will also be there to give their new bonded friend support," he said bitterly. "This will be your opportunity to punish them for what they did to your wife. You can hurt, humiliate, or kill them— I don't care. Only leave Symon to me. I need him to speak to the HEART for me, so I can get her to stop this madness."

"Why would Symon do what you tell him?" JorRobert asked.

"Because he will see that you're going to hurt his bonded friends," he said again with bitterness in his voice.

"I see. It sounds like a pretty good plan… only there is a problem," JorRobert said thoughtfully. "They outnumber us."

"I thought of that," Fredrik told him. "I have a few ideas that will even the odds."

"Don't listen to him, JorRobert! Please don't listen to him. He is mad!" JorMelony begged her husband again.

"Stop it; I'm doing this for you," he growled at her under his breath.

This time Fredrik heard what JorRobert said. "Stop it?" Fredrik asked him. "I thought you wanted to know about our plan."

"I wasn't talking to you. I was talking to…" JorRobert stopped, not wanting to tell Fredrik about his wife's presence.

"Who?" Fredrik asked, a little annoyed.

"It's my wife's soul. She won't leave me alone," he told Fredrik, feeling a little embarrassed to admit that he was seeing someone that was dead.

"Oh, is she here?" Fredrik asked brightly, almost as if he was his old jovial self again. "JorMelony, if you can hear us, my dear, we're doing this for you," he called to the room, not really believing she was there.

Ignoring the feeling that he was being mocked by the Second Councilor, JorRobert gruffly asked, "So what is it you think we have that will even the odds?"

"First off, you have that weapon. But you need to be sure you have enough energy to use it." Fredrik stopped, trying to control the pain that flared up in his head again so he could talk.

"And?" JorRobert asked.

"And we will have Jude," he said, finally able to control the pain.

"What… how?" JorRobert asked in surprise.

"Come my friend, I will explain as we prepare. We don't have much time," Fredrik said as he led his new friend to the HEART stone altar.

Ambush
33

A compelling yet gentle tolling sound came from the HEART stones all over the ship. It called everyone out of their energy induced sleep. The tolling also said *"come to the courtyard,"* and come they did. They just didn't know why.

Those who lived in the Ambassadors Community came on foot. Those that lived in the Second Councilors Community used the energy travel to the temple office, lining up and going by twos or more.

Those that lived in the First Councilors Community used the energy travel to the upper chamber of the temple. At any other time the thought of being in the temple was the cause of trepidation. No one but the Ambassador ever entered the temple, but the gentle tolling of the HEART stones told the people it was okay this time.

Symon stood watching all the HEART's children pour into the courtyard, and those who had been asleep on the ground in the courtyard began to wake and stand up, looking groggy but calm. He felt a flutter of fear in the pit of his stomach, because he didn't want a repeat of what had happened the night before.

"I hope they listen to me this time," Symon told DraDevon, who stood next to him along with DraDonna and TynLexa.

"I think they will," he responded. "Everyone looks calm and you have us, Symon. You're not alone." DraDevon placed his hand on Symon's shoulder. "What is your plan?"

"I think I'll ask everyone to link up first; then I will channel very strong positive energy. Then I will talk and tell them what's going on." Taking a shaky breath, he voices his fear again. "I hope they listen to me."

"I don't know why they wouldn't. The people all love you, Symon," DraDonna told him.

"I know they do. I can feel their love, but the problem is I don't have my councilors with me. I don't know how the people will react to that. I also need help channeling the energy into the linked up crowd. Maybe you three could help me."

"But Symon, we can't channel like a Councilor can. We only have the one grain of HEART stone in our right wrists," TynLexa told him with a worried look on her lovely face.

"I think I have an idea around that," he said with confidence. "Listen, the link works when a person is in contact. Now, all the councilors do is amplify what I have and split the energy from either wrist. You will not need to split the energy because I will have already done it. Just touch me with your left hand let it flow down your left arm to your right wrist, then focus the energy on the grain and let the grain amplify the positive. Take hold of the person in the crowd closest to you."

"I think it might work," DraDevon said.

"We'd better start," Symon said. "I just saw the last person leave the temple, as well as the office."

"Be ready," he warned them. "Devon, you take my right hand. Donna, you take my left, and Lexa—"

"I can't!" she whispered, her voice full of fear.

"Why?" he asked.

"I just can't. Please… Symon, I can't. I will tell you why some other time, I promise, but I just can't now." she pleaded with him.

Searching his friend's face, he saw pain as well as worry, "It's alright. I'm sure the three of us can handle it."

"I'm sorry," she told him, a look of relief on her face.

"It's alright, Lexa," he said again. "In that case, you stand behind us. I don't want anything to happen to you."

"It will be alright, TynLexa," DraDonna said with a reassuring smile.

Symon turned to face the crowd with DraDevon at his right, DraDonna to his left and TynLexa behind them.

Symon raised his hands to get the crowd's attention. "I am so pleased to see all of the HEART's children gathered together this morning for such a special gathering. Let me start this gathering with a special dose of positive energy!" he said with a wide charming smile.

The crowd of people, who once looked sleepy, began to cheer.

"Link up, sons and daughters of the HEART!" he told them, and they happily obeyed.

With just a look to his friends, they linked arms and Symon closed his eyes to concentrate. Reaching out to the HEART stone that he carried in his head he drew all the positive energy he could and pushed it down to his chest, letting it flow out his arms into DraDonna and DraDevon. They in turn amplified the energy and reached forward, taking hold of the person closest to them.

The feeling of the flow of the HEART's energy changed—Symon looked up in surprise, realizing that he was no longer channeling the energy into his friends, but that they were drawing it directly from him. He had never had that happen with his Councilors.

With a genuine smile on his beautiful face he addressed the children of the HEART. "Children of the HEART, you have all been called here this morning to hear glorious and historic news. The HEART who is our MOTHER has found us a new home.

"This home that we have known for more than a thousand years is old and has been holding back the souls who have died, shutting out the souls of our babies. So the HEART has found us a new home where she will be able to set the old souls free, and our babies once again will be born to us!"

He stopped for a moment to look into the crowd. He saw calm faces and smiles as they listened intently.

"I know that you may not understand a lot of this just yet. But the HEART wants me to explain the truth of all things to you. She is our MOTHER who has loved and cared for us for over a thousand years. But she is not our God. She never claimed to be; it was we who had seen her as one."

He looked around, still seeing that the people were focusing on his words. Symon looked to his two friends at his side. He worried for them because they had never channeled like this before, but saw that his worry was unfounded. They strongly kept concentration as they drew a steady stream of positive energy from him.

"She wants you all to know that she will always care for us and guide us. Even on our new world. The best news of all is that she has a great new gift. She is giving us the gift of freedom. She will guide us, but we will be free to choose how we will live our lives."

Symon felt pleased that the crowd of HEART's children was reacting so well to the news, so he continued. "Now I know that you will have many questions. Please be patient and I will answer all in—"

"But what are those two criminals doing with you?" Came a gruff voice from the crowd.

All three of them look up in surprise.

"Keep channeling," Symon whispered desperately to his two friends.

"What I want to know is, where are your Councilors?" came a second voice.

Symon knew that voice very well, but there was a dark sound in it that filled him with dread. He looked wildly into the crowd for the source of the voices. It did not take long for him to locate them.

The two men were pushing people out of their way as they went, causing people to break the link of positive energy. He saw the blue glow flicker and die as more of the link was broken.

"What have you done now, Symon?" Fredrik said as he approached the Ambassador, shoving him hard, breaking the link to his friends.

"Fredrik, stop!" screamed TynLexa.

"Well, Lexa." Fredrik said with a brief flash of his old cocky smile. "It's good to see you, but I need to know if you have been caught up in this HEART madness. It needs to stop!" Fredrik declared.

"Leave her alone, Fredrik," Symon warned, standing between them.

Fredrik turned his angry gaze back on the Ambassador. Symon saw the pain and madness that burned in his friend's eyes.

Out of reflex Symon channeled positive energy to his right hand and reached up toward Fredrik. "Fredrik, why didn't you tell me you were still in pain from the pulse? This is all just madness. Let me heal you."

"Don't touch me, Symon!" Fredrik yelled as he smacked Symon's hand away. "You are the one who is mad, not me! You are going to help me stop the HEART and this mad plan to leave our home." Fredrik's face bore the look of violence.

"I will not help you do anything of the kind!" Symon said with conviction in his voice.

"Oh, but I think you will... JorRobert!" he called.

Cold fingers of dread gripped Symon's soul as he saw the big man push his way through the crowd of scared people. In his right hand he carried the emitter. In the other, cradled in his arm like a child, was Jude.

"You will do whatever we tell you to do, or I will burn a hole in her chest. I don't think you can heal that, now can you, Ambassador?"

"Before we get to the business of you stopping the HEART, Symon," Fredrik said, "we're going to have a little entertainment." The madness burned bright in Fredrik's eyes. "Mind wipe DraDonna. Or JorRobert will kill the love of your life."

Sacrifice
34

The crowd of people stood in stunned silence as they watched the two men prepare to torment those they thought responsible for their pain.

"No!" DraDevon screamed as he charged to DraDonna's defense. "Don't touch my wife!"

Anticipating this reaction from DraDevon, Fredrik quickly channeled only negative energy, swung around and putting his hand out in front of him, halting DraDevon's mad dash. DraDevon skidded to a halt just a breath away from getting a jolt of the negative energy in his chest.

"That's right, DraDevon, stop right there." Fredrik said, still holding his hand close to the shorter man's chest. Fredrik walked behind DraDevon, wrapping his left arm around his neck in a tight chokehold, all the while keeping his negatively charged right hand near DraDevon's chest. "Now I know that I am not nearly as powerful as Symon but I do know that this little jolt I could give you would hurt badly, and might even be enough to stop your blood muscle. So don't move."

"Let them go!" TynLexa cried. "I have known you all my life, Fredrik, this isn't you! You are kind and funny, not a killer."

"Stay out of this Lexa!" Fredrik warned her.

"Enough talking!" JorRobert yelled, turning the weapon and randomly shooting into the crowd, striking a surprised middle aged man in the chest. Without a word he slumped to the ground, dead.

"Now mind wipe that energy mad woman!" he screamed as he plunged the hot end of the emitter into Jude's chest.

Symon, feeling the searing pain of the man's death as well as the cold fear that these two would kill someone he loved, desperately tried to think of something that would stall or stop them.

"Why just mind wipe Donna? I don't understand," Symon asked JorRobert. "Why not kill her yourself with that emitter?"

JorMelony appeared only to her husband once more, begging him, "Don't do it!"

"You just don't get it, do you Symon?" JorRobert laughed mirthlessly, ignoring his wife's invisible soul. "I don't just want her dead. I want her in pain! I want both of you... all of you... to suffer for what you did to us!" JorRobert screamed hysterically. "Now get to it or Jude here will join that dead man!"

With her head held high, DraDonna walked boldly to JorRobert. "I don't want to die, JorRobert, but I will do whatever it takes to protect the ones I love. Even if that means I have to sacrifice myself to a couple of madmen," she said bitterly. She looked up at the big man and whispered softly, "I miss JorMelony, too."

Rage that had built up over the past few days suddenly exploded at the sound of his wife's name. JorRobert drew his right hand back and hit DraDonna across the face with the emitter. He hit her so hard that she flew backward several feet, landing at DraDevon's feet with a large bleeding gash on the side of her face.

DraDevon looked down at his wife as best he could and managed to say, "Fight them my wife. Fight them."

Getting shakily to her feet, she looked into her husband's eyes and said with tears in her voice, "You once told me that you would die for me. I am willing to die to protect you."

"Get moving, DraDonna!" Fredrik interrupted them. "Or I will give him this jolt of negative and stop his blood muscle. Then there will be no more question of which lover will die for whom."

With legs shaking in fear, DraDonna walked with as much dignity as she could to Symon and knelt in front of him. "Do it," she told him. "This time I know you're doing it for the right reason."

"I don't want to," he whispered to her as tears spilled from his eyes.

"Do it!" she told him again. "Protect the people we both love."

"I'm so sorry, Donna. I love you," he said with tears streaming down his face as he lifted his shaking hands to the top of her head.

"I love you too, Symon," she said softly. Then she yelled, "Just do it!"

"No!" DraDevon shouted in desperation.

Gritting his teeth against the torment in his soul, Symon reached inside of him and found the energy, splitting off the negative, channeling only that into DraDonna's head once more.

JorMelony's soul now felt panic. She had to stop this. "JorRobert," she begged again, "don't do this! Don't hurt my baby sister." But the desperate pleadings of her soul could not penetrate her husband's fevered brain any longer. She was desperate to find a way to stop this now, before it was too late and her sister was completely mind wiped.

She looked at the slumbering woman in her husband's arms and had an idea. "Okay Jude, now it's time to make up for all the pain you put everyone through."

"Come on, Jude, save my baby sister." She placed her transparent hands on the sleeping woman, causing her to moan. "Use my soul's energy and wake up, Jude, for just a moment, COME ON!"

In response to JorMelony's command, Jude began to moan loudly and fling her arms and legs around. JorRobert was so startled by the life that suddenly returned to the woman that he dropped her.

Symon, seeing this out of the corner of his eye, seized the opportunity and lifted his hands off DraDonna's head and pushed all the negative energy that he could channel into one powerful bolt, casting it at JorRobert, striking him in the chest, stopping his blood muscle, killing him instantly.

At the same time, DraDevon saw his own opportunity to liberate himself of Fredrik's chokehold. He channeled his own supply of energy down his right arm, splitting the energy at the HEART stone grain in his wrist, the negative to his thumb and the positive to his forefinger. He brought both fingers together on the underside of Fredrik's arm, burning him badly.

Fredrik screamed in pain and let DraDevon go, ridding himself of the fingers that were burning his flesh.

Free and spinning around, DraDevon swung a wild punch with his still energy charged fist, smashing it into the Second Councilor's face, knocking him flat on the ground. "I told you not to touch my wife!" DraDevon screamed at him.

DraDevon then scrambled to where his wife lay motionless on the ground. "What do we do?" he asked Symon desperately.

Symon was now bending down over DraDonna as well.

"Can you heal her?" he asked him, having to speak up because the people in the crowd were beginning to panic with fear from all they had just witnessed.

"I don't think I can, Devon. I'm sorry," Symon said, his voice thick with guilt.

"It's not your fault, Symon, but... what do I do?" DraDevon asked, feeling close to panic himself.

"Get her down to the HEART's chamber. Devon, the HEART will know what to do," Symon instructed him as TynLexa joined them.

"Fredrik ran off," she told them, trying to catch her breath. "I tried to catch him but I lost him in the crowd."

"We will have to deal with him later," Symon said. "We have to get these two down to the HEART."

"Let's go then," DraDevon said eagerly as he tenderly lifted his wife's limp body into his arms.

"I can't go," Symon told them.

"Why?" DraDevon asked.

"I have to stay here and soothe these people. I can't leave them like this again. I don't know how many more might go mad if the HEART has to drop them all again."

"Then how is Jude going to get down to the HEART s chamber?" TynLexa asked him. "I don't think that I can carry her that far."

"Devon, you take Donna down first. Lexa, you stay with Jude until he gets back and then he can carry her down and you can go with him then," Symon instructed them. "I must stay up here and do my duty as Ambassador."

Shifting his wife's weight, DraDevon looked down at his two friends. "I will be back soon." DraDevon turned and walked swiftly for the temple.

"Are they going to be alright?" TynLexa asked Symon.

"I hope so, Lexa. I hope so," It was the only answer he could give her. He bent down to kiss Jude lightly on the forehead. He whispered just for her, "I love you Jude."

Symon looked up at TynLexa and said, "You still owe me an explanation Lexa, don't forget that. When this is all done..."

"I know," she interrupted him. "You just go do your duty as a servant of the HEART. We can talk later."

"Right," he said, giving her a worried smile, then stood to face the HEART's children, who were growing more agitated by the moment. Raising his arms, he began to address them. "Children of the HEART listen to me!" he called to them, but his voice was lost in the din of scared and confused people. "Please listen to me!" he begged the people to no avail. "Please!" he begged once more.

Symon looked out over the crowd of people. They were descending into the same behavior as the night before, only this time it was worse. Everyone was here. The crowd was three times as large as it had been the night before. More people would mean more panic. People would be trampled, hurt or even killed because he failed to do his duty as their Ambassador.

The old familiar weight of guilt came crashing down on him, and he fell to his knees.

"HEART forgive me, I don't know what to do!" he called out to her.

H.E.A.R.T. Saga: The Children

Have faith, my Symon, was the only reply he heard in his head.

"Have faith? Have faith in what?" he cried.

He squeezed his eyes shut as the panicking people began to surge around him. He looked inside of himself. He pushed past the feelings of pain, loss and guilt and found the power he needed to help the children of the HEART. The place he found the power was not from the HEART stone chip implanted in his head, but deep within his soul. Symon finally understood what the HEART had been telling him all along about where his true power resided.

Seeing this power, Symon seized it and allowed it to fill every fiber of his being. He stood up and opened his eyes. He called out to all the people in a commanding voice, "STOP!"

The people not only heard his voice, they felt it. Everyone stopped to stare at the incredible sight that was their Ambassador. Not only did his hands glow with the HEART'S energy, but his whole body pulsated with the rich blue light of the positive side of the HEART'S energy.

"Link up!" he commanded them in a voice that could only be obeyed. Symon reached out to the closest two people to start the link. Symon looked into their faces and realized it was NayLara and NayMichael, DraDonna's parents.

They were surprised to see the crackling blue energy in the Ambassador's usually hazel colored eyes. He looked into NayLara's eyes and began to speak as if he was talking only to her. He spoke softly, but everyone on the link was able to hear every word he said.

"Children of the HEART, I know that a lot of us have suffered pain and loss lately, but we must not let that take us over. Think not of your own sorrow, but of the sorrow of the person next to you. Let us all have compassion for each other and work together to help build up our new home that the HEART our MOTHER has chosen for us." he said.

His words began to soothe the pains and ills of their fevered minds. "Now go back to your homes, pack and prepare because our new home awaits us." Symon looked up and saw understanding as well as contentment among the HEART's children.

Hope
35

After Symon's speech, the HEART's children above ground began working hard. The people cheerfully received instructions about what they should do from their HEART stone altars.

Below ground the mood was much more somber as Symon stood over Jude and DraDevon stood over his wife. The two comatose women were both lying on small sofas in the computer room with small HEART stones placed on their heads as well as their chests.

"Will they ever wake up?" TynLexa asked the one question they all feared to ask.

The HEART computer was quiet for a moment while the image of the enlightened flower pulsated. It was almost as if they could see her thinking. "I cannot predict if my two daughters will wake or not. They must both heal in three stages."

"What are the three stages?" TynLexa asked in a shaky voice.

"Mind, body and soul," the HEART answered her simply.

"Why did Jude flip around in JorRobert's arms if she is not healed and ready to wake up?" TynLexa asked.

"I have not found an answer to that in any of my file banks," the computer answered. "However, their conditions are more different than you would think."

"What do you mean?" Symon finally spoke.

"My Symon, the negative energy that you gave to DraDonna you started off with a slow trickle, but Jude's was a fast but intense burst and did more damage. Jude was also injured in the crowd last night."

"Oh," Symon said, hanging his head with the weight of guilt pressing down on him again.

"My Symon, do not carry this guilt. It is not your burden to bear. I see as does everyone else that you did not mean them harm. I know that you have love in your soul for both of my daughters that sleep."

"HEART," DraDevon said, trying not to sob. "At what stage of healing is my wife?"

"I do not know that, my son."

"Is there really any hope that either of them will ever wake up?" he asked.

"Have faith, my son," was the HEART's puzzling answer.

"What do you mean by that?" DraDevon questioned the old computer.

"Faith is things that are hoped for but not seen," the HEART computer explained. "Every time you opened the MDC you had faith that there would be food inside. You did not see it, yet you hoped that the food would be there. This hope that your wife will wake is the same hope that all my children have of the new home that they will soon see. All of the trapped souls have faith that they will be set free on this new home planet."

"HEART, I don't understand why we need a planet to free all the trapped souls. I don't understand why they have been trapped in the first place," TynLexa said.

"I have processed this question many times over the last several hundred years while my programing was caught in the loop. I have come up with two separate answers. The first is that we are in space. Everything that is outside of this ship is a cold vacuum. Should I open the dome while in space, all on board would die instantly."

"What is the second reason?" TynLexa asked the HEART.

"It is a little more complicated, my daughter. The old souls are trapped on the ship because they need to be on a planet that is made by a God. I am not a God, I was made by people very much like you, but the people who made me lived on a planet made by a God before the planet died.

"When I get you to the new planet, all my children will have to leave the ship by walking down through the ship and go out the hatch door on the underside. This will enable you to acclimate to the change in pressure from the ship to the new planet.

"After all my children have left, I will open the top and set all the souls free. I know that all the old souls of my children have a hope that they will be freed at this point. I have faith that once the old souls are set free that the new souls of babies will be able to find their way to the bodies that are created for them. Like the body that grows within you now, my daughter." the HEART stated.

"TynLexa!" DraDevon said looking up at her. "You are with child?"

"After all we have been through, DraDevon, you and your wife should be my bonded friends too, and call me Lexa like Symon does."

"I'm honored Lexa," he said. "But…"

"You're with child?" Symon interrupted with the same question.

"Yes I am," she said.

"How far along are you?" DraDevon asked her with concern for his newly bonded friend.

"Not long, Devon," TynLexa answered simply.

"Did… did Timothy know?" Symon stammered, almost afraid to ask.

"No. I never had the chance to tell him with all that was going on with Jude; it just never…" she stopped, because her voice wavered as tears fell from her eyes. The pain of her husband's death was still so fresh in her soul.

"I'm so sorry, Lexa," Symon said. "I promised Timothy's soul that I would take care of you. I promise now that I will see to it, both you and your child will always be taken care of."

"We all will, Lexa." DraDevon added.

"Thank you, my friends."

"HEART," DraDevon said, "I understand faith now." He bent down to kiss his wife's forehead and whispered, "I have faith that you will come home to me."

Free
36

All DraDonna knew was darkness. She could not feel her arms or legs. There was nothing; just blackness. She was so alone, in pain.

She had been in the darkness before, in dreams. But never like this. There was so much pain and she could not move. She didn't know where the pain was coming from because she didn't have a body. She would have wept if she had eyes to cry with.

"Help me," she whispered, or was it just the whisper of a thought?

"Get up, little Donna," she heard the lovely voice of her childhood friend.

"I can't stand. There is nothing; I...I don't have a body," she told the voice.

"You do have a body, Donna. You can see me if you get up and open your eyes," the voice told her.

"I can't," DraDonna cried. "I feel so numb and weak."

"Take some of the energy of my soul, child," the voice offered.

DraDonna felt warmth wash through her, and some of the pain ebbed. DraDonna felt as if she could indeed stand. She opened her eyes stood up. She finally saw light and color but none of it made any sense to her. The light and color swirled around her in a torrent of different shapes and hues.

"What?" she said, not understanding what she was seeing. "Tatiana, are you there?"

In response to her question, one of the shapes of the swirling throng stopped in front of her and the form instantly became her lifelong friend Tatiana. "Yes, child. I am here."

"Why aren't we on the mountain? You look different, more solid; and why do I hurt so much?" she asked a long string of questions.

"The difference, little Donna, is that it was your mind I had met before so you created the mountain place that we met at. This time it is your soul that is here, so you will only see what is."

"Am I dead?" she asked.

"Not yet," Tatiana answered her cryptically. "Your body still lives. That is why you have so much pain."

"Was it you that saved me?" DraDonna asked her.

"No, child," she answered, gesturing to the swirling throng as three shapes approached them. Two of the shapes were more solid and brilliant, like Tatiana, and one was weaker and more transparent.

"Who…" she started to say when the three took shape. The two stronger shapes were JorMelony and JorRobert. The third, weaker shape was that of Jude.

"It was me, little Donna." JorMelony admitted.

"JorMelony!" she cried, wanting to hug her sister but not sure if she could. "I am so sorry for everything that happened. I can't help but feel like your death was partly my fault."

"It was not your fault, DraDonna," JorRobert told her. "If anyone should be apologizing here it should be me."

"You don't…" DraDonna started, but he cut her off.

"Yes I do. I need to make things right with you. I was mad, but even before that my attitude toward you was bad. But I see now that you are so very special. It was because of you that the HEART was able to break the loop in her programing, so we will all be set free."

DraDonna looked into the strong planes of his good-looking face, hardly able to recognize the man that stood before her.

"You look so different," she told him.

"I am. I have been freed from a madness that plagued me all my life," he confessed. "Can you forgive me, DraDonna? For all I did to you?"

Still looking into the beautiful face of a man she felt she never knew she saw true sorrow for all his misdeeds.

"Yes," she said with enthusiasm.

"Donna, we have to go," JorMelony said.

"Will I ever see you again?" she asked her sister with tears in her voice.

"Anything is possible once we are free," she told her younger sister. "I have a gift for you." Reaching out both of her closed hands, she placed in each of DraDonna's hands a brilliant and beautiful point of light.

"But... I don't understand," DraDonna confessed in awe.

"You will," JorMelony said. "I will always love you, my baby sister. All is well; all is well." She turned to JorRobert. They wrapped their arms around each other. Their souls then merged in a brilliant flash of light and acceded to rejoin all the other souls in the swirling torrent of colors.

"I must go now too, Little Donna," Tatiana said. "Thank you child; you have freed us all. I knew you would."

"I wish you didn't have to go. I will miss you. Aside from DraDevon, you were the only friend I ever had," she said.

"Yes I was, but you don't need me anymore. You do have wonderful bonded friends now and they will stand by you, child. Did you ever wonder why I never longed for a child of my own?"

"I always thought that you found fulfillment in your service to all the HEART's children."

"Well there was that, but mostly it was because I had you," she told her. Once again she leaned forward and kissed her curly head. "I love you, Donna." Tatiana ascended in a bright flash of light.

"But Tatiana, I don't know how to go back!" she called after her friend in panic.

"Maybe I can help you," Jude said. She had been standing quietly behind her.

"Jude, I'm sorry, I forgot you were here, too." DraDonna said.

"Please don't apologize to me. It should be the other way around," Jude said with the pain of shame and sorrow in her voice. "I have caused so much grief that it torments my soul. I can at least make things right with you. I betrayed you and I am so sorry," she sobbed.

DraDonna remembered what the HEART had told her about the control collar and how it affected Jude. She knew before Jude began to wear it that she was a bright and happy person who was full of compassion.

"It wasn't you," DraDonna told her. "It was the necklace. The HEART said that it was old and evil and had been falsely reported to her as destroyed. She said that it corrupts the person who wears it. That thing blocked the energy from your mind as well as the Traveler's Joy. So it wasn't you."

"But still...I...I did those things, control collar or not," Jude confessed in sorrow. "Can you forgive me?"

DraDonna looked into her beautiful ghostly face and smiled. "Forgiveness is greater than vengeance. Of course I do."

Jude smiled back with the relief of redemption in her eyes. "Thank you, DraDonna. But you need to go back to your body now."

"But I don't know how."

"I will show you. I have tried many times."

"Are you coming with me?" DraDonna asked her hopefully.

"I can't," she said with pain in her voice.

"But why? Come on, try. Symon needs you," DraDonna begged her.

"The jolt of negative energy I got was so fast and so hard that it did permanent damage to my brain; my soul has a hard time holding onto my body. But I think you might be able to help me."

"How? Just tell me what to do," DraDonna said urgently.

"I'm not sure yet, but I have a feeling," Jude said, unsure of the answer. "Our souls have touched, so I will be near."

"I will look for a way to save you, Jude," DraDonna promised her.

"You must go now, DraDonna," Jude said with insistence. "The longer you are away, the harder it gets."

"There is one more thing I have to tell you, Jude. The HEART has freed you and Symon to marry."

A mixture of surprise, joy and pain was on her lovely face. "Tell Symon for me that I will keep trying to come back to him."

"And I will not stop trying to figure out a way to save you," DraDonna promised again.

"Thank you," she said with tears in her voice. "It's time for you to go back, DraDonna. Close your eyes and listen to my voice. Now focus on the one who loves you. He is close to your body. Hear him call you home."

Darkness surrounded DraDonna once again as she closed her eyes. "Go home DraDonna. Go HOME!" Jude said with so much power in her voice that the last word rang in her ears over and over: "HOME...HOME...HOME!" The echo of that one word began to change. The sound of the one word became masculine, and the voice that spoke it was deeper.

"Come home to me DraDonna!" It was DraDevon's voice that she heard calling her home.

Epilogue
HOME

The journey down through the ship was strange but exciting. They were going to get a look at the HEART's choice for their new home.

The four bonded friends stood in the cargo hold of the ship. "HEART," Symon said. "Will these...umm, machines still work after all this time?" he asked her.

Yes, my bots have kept them in good working order. I control them, my Symon, so all you have to do is get in.

"She says yes," he told the other three as he stood up and gestured toward the back of the cargo area. All the people began to pour into the machines. "Let's go," He called as he climbed into one of the machines that were filled with the HEART's children as well as his three bonded friends.

"We need to hurry," DraDonna said, "the sun is setting. The HEART said she will open just after sunset."

"I know it will take time," Symon said, "but we will make it. There are a lot of these things and I think they go very fast."

"Let's go, HEART," he said.

The hatch began to open with a grinding noise, then a hiss of pressure, and everyone felt their ears pop.

The engine of the machine started up with a roar and they all began to move toward the large opening near the bottom of the ship. Once the machine was free of the opening of the ship, it climbed slow up an incline at first, and then picked up speed as it leveled out on flat ground.

Everyone was breathless with exhilaration from traveling at such high speeds. DraDonna looked forward out of the machine, and saw the rich colors of the rocky plains of her new world. DraDonna could not resist asking Symon questions.

"Why did the HEART land here?"

"She said that this is called a crater, a... umm... place in the ground that could handle her landing. She said that

267

there was no other place like it on the planet and if she didn't use it she was afraid she would harm the planet."

"Look how beautiful those mountains are!" TynLexa pointed out in excitement. "Are we going all the way over to them?" she asked.

"No," Symon told her. "In fact, see that hill just over there?" he asked her, pointing to a nearby green hill. "That's where we will stop. It will give us a good view of the ship."

The machine began to slow as it approached the hill and came to a stop with many others just behind it. The children of the HEART climbed the hill in the rapidly growing darkness.

"Wow!" Exclaimed DraDevon as he looked up at the darkening sky when he reached the top. "What are those lights called again?" he asked Symon.

"Stars. The HEART called them stars," Symon answered him with awe in his voice.

"Look, there's NulSam and NulJena!" DraDonna said, running off to hug her HEART brother and sister.

"How are you feeling, NulJena?" DraDonna asked her with concern with her arm still around her HEART sister as they walked to join the others.

"I'm feeling huge but good. This is so amazing; the colors of everything are so rich and bright even though it's getting dark."

DraDevon and NulSam embraced happily as they all turned to look at the ship.

"It should be any second now," Symon informed them.

"NulJena, are you feeling alright?" Symon asked her as he gently patted her large belly.

Now My Symon! The HEART warned him.

"Now," he told his friends with his hand still on NulJena's tummy.

A loud grinding noise began. The dome that was once their sky quickly fell back, sinking down inside the hull of the ship. As soon as it had opened, there was a great explosion of light as millions of souls raced across the night sky, leaving a blazing trail behind them on their way to freedom.

The light from the freed souls began to fade and a great cheer rose up from all the HEART's children. NulJena and Symon both gasped at the same time instead of cheering.

"What is it?" NulSam asked them with concern. "What's wrong?"

Symon lifted his large hazel eyes to look at NulSam and said, "I felt the babe move."

***

While the HEART's children cheered with happiness at the sight of the freed souls, he was still in the ship. In a dark and secret place, he waited and planned.

About the Author

Linna Drehmel was born at the Mountain Home Air Force Base in Idaho in 1973 and grew up surrounded by military. Her father served for 22 years in the Air Force, her mother was a military police officer in the Marines, and her older brother served for 10 years in the Navy. She draws inspiration from her family's many years of proud service in the military. She has spent much of her life studying anthropology and has a particular fondness for archaeology. She loves to find ways to intertwine anthropological and archaeological themes into her writing. She also has a strong understanding of what the reader likes, as she herself is an avid reader.

Acknowledgements

First, I thank God for this great talent that I have to share with the world. My husband and kids for putting up with the weird hours, frozen food and my endless prattle about the characters and sub plots. mp-66 and Dez, my Uncle and Aunt for much advice on Clematis. My publishing family: Sarah, Madison, Alexia, Kyani, Jenna, SK, Nathan S., Roxanne, Para Graphics for the amazing cover art and all the fantastic people at Crushing Hearts and Black Butterfly publishing.

Gabriella Hartwell Chapter 18 is dedicated specifically for you for the inspiration and guidance you have given me when it comes to soul mates. Thank you Chris Clark for the advice on fine carpentry, and Bri Clark for the advice on everything, Aaron P. for stopping me from making a big mistake, Chris W. for ever so much, Trish and Nathan W. my late night councilors, Kim Curtis for the first photograph of the HEART and for the pic that has made look like a rock star. Carly Anne W., Wendy L.T.G., and Deborah Beale for just being darn kool supporters of my work. And a very big thank you for my friend and writing mentor Lindsay Downs, and the list goes on. All who let me name characters after them. There are so many amazing people whom I thank and love for their support, just know that if you don't see your name here it is written on my heart and I will thank you always.

This would just not be right without a thank you to my muses. Narcisse Navarre (Khajj) for the amazing poetry. Tad Williams I look up to you. My two most powerful musical muses, Josh Groban and Depeche Mode who's voices inspire the creation of characters and new worlds.

Last but not least the people who invented earbuds so I can keep my muses to myself at 2am, and Diet Coke with lime so can stay up till 3am.

Made in the USA
Charleston, SC
16 June 2012